A CROSS TO BARE

A CROSS TO BARE

James Allan Fredrick

For Denise,

I imagine you putting yourself in debt when buying your first baking and
distribution plant, then coming to your senses and selling this signed copy
on ebay (its value having appreciated astronomically after the author had
been publically executed) Here's to success.

Love & friendship,

Writers Club Press
San Jose New York Lincoln Shanghai

A CROSS TO BARE

Writers Club Press
an imprint of iUniverse.com, Inc.

For information address:
iUniverse.com, Inc.
5220 S 16th, Ste. 200
Lincoln, NE 68512
www.iuniverse.com

ISBN: 0-595-19701-9

Printed in the United States of America

DEDICATION

This book is dedicated to the Triumvirate who made it happen:

For Jim Fisher
Who coaxed the story from me and convinced me it needed telling.

For Jason Schnabel
Who seemed as genuinely enthusiastic to read each chapter as I was to write for him.

And for my wife, Nadine
Who was the first to see the potential within me.
(*Look honey, it only took a decade!*)

ACKNOWLEDGEMENTS

For my readers (in no particular order): Sarah Schnabel, Michele Richardson, Anne Kane, Beth Greenfield, Cindy Schauer, Maria Polgano, and Heather Grattan. Your enthusiasm and support helped make this possible.

Thanks to Ken Aguiar of Aguiar Photography for the pictures.

For Jeanne Kalogridis. You must have been digging through a ton of dirt to consider me a diamond.

And for the original Triumvirate: David Bernstein, Denise Treco, and Steve Levoie. Maybe they'll read it someday.

PROLOGUE

A few dozen men gathered at the West banks of the River Jordan, just outside Pilate's city, Archilais. It would later be described as hordes but, in truth, it was a polite and curious crowd.

John was in the midst of his standard rhetoric: dipping the heads of recent converts into the lukewarm muck, calling out for the others to repent, and yelping and spitting in agony each time he bit his tongue, swollen from dehydration, with his cracked and snaggled teeth. Understandably, not everyone attending was eager to have his head lowered into water that was tainted at best, by this zealot who was alarmingly eccentric at least.

There were no fewer than four representatives of Herod in attendance, anxious to report any serious offense that could lose John his head. A handful of young men present were actually disciples of John, this "Baptist," poised with papyrus, ready to scribe any pearls of God-granted wisdom that could spew from the man they called "Master." Much to their disappointment, he mostly repeated himself.

"Repent! For the Kingdom draws nigh! Know He is watching!" You could actually hear the upper case letters in all the really important words.

The fact that some of the crowd began to murmur and snicker didn't help to reassure the followers that they were choosing the correct career path.

"Seems like a lot of fear and intimidation to me," commented one onlooker.

"If this is the best form of representation this religion can afford, I don't see it as having legs," sniffed yet another critic.

Suddenly something caught John's eye, and he stopped caterwauling and gyrating. The crowd followed the madman's squinty gaze to see the outline of a small group form in the hazy distance. They were approaching the service. Though indistinct from any other such group of men that had come to witness John's antics over the last several weeks, the prophet was busting with vindication.

"It is He," the malnourished seer began shouting. "The One I've told you about! The One who will Baptize us all in Fire and the Spirit!"

The crowd parted—more from curiosity than any real reverence. The men walked through, right up to the edge of the weeds. One man broke from the small pack and slowly, quietly waded out to greet the haggard-looking minister.

"How goes the war, John?"

"Perfect, Lord! Our Father provides locusts and wild honey, and I am nourished by His Word!"

Jesus' face pinched a bit. "I'm happy I asked."

He began to put his arm around the mad monk's shoulders, took a whiff and thought better of it. Instead, he leaned in as close as he could tolerate. "Look, cousin, we should get this thing moving on. The people came out here for a show…"

John's hands snapped out like an asp, grabbed Jesus' wrists and pulled the Messiah's hands to his lips.

"I only pray that I might be worthy." John spoke in-between knuckles. "To be baptized by you, my Christ, means having God's Own Blessing!"

The soon-to-be savior tore his hands from chapped lips with considerable effort.

"I know this seems a little 'outside-the-box,' John," Jesus felt compelled to explain to this man who was integral in launching Christ's own movement. "You're going to have to trust me. I've been going over this with my people for weeks now. You need to do this…thing you've got going on…to me. On me. Whatever. It's like an initiation. It's symbolic. And it's the best way to create an impact right now. Y'know, it's humbling and non-aggressive and all of that. Our research shows that this is what Palestine is craving. Do you follow?"

When he became aware that the concept was far outside the scope of John's limited focus, Jesus brought it back down to his level.

"My Father told me we should do it this way, John."

●

The Baptist was uncharacteristically silent as he cupped his Lord's head and slowly lowered him back into the water.

He honestly couldn't think of any words to commemorate this historic event (although Christ's disciples were scribbling furiously, so it was a given that history would remember John to be quite expressive, indeed). He remained speechless even as he gradually raised the man who would be King upright.

This time it *was* reverence that kept the small crowd orderly. Everyone stood stock still…waiting…listening for the other (possibly divine) shoe to drop.

The sound was something like thunder. It started very low before building; not coming from any particular distance, yet growing in intensity as if closing in on this curious crowd.

The air became electric. And, as every strand of hair on every man's body tugged skyward, it finally dawned on everyone present that something was approaching from above.

In unison, the entire congregation snapped their eyes toward Heaven. They were immediately blinded. To a man.

BOOK ONE

A

Days

In The

Lives

Chapter One

I've got no money, no job, no friends or family (even if I could afford to spend the nickel-a-minute), and only a fuzzy notion about where I am and what year it is. But I tell you this: I can remember everything that happened yesterday, and 2,000 years ago, better than I can remember my own mother's face. So the one thing I do have is purpose.

But the part that really kills me…I mean, the one thing that just ties my panties in a knot, is that it began so simply. So tritely. Like so many thousands of other stories, which have begun exactly the same way.

Memorial Day weekend. Coming out of a peepshow in Times Square.

Jackson Cross
The Judas Conspiracy

A dirty-gray morning in Manhattan—Thursday, February 16, 2012. Jackson pushed his way through the crowd with the neon-blue faces. His destination being just a few more blocks west, everyone facing him was bathed in the illumination of the giant Apple® advertisement. Flying from his second joint before 8:00 A.M., Jackson felt as if he had taken a wrong turn and stumbled into a Fellini film.

Passing the Virgin/Nova Center, the stocky, wide-shouldered man with the classic Roman nose came to a stop in front of a conflagration of color and brilliance that tore him from his cinematic reverie and plopped him down into an entirely new one.

GIRLS * GIRLS * GIRLS
ALL LIVE—ALL NUDE
XXX—ADULT ENTERTAINMENT—XXX
Jackson smiled and sighed inwardly.

"Memorial Day weekend. Coming out of a peepshow in Times Square," he stated dramatically to himself while shrugging his hemp-and mylar-covered shoulders against a stiff winter gust of wind.

This was the moment. His life was in exactly the place he knew it would be in the early summer of 2009, when the germ of the idea for what would ultimately be called *The Judas Conspiracy* bitch-slapped his right brain.

He was already late for his appearance on "The Tom Green Radio Hour," but Jackson's first HBO Comedy Special was being taped that night, and he was widely considered an artist at that point. So, if the early nineties were any lesson at all, Cross could just about get away with murder, let alone being tardy for a nationally syndicated broadcast. They loved him. They could wait.

While this was only his fourth trip to New York, the mere fact that it played such an integral part of the beginning and end of his novel was enough to convince people that he was from "The City." In truth, he couldn't stand the town.

It wasn't the crime, because *it* had been all-but eliminated. In the new, corporate New York, everyone on the island wore ID, and you could only get that with a work visa or a Tourist Request Order, confirming employment elsewhere. If you were caught committing a crime, you were fired. Unemployed people were not allowed on the island.

It wasn't the attitude. When corporate executives run the entire city, you never know how to act. One day being aloof and apathetic is in, but the next day it could get you canned. Civility drew the least amount of attention from the Suits, and could sometimes call for a Favorable Recognition, so it pretty much paid to be nice.

And it wasn't the grime. All Apple® transportation hovered over the city's magnetic grid, fossil fuels were banned over three years previous, and littering was a crime punishable by termination—of your job, of course. All in all, it was a pretty clean city.

It was primarily the feeling of insignificance that wanted to shackle his ego each time he walked within its canyons. It was all-but impossible to feel unique in a metropolis that was forced to construct multi-billion-dollar hydraulic supports which were supposed to prevent an island, with 24 million people on it daily, from crumbling…somehow. He had no idea how. What he *did* know was that there were very few "special" people in this town. And Jackson was not one of them. Yet.

But on this cold and blustery morning, amidst all the traffic and hustle of rush hour, Cross was somewhat grateful for the chance to be anonymous. His book secured a position in the top five of every bestselling chart, *internationally* (a pleasant surprise, for the novice wordsmith never considered that the system at the publisher's house could have translated the novel the moment he uploaded it). The Religious Right began protesting within three hours of the book being issued to the servers. He was notorious by nightfall.

Fourteen months had passed since his "inflammatory piece of provocative trash" had been released. His book had been publicly flayed; laid bare for anyone with a keyboard and a bible to criticize and/or openly ridicule. Cross' writing abilities had been scrutinized to the point of non-existence. No one bothered him here though, standing in front of the gaudy, flashing lights of the corporate-sponsored skintique. Being "no one special" here was a nice break.

Even his most ardent detractors had to admit, if only to themselves, that Jackson took the seemingly insurmountable sniping in stride. He remained cool-tempered, never allowing himself to be drawn into a public fight. He kept his comments light and witty. Soon, the writer parlayed his sudden celebrity into enough talk shows and live chats as to be a little more than intriguing and a little less than annoying. And, with those appearances, the writer's plan began to bear fruit.

Implausible as it seems, the book was conceived as a tool to introduce his humor. His goal had always been comedy. Unlike the self-indulgent stand-up comics of the mid-to-late nineties who cashed in on their names by selling an extended deconstruction of their own routines, Jackson was an insecure yet attention-starved writer. He was sure that his own material could be performed with great comedic results. He just lacked the nerve to get on stage and try. If the world wanted to see Jackson Cross, comedian, the world would have to ask. That was how deep both his pretension, and lack of self-confidence, ran.

And it worked. He turned all the small-minded, vicious attacks on his work and his person into strikingly funny anecdotes to be delivered during his almost-constant public appearances. A year after being voted public enemy #1 by the Southern Baptist Convention, the humorist was appearing at the Neil Simon Theater on Broadway.

New York City and HBO wanted to see Jackson Cross, comedian. The world was sure to follow.

He was so enraptured with the flashing neon and self-congratulatory meditation, that the writer/comic barely reacted when a magnecab ripped itself from the grid, jumped the curb and scraped to a grinding halt mere inches from his own boot heels.

"Jacks!"

Daniel Epstein exploded out of the driver's seat. His flack jacket waving in the wind, Daniel's "Get Off The Cross" t-shirt attracted more immediate attention than the curbed taxi. Daniel was independently wealthy and a friend of Jackson's since high school. Jackson couldn't place a finger on when it was exactly that Danny started driving a magnecab in his spare time.

"You were supposed to be at the station over an hour ago! They've kept Seinfeld on for an extra ten minutes already, and who wants that?"

Beth, the publicist, stepped out of the passenger side with her emotions slightly more veiled. Rancor and distaste were thinly concealed with a desire for public decorum. Her anger was under control, but only like that of the refrigerated spaghetti sauce getting warmed up on the stove. You just know that even though it still looks cool on top, it's boiling underneath. It wouldn't be long before that sauce skin is going to give into the pressure of hot tomato paste. That's how Jackson saw it through his marijuana-induced fugue anyway.

"I *knew* I should have sent you the car," she hissed through a prosthetic smile she displayed for the onlookers. "'No,' you said. 'I love the walk,' you said. 'I'll be there before Tom comes in with his first cup of decaf,' you said. Now we owe I-don't-know-how-much for this stupid fucking cab fender, you may never be invited to do Tom's show again, and I look like a total SHIT of a publicist."

I'd say that pot's on the boil, Cross thought.

The writer took his verbal medicine silently, trying to ignore the crowd that began to gather and take notice of him, and helped his friend push the 400-pound vehicle off the sidewalk until it was hovering over pavement once again. The 40-something, incensed and artificially blonde woman continued to usher her prepared chastisement.

"If you want to throw away *your* career, that's *entirely* up to you. Just do it a-*fucking*-lone. Understand?"

"A-fucking-loan? Wonder what kind of interest rate you can get on something like that," Danny pondered while getting back into the driver's seat. Jackson quietly settled into the warmth of the plastic car next to his friend. Beth slinked into the backseat, waving her Pocket-Mac™ and continued to express her disappointments at her client.

"Some of us aren't fly-by-night successes, you know. Some of us actually *worked* to get a career. Maybe *I'll* write a book. Maybe I'll call Moses a *faggot*. Then maybe *I* can do whatever the hell *I* want. Huh? What do you think about that?"

The cab pulled unsteadily back into the magnetic flow of Times Square traffic, away from the gathering crowd, and headed Uptown.

Chapter Two

For those of you who think having your consciousness fired from a hydro-powered cannon and projected millions upon millions of miles over time and space only to crash-land inside someone else's brain is some kind of joy ride, I'm here to say that you're wrong. It sucks ass.

I hurt from the tip of my new body's scalp to the balls of my new body's feet. Actually, any balls in or on the corporal property were throbbing almost beyond toleration.

It couldn't have been too much fun for the previous occupant, either. The scientists warned me about a lot of things, but they never prepared me for the death rattle that echoed for days after the transference. The man I effectively killed, by forcibly ejecting his consciousness from his body, thought the whole circumstance was very unfair. I was in no position to disagree as I tore my face out from the muck and grime in which the body had been plastered as a direct result of my impact.

I must have made quite an entrance too. Everyone around me was also prone on the ground. I remained silent as they asked understandably curious questions as to what knocked them all down or who remembered anything.

One man seemed unaffected. While we were all picking ourselves up from the reeds and silt of the shore, one man was standing perfectly erect several yards out into a body of water of some kind, helping his companion to stand. My stomach tightened as he began to approach.

"I heard it!" One of the young men who had regained his footing began writing on some kind of parchment. "Jehovah's Own Voice saying, '*This* Is MY SON!'"

Glancing up at another young man with parchment, the excited boy asked, "Isn't that what you heard?"

The second boy's expression turned from confusion to certainty without the hint of a second thought. "Absolutely," he confirmed. "I *too* heard Him." He began writing. "And He *also* said, 'I have Approved Him!' Remember?"

The first one began crossing out something furiously. "You! He said, '*You* are MY SON,' and, 'I have Approved YOU!' *That's* what He said," he finished, nodding.

The second one fell into the same rhythm of nodding. "Yeah," he smiled. "That's what I heard, too." Then he looked up at all the young men with quills and fragile paper. "And that's what *you* heard, too!" They immediately began writing and nodding.

I hadn't found the strength to get up before the man in the water was standing at my feet. He was a dark man, made darker with the light to his back. His head just blocked out the sun as he bent down to offer me a hand. This illumination sprang out from his head like some brilliant crown, almost blinding in intensity.

"Jesus," was all I could say about the startling light.

"Let me help you, Judas," was the dark man's reply.

●

Danny and Jacks sat facing each other, a small coffee table separating their couches within the little turquoise room.

"I can't believe you jacked a cab," Cross observed, while leaning forward to tap his cigarette into the ashtray on the center of the table.

"I gave him like $200 and promised that the radio station would reimburse his company if we wrecked the thing. He thought it was some kind of radio gimmick." Danny scratched dead skin from his goatee. "*He* wasn't upset."

"You can get fired for shit like that nowadays, Mr. I-Luv-The-Apple."

"Check your WHPs. I'm working for *you* now, Dopey."

"Really." Jackson exhaled a copious amount of smoke, stubbed out his cigarette while getting up, and moved over to the courtesy bar. "Why do I think you're costing me a fortune?"

Epstein stretched out on the couch. "I'm your Vice President of International Marketing. You filed the paperwork the day you called to tell me you were going to be in town. I head-up your New York office."

"And how many employees do I employ at my New York office?"

"Just one."

"Salary?"

"Fifty G's. Annually."

"Heh. That seems almost insulting for such an executive position," Jacks responded before devouring the better part of a cheese danish with a single bite.

"That's the most I could legally launder, if there is such a thing."

"So, I'm *not* actually giving you all my money," the writer confirmed between chews, marveling at the fact that Danny had his head back and was talking while holding a cigarette straight up between his lips.

Doesn't he get ash in his mouth?

"Would I do that?" Daniel sat up, dislodged the cigarette, spit some ash on the floor, took a sip of coffee and continued. "It happens that your company is fortunate enough to meet the single requirement necessary to receive the Daniel Epstein, Esq. Business Grant. It's a foundation established to help new small businesses thrive in this cold, corporate-choking-the-underdog society in which we live. It pays fifty G's."

"And the one requirement?"

"Employing Daniel Epstein, Esq. Where did I lose you? You're not going to have to pay taxes on me next year and I demand to be sexually harassed. What more could you ask of an executive?"

Beth stuck her head in just as Jackson was lighting a joint.

"I've smoothed it over with Tom's people," she said. Her face was smiling the smile of a serial guilt enforcer. "You're on in about five, so let's get moving, 'k?" Her attitude shifted from conciliatory to den mother when she caught site of Jackson's smoke. "Oh, no! We're not doing that!"

"Who *are* you and what power do you *think* you have?" Jackson pushed past the stunned publicist and marched in the direction of the control booth.

"'We're not doing *that!*'" Danny mocked while slithering past.

"You're not going with him, *Mr. Epstein*," she responded coldly, desperate to maintain some control. "I'll have the studio pipe the show into the Green Room."

"Don't mess with him, lady," Jacks called without turning around. "He's my Vice President of International Marketing."

CHAPTER THREE

I was able to contain my amazement and confusion for the most part of that first day, but I still couldn't get over the fact that alien technology had downloaded me into possibly the most nefarious traitor in recorded history. Maybe that would be no big deal for you but, for me, the compulsion to curl up into a fetal position and begin drooling explosively felt more and more like the most logical option.

Jesus could tell something was up, but he had a lot on his plate. At one point he called John (the Apostle, not the Baptist or, say, the Beatle) over and whispered something while motioning toward my direction.

John, the man who would become the spiritual Father of Catholicism, the man who wrote the Book of Revelations which laid it all down, was, and I don't say this lightly, completely insane. He had wild eyes, always sizing you up, always calculating his odds of success should he suddenly feel the need to strangle you. He was one swastika shy of being a Manson. No joke. When he got Word to watch me (which I'm sure he did), I knew I'd have to straighten up and start acting like a real religious fanatic before I became history before becoming history.

Right after the Baptism (an unparalleled success thanks to my timely arrival), Christ announced that he was taking a pilgrimage to pray and face temptation. I found it kind of odd that the New Testament never mentioned him taking a pair of young clerks with him during that fast. These "disciples" were said to be helping Christ prepare the big sermon tour. Timothy and Paul had both previously worked at the House of Caiaphas, with the Event Coordinator. They were said to have a terrific feel for what impressed the Palestinian people, which is why Jesus felt compelled to bring them into his camp. They had about a month, and he really wanted this thing to "pop." Within just a few hours of my arrival, I was standing with a small group of Arabs (we looked like a bunch of cabbies at a union meeting), waving goodbye to the Messiah.

Once Jesus was out of sight, John and Peter were in charge. James, Andrew and I were the only other followers at that point. I quickly determined that John was the "brains," while Peter was pretty much a hired thug. I liked Peter, though. He'd kill you if John told him to but, other than that, he was a really nice guy. He was sweet in that "feel-no-guilt-if-I'm-killing-for-God" kind of way.

We walked for what seemed like forever. It was all pretty much arid wasteland. There was this path in the sand that sort of resembled a road. We followed it north.

They left me alone for the most part. I appreciated that because, let me tell you, hygiene was not a priority for these people. I was having a hard time tolerating my own stink; I didn't need it churned up with the overwhelming stench of the group. Of course, the pounding sun and dizzying heat weren't helping matters.

Peter and John kept going over plans as to how they were going to rig the well at some guy's house in Cana. It was a wedding we were all invited to, and it was the first place we were going after hooking up with Jesus again. I was less interested in the details than I was in the fact that I could speak and comprehend ancient Hebrew as if I was raised with these men. Who knows how many times the aliens had infiltrated our planet? It was flawless! I looked like them, spoke like them…there wasn't a speck of evidence to suggest that I might be an alien consciousness inside this body—with the possible exceptions of the cascading light, explosive thrust and sonic boom on impact, of course.

We camped about midway to Nazareth, outside the city of Aenon.

I desperately wanted to find an inn with a bath, but James convinced me that our destiny rested in the stars.

"We'll be seeing God tonight, brother," he whispered. Then he opened his fist to reveal what appeared to be two peyote buttons. James and I were pretty much friends from that point on.

●

Excerpted from transcripts:
The Tom Green Radio Hour
February 16, 2012

Tom Green: OK, I think we're finally ready. My next guest is the author of the hugely successful, and greatly controversial, piece of fiction, *The Judas Conspiracy*. He's been both lecturing and working comedy clubs for the last couple of years, and he'll be opening his new one-man show, *Just Another Crucifixion*, tonight at the Neil Simon Theater on Broadway. If you miss him tonight, you can catch the digital feed later this month, February 22, at 10:00 PM EST, to be exact, on The HBO Comedy Hour. Anything else?

Jackson Cross: I think that's everything.

TG: Jackson Cross, everybody.

JC: I'm sorry I'm so tardy. I do have a note from my mom, if that means anything.

TG: Well, we were told that they found you, in some kind of trance, in front of a skintique. So, your mother…?

JC: Oh, she was working. They've put her on the morning shift since the amputations. The tips aren't great, but she's finally got a steady clientele.

TG: Now it's been a while since I've tried to read your book but, if I remember correctly, didn't it begin with one of those places? Memorial Day weekend…

JC: Coming out of a peep show in Times Square. Yeah. That's like the only non-fiction part of the book. See that guy in your producer's booth? That's Dippy. How they treatin' ya in there, Dippy?

Production Microphone: Like an executive, Dopey.

JC: He and I went to school together and, the very first time I came to NY, Dippy there takes me to his dealer in the Village. That was before this stuff was legal, you understand.

TG: I noticed you and your friend are believers in the home-roll.

JC: Well, I want to give a heartfelt "thanks" to Mrs. Sagan of the legalization committee, not to mention the federal government, for coming to their senses after too many years of committed ignorance. But, by the same token, I can't abide by filtered joints. Call me a rebel…

TG: You're a rebel.

JC: Be that as it may, Dippy drags me up one of the few pre-war, six-floor walkups that were left in that side of town. This place was a complete and absolute pit. Maybe 400 square feet, it had one small bedroom and a kitchen/dinette thing and a toilet. And that was it. His dealer, Jake, was a refugee from that old '80s band, ZZ Top. But in that little kitchenette were well over a dozen, gallon-size plastic containers. Each was filled to capacity with every kind of marijuana known to man. All you did was pop the top and consult the 3 x 5 card inside to find the nation of origin and price-per-ounce of the contents. The first one I opened was from Brazil, I think, and the price was $1,200 an ounce. I was very careful putting the lid back on that thing, let me tell you.

TG: And, what? Did this guy strip for you? How's this tie together with what we were talking about?

JC: Give me a second. See, I had these other friends, Scott and Darlene, who were watching the latest Godzilla movie at the Virgin Complex. They're not smokers or anything, so we wanted to take care of business before meeting them. Y'know, get a little buzz-on before having dinner with some straights. So we made our purchase and started hoofing it. We smoked and walked up to 44th Street pretty fast. We noticed that we were left with some time to kill as we passed the peepshow. They weren't corporate-regulated then. They were good, old-fashioned, blue-collar American filth. We were just baked enough to go in. Next thing I know, I'm standing in this tiny room, giggling madly, looking through what I imagined to be bulletproof glass into an equally small closet where this nubile, young Hispanic girl maneuvered herself in elaborate contortions around a bar stool, offering me views traditionally reserved for gynecologists. The only thing she said during our entire relationship was, "you masturbate." It came across as like a rule or something.

TG: And it was under these conditions that you came up with the idea of flipping off all Christianity?

JC: Not yet. Actually, Dippy and I met back outside. We didn't shake hands for obvious reasons, but we were falling over each other in minor hysterics. I remember he said to me, "Do you have any idea how many vices we've succumbed to while Darlene and Scott are watching their movie?" And then I remember thinking that some story should begin with this pit-of-your-stomach, spent-testicle, guilty-pleasure feeling of walking out of a peepshow. It just happens that the next piece I wrote was received as "flipping off all Christianity."

TG: Well, you do make Judas out to be a patsy and call people who follow conformed religions, and I think this quote is accurate, "mean-spirited, narrow-minded mouth-breathers who can derive joy solely from the suffering of others."

JC: That's right, focus on the negative. I mean, that's only a small portion of the book.

TG: It's true that part three of the novel gets the most scrutiny, but the first two parts are primarily preamble. True?

JC: Not at all. What most people don't get was that I was retelling Dante's *Divine Comedy*. It's something I'd wanted to do since high school.

TG: Well, the *Inferno* was obvious. Your characters actually descend into Hell, as Dante did. Your Hell was especially interesting, being that it was managed by deceased stand-up comics.

JC: My brother had Sam Kinison tapes when we were growing up. When I was thirteen, I wanted to be a priest. When I was fourteen, I wanted to be Sam Kinison. With the possible exception of the head-on collision in the middle of the night on a Nevada highway.

TG: I remember you had Lenny Bruce and Groucho Marx and John Belushi among others, all torturing the damned in various ways. And Howard Stern was Satan. What's that about?

JC: Well, obviously I wrote that before that whole, disturbing, strangulation incident.

TG: He still says it was the only time he cheated on his fourth wife.

JC: One time too many. Anyhow, at the time that I conceived this piece, Howard had the whole thing going on. He was finally accepted as an artist, and his production company was going gangbusters, and he had a new wife every six months, each more beautiful than the last. It just seemed apparent to me that he was, in fact, Satan. Nobody else could have it so good. Don't forget, there were multiple Satans. Everyone creates their own. There was Bill Gates Satan, Michael Jordan Satan, Tom Cruise Satan and others. There was even a Your-Boss Satan, for the self-centered pricks who can't see past their own paltry existence and believe that their employer is evil incarnate.

TG: And having the comedians run things allowed for some flavor. I'll never forget the image of some group of people, naked, with their ankles tied back behind their necks. Then they each had a spoon sticking out of their anuses. What were you thinking there?

JC: That was the Circle of Vanity. I figured, how could you be vain with your feet tied behind your head and a spoon sticking out of your ass? My favorite part of that was the fact that they had peas all over the surface, and goals on each side of the circle. They had to figure a way to use the spoons to scoop the peas into the goal. Then, once every hundred years, they would get untied. The amount of peas you got in the goal determined the amount of seconds you could stay untied that one time that century.

TG: Really? I don't remember that part.

JC: I think I had that in there. Maybe I planned to and never did. It's all a blur.

TG: So, these four characters tour Hell…

JC: Right, right. Making a long story thin: The main character turns down the chance to be the new Judge of man's souls. Unfortunately, being taken into Hell meant that he lost corporal life. So Death gathers him from the devil's throne room and reincarnates him into an alien life form. But his human consciousness essentially prevents him from becoming an alien being. He remains human, can't possibly comprehend this alien existence, and he effectively becomes the village idiot. I mean, they're super-evolved, while he's like this moderately well-trained marsupial, so they ship him out to help a missionary on some distant mudball, and he lands smack-dab in the body of Judas Iscariot. And everybody's pissed at me.

TG: At least it's not complicated. Listen, I want to get into your show and what you'll be doing next, but my producer says that the lines are totally blocked, so we need to take some calls. But, before we do that, let's hear some words from our sponsors. We'll be right back with more of Jackson Cross on the Tom Green Radio Hour.

CHAPTER FOUR

The most amazing part about tripping with apostles was how stupendously unimaginative they were.

We had the desert night, a fire, and a sky untouched by industrial pollution. I had never imagined so many stars, even when I lived among them.

Yet all John and Peter were capable of focusing on was their fantastic, merciful yet ruthless, tolerant yet judgmental, omniscient and loving god. "Our Father is stronger than anyone! Our Father cannot be seen or heard, but He knows everything!" John would shout at the heavens. "Amen. I love my Father," was Peter's muted reply. Whereas John became expressive while under the hallucinogen, primarily in monosyllables, Peter became introspective. He sat at the edge of the fire, giving John the occasional, "Amen. I love my Father," stared into the flames and rocked back and forth.

For no good reason, I began to envision John as some huge raven; cawing and flapping and raging around the burning, snapping wood. Whenever he turned toward me I shuddered with an overwhelming fear of having my eyes pecked out.

Peter was right around my age, but I began seeing him as the old and abused and misused mutt that finally found a family to take care of it. He sat docile by the fire, responding when it was expected of him, like a good dog.

"My Father loves me! My Father will destroy anyone I don't like! My Father can do anything! He's better than any other god!"

"Amen. I love my Father."

These were the guys who started this movement? These were the men who wrote the New Testament? There are thoughtful and compelling letters to be written to whole communities and heads of state, and a book detailing the end of all existence. I couldn't understand how it was possible for these simple, narrow-minded fishermen to accomplish everything history has credited to them. It didn't sit well for me at all.

I finally laid down in the sand and tried to focus on the stars. I thought about the first time I looked deeply into space with my cousin's telescope. But the moment I remembered existed two millennia in the future, to a completely different person. Ironic that I never felt homesick when I was on an alien planet. It wasn't until I returned to Earth that I truly ached for the life that had been stolen from me.

I was going to die 2000 years before anyone who knew me would be born. And here I was—essentially a hired assassin, sent to create the single-most effective martyr in all recorded history. The cornerstone of Western culture right up to the invention of television hinged on my actions. The weight of my circumstance settled on my mind. John's declarations and Peter's affirmations drifted twenty centuries away.

I was scheduled to betray a man who, by all accounts, had nothing but kind and hopeful wishes for everyone. He would be beaten, tortured, pushed beyond the limits of endurance, displayed, ridiculed, stripped of his followers, his dignity and, ultimately, his life. It was a messy death ahead for this man with the thick, black curls and the dark, rough skin. I had to admit, when I thought of his smile, his agonizing death sickened me.

Then the faces of thousands of followers who've died for Jesus began to appear in the stars. Those who believed against all odds and allowed themselves to be killed for their faith.

Next came the millions of converts, beaten and stripped like Christ, forced to pledge allegiance to this "Son of God." They all appeared before me in the sky, levitating from horizon to horizon, crying out for justice. Crying out for retribution.

I can safely say that it was from that very first night that I considered the possibility of changing the course of things to come. This was a unique opportunity to make a fundamental difference in the world. Literally...the world! History was mine for the making! I could save everyone ever persecuted for believing in him. I could prevent the countless murders committed in defense of some doctrine of the Church. I could become the unseen avenger of the "heathens" converted by the sword. I could prevent the resentment of any particular nationality directly attributed to his death. I could do all of this, merely by *not* betraying him.

But what if more people suffered *without* his sacrifice? What if the lack of a cohesive religion, based on the martyrdom, prevented some natural evolutionary path?

And how was my knowledge of the fact that he's really from an entirely different race and galaxy going to affect the way I would conduct myself?

I was still sifting through that last one when James began nudging my right arm. I looked over and met his glassy gaze. He was lying right next to me.

"It's hard to focus on your own prayers with the two of them being so odd, don't you think?"

The question struck me. "You're not quite so...focused on this thing yourself, are you, James?"

"Well, John's my older brother. I've been having to keep him out of trouble since I remember anything. He's mostly harmless, but he can turn ugly when you least expect it. I have to admit, Jesus has been the most positive influence John has ever gravitated toward. His teaching is primarily about love, so that *has* to be good. Right?"

I found myself without an answer.

Anyway, John interrupted.

"Our Father is listening; Andrew, James, Judas! Our Father knows everything! Our Father wants to hear His praises sung!"

"Amen. I love my Father."

My saturation point overwhelmed, I offered my first dissension.

"How do you know so much about the Father, John?"

The fiery eyes darted from my gaze to that of Peter and then James.

"Jesus is the source of my knowledge!" he stated matter-of-factly, as if the answer should be obvious to all of us present.

I fought the compulsion to flinch against being pecked at, and looked the mad black bird straight on.

"So you don't really know. You were merely told," was my return.

The gaze turned cold. Doubters were not welcome at this fire, *that* much was certain. "I know Jesus is my savior. I know he'd die for me. I know he *will* die for me! What do *you* know, Judas?"

I looked back out at the stars and considered that for a moment. Then I took a deep breath and said, "I know that this thing we live on is called the Earth, and it's round, and it rotates around the sun; instead of the other way around. I know that hurting someone because they see things differently is the only real sin. I know that the primary reason men do things is to get laid, which makes what you guys are doing even more of a mystery. I know that ducks float, but witches don't because there aren't any real witches and a lot of independent women will die needlessly. I know that there's a race of beings living in the stars who have been evolving longer than our planet has been cooling, and it seems they can't resist the chance to fuck with everyone else in the multiverse. I know that, for better or ill, the things we do in the next three years will affect the future of everyone on this world—some directly, some indirectly. And I know I'd give my right testicle for a shower, some air-conditioning, and a beer. That's everything I know right this second."

I guess I had made up my mind about what path I was going to take. As usual, I was the last to see it coming.

Feeling three sets of eyes staring at me with both confusion and growing concern, I turned my back to the campfire and tried to ignore the millions of cheering voices in my head.

●

Excerpted from transcripts:
The Tom Green Radio Hour
February 16, 2012

Tom Green: Welcome back! You're listening to the Tom Green Radio Hour and that's it. Just me. Just Tom. I've fired all the dipdoodle side-kicks and sycophants and it's just me and you, webhead. You're probably getting this feed live off our site, unless you're one of those troglodytes who still listen to that radio contraption. In which case, you'd be listening to 98.8, KFX2 FM, just another happy acquisition in the Murdoch family's bid for corporate dictatorship and world domination.

Jackson Cross: Wow. You can say that and stay employed?

TG: As if any of the Suits even listen to this thing. Now! The gentleman interrupting my after-commercial soliloquy…

JC: Sorry, sorry.

TG: Twice, no less. This rude bastard's my guest this morning. Writer, comedian and rabble-rouser, Jackson Cross.

JC: I'm not surprised that "bastard" was on the publicity kit you guys were downloaded. My publicist hates me. See that middle-aged cheer-leader in your producer's booth? The one giving me the finger? That's Beth, my publicist. Hi, Beth! I bet Kevin would love to know what a bitch you've been to me over the last three weeks! How 'bout you?

TG: Jeeze, Cross. Don't let a national audience get in the way of you fulfilling some vindictive fantasy. My podium is your podium.

JC: No. Kevin Smith's producing my HBO special, and his office forced her on me for the duration of the publicity tour. And she's just mean, man!

Producer's Microphone: I don't have to be publicly ridiculed! If this costs me my job…

TG: Lady, get off my show! Bobby! Get her off the mike!

Prod. Mike: I'll sue that [expletive] [censored]!
    I don't want to get security, Ms. Krumper. Let's turn this…

TG: You're in Public Relations! Taking abuse is part of your job! Maybe you can yell at an intern now and again but, other than that, just smile and nod. Where did you go to school?

JC: That did it. She's gone.

Prod. Mike: Hey, Dopey. Don't pull that kind of stunt when I'm in the shark cage with the shark! I have total confidence that she can kick my ass.

JC: Sorry about that, Dippy. Guess I wasn't thinking ahead.

TG: Hey Billy! How many times have I told you? You're Secret Service to these people! You are to happily, cheerfully, almost maniacally defend their lives with your own! Seriously, though. That lady shouldn'ta got on the mike, but I don't know if she should be unemployed just because she lost her head.

JC: Forget it! She's spent the last three weeks belittling me during the day, and then I tell her off at night in the clubs. It's become part of the act.

TG: Really?

JC: No, not really. I *really* don't like her and she *really* wishes I was dead. So this was the best possible way to part company. Now, should anything happen to me once I leave the studio, the cops will know exactly who to investigate first.

TG: How Machiavellian. But, in Hell's corporate structure, it wasn't Public Relations that got the worst treatment. I remember this pretty clearly. You were brutal to Human Resources.

JC: You mean just because people in Human Resources in this life had to spend eternity with their heads stuck up Satan's ass while masturbating lessor demons? Or because the demons were all eunuchs, so it's not like they were going to finish? Ever? You think that was too much? Because I disagree. Tossing the boss' salad while perfunctorily servicing the staff is, to my thinking, exactly what HR does.

TG: Well, heh, I guess we should find out what everyone else thinks. All lines are taken, but we'll be making space soon, I'm thinking. So go ahead and dial, toll-free, 777-343-KFX2, and say whatever you like to Jackson Cross, Humanitarian. And, check this out! We've got Patty on line 3! And it says here that Patty works in, get this, Human Resources! What's on your mind, Patty?

Line 3: Um, I've been holding for like twenty minutes to tell Mr. Cross how much I loved the book?

JC: You don't sound very convinced, Patty.

Line 3: Well, I assumed you meant what you wrote to be a joke, but…

JC: And your first instinct was right. But now you've got me worried, Patty. My intention was to play with people who generally take themselves too seriously and show them how silly they are. Do you think I wish everyone in Information Systems to spend the rest of all time cleaning the sluice channels that carry the excremental waste of the gluttonous? No! It's just that I found it ironic that these primarily introverted, social midgets who appear to have little or no ability to interact civilly with the rest of us lowbrows, consider themselves such hot[censored] because they can do a job that no one with even the slightest interest of having a real life would accept.

TG: Systems Analyst on line 4. Just kidding!

JC: Of course, I'm not saying all MIS people are this way, just all the ones I'd ever worked with in the eight years I put into various corporations.

Line 3: Oh, so they're antisocial, but you can't even hold a steady job!

Prod. Mike: Me—ow!

JC: My problems were more with authority than being able to deal with people in a social environment. I suspect your issues have more to do with an inability to relate with people if the fate of their future employment and maybe even viability isn't affected by your appraisal of them.

Line 3: I know that was meant to be insulting, but I didn't really get it.

TG: Have to admit, you completely lost me there.

JC: Shoulda passed last round. Let me try again. You're right, Maddy…

Line 3: Patty.

JC: Patty. You're right. Human Resources constitutes the finest, most righteous employees of any corporation. And, without exception, each of these pure, angelic creatures are solely committed to preserving the rights of their fellow employees—selflessly putting their own heads on the chopping blocks, if need be.

Line 3: I've never understood why employees are under the impression that HR is supposed to throw themselves on the sword. I mean, ideals don't pay mortgages.

TG: Fantastic! I have to admire you. The beauty of that was she's going to be the last person to understand that she just proved your point. Let's move along to Don on line 1. Hi, Don!

JC: Hey there, Don.

Line 1: You're going to die, you kike bastard.

TG: You think that's for you or me?

Line 1: He knows who it's for.

JC: Well, I'm not Jewish, but I wrote about this Jew once; he had really dark skin and supposedly forged a whole new class of bigotry and hatred under the guise of love and understanding.

Line 1: Keep talking, you [expletive] faggot. Keep sullying the name of our Lord.

TG: Not often you hear "faggot" and "Lord" in the same breath. I still think he could be talking to me. I *am* a member of the tribe, after all. Maybe he hates you, but I brought you to national radio. I believe I might be the kike in question.

Line 1: Keep spreading your poison, whoresons. People are dying while you talk. Dying because of you.

JC: What are you saying?

TG: Ok, that's enough of Mr. Happy…

JC: Wait a sec, Tom. What are you talking about?

Line 1: Open a window. Listen.

JC: [censored]

TG: Don't give this cretin any credence.

Prod. Mike: Jacks.

TG: He's a crank! You're a crank, a loser and a moron, Don! You have no power, no brains and, look at this, you're calling from Jersey!

JC: Danny?

TG: I'm hanging up on you, Don! I'm condemning you back into powerless, harmless obscurity!

Prod. Mike: Jacks, we've got a live feed here on the monitor. There are people being assaulted all over the country. They're being dragged out of their cars…

Line 1: We will proclaim liberty to those taken captive and proclaim the year of good will and a day of vengeance for our God.

JC: I didn't think they'd do it.

TG: Do what?

Prod. Mike: Dozens of underground religious groups are taking responsibility for this action. 35 cities have been affected so far. And, Jacks?

Line 1: We're setting free the souls you have corrupted. But, you? You will be punished.

Prod. Mike: Jacks, they've got the building surrounded.

Chapter Five

Day two.

I awoke, stiff and numb from the desert cold, with visions of manna, God's own breakfast. Instead I found John, sitting on the opposite side of the remains of our fire, staring at me.

"Where's breakfast?" I asked, stretching and trying to appear nonplussed by the implication that this lunatic could have been staring at me, tripping and paranoid, for the entire night.

"The same place it was yesterday, boy." It seemed my monologue from the previous night hadn't gone over well, either.

Believe me when I tell you this: It personally shames me to admit that, as a child, I liked to poke angry dogs with sticks. My only defense is that it's ingrained into my personality. So, as Lenny Bruce used to say, "the fault lies in the manufacturer. It's just that cold, Jim."

"I was just thinking God would provide. I mean, we're out here doing His work, right?" Even if you *asked* me, I couldn't explain why my mouth does what it does in moments like those. I mean, if you offered me real money, I couldn't explain it. It's possible I never outgrew the suicidal tendencies of my adolescence. I just don't know.

"You Dare!" He stood. He pointed. He took every stereotypical posture and gesture conceivable. It was hysterical!

"John. Calm yourself, brother. It's far too early for such drama." James attempted to cool tempers without even turning or looking up from his sleeping position. I imagined that this was an all-too-familiar scene for him.

"He wants Our Lord, Jehovah to cater to him? Blasphemy!"

"He did set precedent back in Egypt, you know. We're Jews, we're in the desert, I just kind of assumed there'd be manna." I got up and dusted myself off.

That actually knocked the wind out of John for a moment. He was still pointing and posturing, but the only thing coming out of his mouth was, "He…" and "Ut…I" and other incoherentness. He looked to Peter for support, but the big man was still snoring deeply a few feet behind him. James, however, turned around then.

"Judas, did you take a blow to the head recently?" He covered his eyes against the rising sun and cautiously surveyed me.

"If I did, I think I've got a suspect." I looked John straight in the eye. The fact that I didn't burst into flames before falling back into a chasm which opened directly to Hell was shaking John's faith to the core.

"Because I've spent almost every night in the desert with you for the last month and you've never acted like this. Besides," he continued as he sat up and slapped the dust off his legs. "You know we had our manna last night."

That caused me to pause.

Could it be true? I considered. *They wandered in the desert for forty years sustaining themselves on hallucinogens?*

Then I realized that it would explain the long, strange trip, and resumed packing.

Peter woke up. "What's for breakfast?"

John stormed off, kicking Andrew's feet to rouse him as he went. About twenty yards out of camp, he picked up some stones and began throwing them in the direction of a nearby mountain. He stayed out there until we were ready to walk again.

# # #

A few hours into the trip, I asked Andrew how much further it was to Nazareth.

"Why, Judas," John interjected. "Did you not expect Jehovah to create some great puff of wind to blow us there?"

I let that one go. Peter, on the other hand, was appalled.

"John! You know better! Using Our Lord Jehovah's Name...!"

"But...he...! I didn't...! You weren't awake!" John sped up his stride to escape the big man.

"We'll be in Nazareth some time before dusk," Andrew said, a bit disdainfully. I looked to John up ahead, searching for signs that he might have heard Andrew's tone. He seemed to be preoccupied in his own thoughts while trying to ignore Peter's lecturing. So I quietly altered my pace and direction to sidle up to Andrew in as casual a manner as I could manage.

"Have I offended you, Andrew?" I posed the question with genuine sincerity. Too often, my rallying against the powers can offend a third party I never considered. I'd gotten to where I could pinpoint the signs almost immediately.

"I don't know what has happened to you." Andrew looked at me without slowing his stride. His tone was measured. "Jesus' teachings are important to me. They were important to you. It's fine if they're not anymore, but that doesn't mean you should stay here and mock us."

I felt like a schmuck. Up until that moment I had been reacting on pure righteousness, from some overpowering moral imperative. It's easy to tear down the nutballs while educating those who simply don't know better. Did I have the right to question people, like Andrew, who had possibly made a thoughtful and informed choice about where to place their faith? Did I have the right to shatter that faith which, right or wrong, they rely on so heavily in their day-to-day lives? I decided I wasn't in any shape to answer that question there and then.

"Jesus promises me a future outside of fishing, Judas. Jesus believes in me as a man. When we work with him, I feel like someone who can make a difference. A contribution. I thought you felt that way too."

"I apologize for any offense, Andrew. We're doing something that will affect a lot of people here. I'm having some problems dealing with that, but I'll try not to be so flippant."

He nodded in acceptance of my statement before veering off to our left. I understood that the discussion was closed and slowed my pace to separate us even more. I reached into the leather pouch on my waist, pulled out a small piece of salty, dehydrated meat and stuck it on my tongue. I hoped that would be enough to keep my mouth shut for a while.

# # #

About mid-morning we instinctively moved into a single file, each pulling out two small sticks from our bedrolls. We tied some thick scarves to the ends, and looped the other ends into our belts, all without having to stop or even slow our pace. Within minutes we were our own little caravan, walking in step, with our heads protected from the midday sun by a small, traveling tent. For all our foibles, I walked in time with these simple, smelly fishermen, and glowed with pride for our species.

I was back on Earth, among humans, for the first time in something like twenty years. We walk, we talk, we plan, we create; we evolve. And I had a choice, as a human being, to allow history to develop as it had originally unfurled, its destiny created by aliens, or to give us a fresh start to develop our own myths.

The memory of my closest friends hit me like a dialog box announcing a crashed server. (Judge) Scott, (Convention) Darlene and (Excess) Danny: the Triumvirate. What would have happened if I accepted Lucifer's offer to become the Judgment of all Humanity? So ironic that I declined then, only to find myself now having to make exactly the kind of decision I had wanted to avoid.

I kicked at stones in the road and watched Peter's feet as he walked ahead of me. A warm breeze blew through our little makeshift tent. I immediately flashed to being a boy back in Ft. Wayne. Some miserable-hot summers in Indiana, let me tell you. And my grandparents didn't believe in air-conditioning, of course. Visiting my grandma meant sitting real still in her perfect, doily-and-plastic wrapped living room while she knitted. The sweat slowly trickled down our faces, arms, legs and back, while we listened to the music from "her generation": Kenny Rogers, Lionel Richie, Barry Manilow. Ugh. I don't know how such a useless and arduous time in my former life brought such a broad smile, but it did. Sometimes she'd let my brother and me read comics, so that was cool. And, as much as I hate to admit it, some of the music I liked. James Taylor. He was OK.

I looked up to make sure no one was talking. Let me stress: this seemed like a REALLY good idea. I knew songs from over 2000 years in the future! I mean, technically I knew songs from another planet, but you have to be underwater and breathing through osmosis to recreate those notes, so my excitement remained steadfast on Earth. I probably knew a song for every situation. I could be a great singer/songwriter in this life, relying on songs stolen from the future. It just seemed really cool. More than slightly unethical, but really cool nonetheless. Right then, the perfect James Taylor song was jumping around in my head. I nodded to myself, took a deep breath and, quietly—not broadcasting for the whole desert, or anything—began to sing.

"Moving in quiet desperation—Keeping an eye on the Holy Land"

"What! What did he say about 'Holy Land?'"

"A hypothetical situation—Who is this walking man?"

I had my eyes closed, but I could feel a ruckus in our tent poles. Someone was stepping out of line. I didn't care. It felt good to sing this song my grandmother made me listen to when I was a kid.

"Well the leaves have started turning…" was as far as I got before being shoved roughly to the ground. I looked up to see John, furious as usual, being held back by James and Peter (which *was* a bit surprising).

"That is not a song taught in the synagogue! Songs *not* from the teachers are from Satan! I say we leave him out here in the Hell he's made for himself!" He anxiously looked to the others for support. Considering how upset he was with me earlier, I was taken aback when Andrew stepped up to my defense. "John, we'll be in Nazareth by sundown. That's the first thing. Second of all…" Even though it was my ass on the line, it was fun to watch him come up with some other point. "Second of all, Jesus has told all of us that we will be the new teachers, did he not? Judas was just preparing a new song in praise of Jehovah, weren't you, Judas?"

James was giving me a hand up while Andrew stood between the still maniacally irate John and myself. "Yeah, that's right. Just trying to be a good teacher for Jesus." I dusted myself off.

"Get in line," was John's only response.

"Um, I've got some business to take care of first," I said. I strolled over to some ragged brush, tugging at my robes as if to pee.

I didn't have to pee. I was pissed! Son-of-a-bitch took the first opportunity to lay his hands on me and wanted to leave me to die! Of course, having my (or, Judas') penis in my hand, waving it out in the air, made me have to piss after all. I looked around at the three men trying to placate the one madman, watched their shadows straining toward me, felt how full my bladder still was, and decided it was time for another song. This time, I *did* broadcast for the whole desert.

"What if Jehovah was one of us?—Just a slob like one of us?—Just a stranger on a bus, trying to find His way home?"

I heard the primal, guttural noise that he made when breaking away from the other men. I kept my back to them, even as they yelled to warn me that he was coming, and even as the hurried, angry footsteps came nearer. I waited until I saw his shadow overtake my legs. That's when I turned to greet the maniac, pissing on his feet as he rushed up to assault me again. He stood there, trying to process what had just happened, when I clocked him with a roundhouse.

I tapped, stepped over him and quietly joined the rest of the apostles.

James was legitimately concerned. "Did you just kill my brother?"

I looked back. John moaned and grabbed his face.

"He'll be fine. I, on the other hand, don't think I'll be joining you the rest of the way to Nazareth."

Andrew pointed to the East. "Go that way. There's a town called Nain. It's actually less time there than Nazareth, it's just not on our route. Our Aunt owns an inn there. Her name is Sara. Peter was named after her deceased husband, Simon. Tell her you're a friend and you can stay for the price of labor."

"Thanks, Andrew. I'll see everyone in Cana, at the wedding. I think it'd be best if Jesus was present the next time John and I met." Everyone nodded, including Peter (although I don't think he really understood).

I hurried off into the desert as the sun cooled and a groggy apostle heated up.

●

A life should be made out of countless significant moments. Unfortunately, some lives have had only one or none at all. Don Owens lived 38 years before having one. His life would have a total of four. Not so bad really.

In July of 1998, Don Owens was living in a 400-sqare-foot trailer home in Clearwater, Florida. He made a living selling antiques and collectibles on weekends, in shopping malls around the Southeast.

At 38 years of age, Donald P. Owens weighed 375 pounds, drank an average of a case of beer each evening, had already passed three monumental kidney stones the hard route, and lived with a woman who may or may not have had his child a few months prior. She had a child. It may or may not have been his.

On this particular Monday morning, Don struggled to roll out of his permanently concave double bed. His right shoulder blade spasming from uncomfortable sleep, he grabbed the Formica counter and hoisted himself up.

"Andrea!"

No answer. It wasn't like she couldn't hear him from the other end of their home. She must have gone to work.

She better've moved those cases of Playboy from the truck to the shed. I shouldn't have to do every fucking thing myself.

This morning, as incalculable mornings had before, began with Don delicately peeling his ballsack from his inner thigh, hiccuping and belching simultaneously, removing a Red, White & Blue beer from his 10-cubic-foot refrigerator, popping the top while toasting to no one in particular, "Hair of the dog," and swallowing a significant percentage of the can's contents before shuffling to the closet/toilet to deposit used samples of much the same liquid. It was the note taped over the toilet seat that made this morning different from all the rest.

Hi Hon,

I hope your not pissed about me dropping Celia on you. She gets cranky if she's not with you all the time. You need to get her to her ped doc at the clinic at 2:30. I couldn't get my shift changed. I'll be home bout 4ish.

xxoo Andy

Don swayed at the note, one hand holding the door frame, one holding his prick, both attempting unsuccessfully to work in unison to keep him from pissing on his own seat and/or feet.

He couldn't make any sense out of it. He looked back over his shoulder to the empty bungee swing attached to the trailer door. She wasn't there. She wasn't crying like she does when she's *not* in the bungee swing. She wasn't in the trailer. What the hell was Andrea playing at?

He swung his head back to read the note again when his shoulder cramped like it had when he was getting up.

That mattress is terrible, he thought. *We've got to get a new one.*

"We've got to get a new mattress, Don," was exactly what Andrea was saying when she was in the trailer that morning. The memory faded-in as he concentrated on the last few shakes of urine.

Andrea was complaining about the lumpy, piece-of-shit mattress when she was dropping off Celia. She put the baby on his enormous stomach and ran out. Someone had driven her to his place and they were outside, revving an engine. She was frantic to go.

I dreamed that.

His shoulder flared in pain again.

I dreamed she brought little Celia and put her on my belly and she crawled over and over and then I was dreaming about sunbathing on a cruise ship.

And I was all stretched out.

And his shoulder hurt, as if he slept on it wrong.

Don's mind immediately reverted to the previous year when Andy told him she was pregnant. He had no intention of taking on that kind of responsibility, but there it was. She may as well have driven over him with his own truck. He ran from the trailer that day. He felt trapped, like he couldn't breathe. Getting her pregnant was the dumbest thing he'd ever done, in a lifetime of doing dumb things.

As bad as he felt on the day Andrea dropped that father-thing on him, he longed to return to that day with every pounding, frantic step toward the rumpled, lifeless bed.

Fathering a child, it turned out, hardly changed his life at all. Smothering the baby, accidentally or not, had consequences.

CHAPTER SIX

It was dusk before I stopped looking over my shoulder to see if some enraged apostle was stalking me.

The sun was setting to my back and the stars faded into view as if someone was slowly turning up a dimmer switch.

It really was gorgeous. Without electricity, or even a major populace to speak of, there was no haze or atmospheric interference. The cosmic light shone with an intensity that I would have not found anywhere on the planet in my day.

Of course, thinking of that forced me to recall the fact that I was truly alone, out of time and place. I knew the language, sure, but I had only a rudimentary understanding of how life functioned in this age. How was I going to survive? What were the social rules I needed to follow? Did I have a job? A wife or family? The more time that passed since the transference, the less I was able to connect with the memories of the man whose body I now inhabited.

It brought to mind the anguished eviction of Judas' soul. Was that what death would be like for all of us? Were we all destined to be unceremoniously ripped from our corporal forms and cast out into the ether?

It was a depressing thought. Walking across a strange desert to a town I didn't know and a life I never made, singing to myself seemed the best defense against a nervous breakdown. I felt no compulsion to translate, opting to sing in English instead.

"A stone's throw from Jerusalem, I walked a lonely man in the moonlight, "And though a million stars where shining, my thoughts were lost on a distant planet, "Which whirls around an April moon, whirling in an arc of sadness…"

"What language is that?" The question came from directly behind me.

"Jesus!" This was my standard response to being surprised. As I spun around to see who could have snuck up on me out here, in the middle of absolutely nowhere, I realized I would have to learn some new form of expression.

See, I got it right on the first guess.

●

Tears flowed freely down Don's face as his rectum was torn even wider. *Getting fucked by a nigger. I'm so sorry, daddy.*

Prison life had not been good to Don.

The prosecution had little problem convincing a jury that the smothering of little Celia had been anything but an act of depraved jealousy. Don's own Public Defender was ill-equipped to fight the years of tabloid fodder at the close of the twentieth century—where heartless parents murdered their own children and then hid behind pleas of temporary insanity due to their own tragic upbringing. It didn't help when, after learning that the person waiting in the car for Andrea that day was her boss (who also happened to be Celia's real father), Don threatened to kill him *too*.

He wasn't rich. He wasn't a celebrity. He got the maximum.

Ten years later, Don was bent over a workbench in the janitor's closet of the Stark Correctional Institution's rec room, arms held out by two burly inmates, each waiting his turn.

Grover, a massive, violent lifer, was the lead dog of their grounds. Whatever your jones, Grover was the connection. But, sometimes, payment was a real pain in the ass.

Don had years of self-loathing, regret and despair, which translated quite neatly into a hard-core drug dependency once he got put "inside." He wasn't choosy about his anesthesia. Whatever herb, pill, powder, injection or inhalant became available, he found it. He gave up meals for drugs (and lost over 150 pounds), performed innumerable, mindless chores to curry favors from dealers, and even beat a complete stranger nearly to death with a lunch tray in an effort to make payment. This hot August day he was reduced, for the first time, to sacrifice what he saw as his last piece of self-respect, for a weekend's worth of crank.

Grover's nails almost broke the skin on Don's thighs as he pounded away. Sweat poured from the giant's forehead, dripping onto Don's bare back.

Oddly, the dealer was preoccupied with discussing the quality of the heroin he was expecting the following week.

"You'll be back, cracker," he said, still pounding away. "Once you've had a taste of this shit today, you'll be beggin' ol' Grover to lay his pipe on ya'! But the shit my bitch's bringing in next week is so fuckin' good, I might be raisin' the price!"

Grover stepped up his thrust as if to punctuate, grunted and released, just as the door to the closet was yanked open from the outside.

"The fuck?" Grover turned, still dripping, and faced the intrusion.

Don couldn't decide if he was embarrassed, scared or relieved.

I just need a hit, was his mental mantra.

"What'cha doin', Grover?" The figure of a slim man leaned comfortably in the doorway.

"Preacher?" Grover shielded his eyes against the midday rec room's overpowering light. He expressed no immediate remorse, or even a need to hitch up his pants from around his ankles. "You need to be more careful 'bout which doors you openin'."

"Oh, I've got the right door. All finished I see?"

"I'm done. But Nailz and Orangejello (pron. Ore-AN-jilloe) gots to get their jimmies shined yet." He finally reached down and pulled up his prison togs. Once fastened, he gripped one of Don's red butt-cheeks. "You want sloppy fourths? Don't know how much'll be left…"

"No, no," the unassuming man waived off the invitation. "Actually, I'm here to take him off your hands."

Nailz and Orangejello bristled at this, pulling Don's arms even more taunt. Grover looked back and told them "no" without saying a word.

Letting the door close behind him, the man with the clerical collar reached into his jacket breast-pocket, pulled out an envelope and handed it to the lead dog.

Grover fingered through the envelope and smiled broadly. "I don't know how and why you do this shit, preacher-man. But I ain't much for caren', either. Lez go, bitches."

"That's wack, G! I got work here, bro!" Don didn't know if it was Nailz or Orangejello that protested. All he wanted to know was how and when he was getting his hit.

"Fuck your work, bitch! I say so, you're sucking my ass in the fuckin' yard, mutherfucker! Get the fuck out of here!"

The middle-aged man stepped away agreeably while Grover prodded his men out of the closet with rabbit punches to the backs of their heads.

"Don't you ever face me in front of some crackers, bitch!"

The door closed, leaving Don, still bent over the bench and silently crying, alone with the stranger.

"Hello, Don," the man began. "My name is Max Swanson. They call me Minister Max."

"What do you want me to do," Don asked, sniffing back tears and trying to sound business-like.

If he doesn't like you, you won't get the hit.

"First I'd like you to pull up your pants, Don. Then have a seat."

Don did as he was told. He fastened his own togs, started to sit on the stool next to the workbench, winced, and opted to lean.

"Sorry," said the handsome, kind-looking Max. "I wasn't thinking. Want some gum?"

"I need a hit."

"Yes, you do," said the minister. He pulled out a piece of Wrigley's Spearmint and drew it into his mouth, biting it into three pieces as it went. "But I'm hoping you won't need any more after that. Are you aware just how badly life can get for you from this point on? Not just what Nailz and Or-ange-jello would've made of you if I hadn't come in. Grover will force you into more and more acts of degradation until you're permanently damaged…or dead. Do you get this?"

"I guess."

"But it can stop right here. And do you know who's going to help you stop?"

"You." Don stated with a fatalistic sigh. He didn't want to be saved. He wanted a hit.

"Jesus, Don. Jesus is going to help you. It's going to be a long road, but Jesus will see you through."

Don shifted. He was raw and leaking uncomfortably. If the preacher wasn't giving him a hit, he figured, the preacher had better damn well shut the fuck up.

"Where's Jesus been up 'till now? Where was Jesus when Celia died? Where was Jesus *before* that nigger fucked me? Fuck Jesus! I need a hit!"

"Be careful, Don. Jesus was with you through all of that," Max said, while again reaching into his breast pocket. This time he produced a full syringe and a packaged alcohol swab. "He's just waiting. Waiting for you to reach out. Waiting for you to finally admit that you need Him."

This time the tears welled up from relief. "I need him. Bad."

Keeping the needle just out of Don's reach, Max made sure he had his most recent convert's attention.

"I've been talking to Dr. Harrelson, the prison psychiatrist. He doesn't think you meant to smother your daughter."

"She wasn't mine. Can I have the needle, please?"

"You don't even know what's in it, Don."

"Doesn't matter. Can I have it, please?"

"Did you mean to kill her, Don?" Max held up the syringe to Don's eye level. "Yes or no, you get this either way. I promise."

"No. I was still drunk when Andy dropped her on me. I would never have…" Don lowered his head, but he continued to hold out his hand. "May I please have the needle?"

"I need you, Don. You and more like you. The broken and beaten, honest and loving Christians who've been forgotten and neglected by society. You will help me lead them by example. I want you to be a soldier. I want you to lead by examples both bitter in failure and exquisite in success.

"Folks have washed away from the flock in waves. When that whole Y2K scare fizzled, people lost sight of the fact that Our Lord keeps His own organizer. Just because he doesn't show up when it's a convenient date on their calendar, doesn't mean he doesn't have us penciled in up ahead somewhere. It's my feeling that we need to put the fear of God back into these folks. It's the only way to get society back in line. And God only helps those who help themselves, y'know what I'm saying?"

"Please?"

"Are you with me, Don?"

"Yes." He had no will to spare. The shakes were coming, and his anus hurt so bad.

"Do you accept Jesus Christ as your Lord and Savior?"

"Yes. please. anything."

"Here ya' go sport. A little methadone to take away the hurt, courtesy of the Church of the Modern Light."

Max extended his hand a bare few inches. Don gratefully snatched the needle, brushing the alcohol swab to the closet floor. Looking around in near despair, he grabbed an extension cord and tied it around his bicep.

"I'll be stopping in once a week to look into your progress. You're up for parole in eight months. Do you want out, Don? I can offer you purpose and a new way of life, but you have to want this."

"S-sounds g-great," was the best Don could manage while gripping the extension cord between his teeth. He was desperately trying to steady the needle.

Can you shut up for a second? I just need this hit.

The minister sighed. "Give me that."

Max stealthily located the vein and inserted the second of foreign objects to enter Don that day.

"We're going to get you cleaned up for a higher purpose, m'man. No more of this getting raped by mongrels for you."

"Uh-huh." Teeth still clenched as the plunger hit home.

I just need this hit. I just neeeed…-

Don poured himself onto the stool.

"There, that's better. You ready?"

"Are we going to meet Jesus?" Don smiled a doped-up, vacuous smile.

"Close." Max helped Don up, supporting his weight on one side. "We're taking you to the infirmary. We'll get your basement stitched up, and get that satanic monkey off your back. You're officially on the road to recovery."

"Hmph. 'Covery," Don chuckled at nothing in particular.

Meeting Minister Max was the second significant moment in Don's life, and he would retain only the vaguest recollection.

"And who's responsible for setting you back on the path, Don?" Max opened the door and gingerly guided his soldier out of the closet.

"Jesus?" His answer echoed in the empty rec room, traveling across the ping-pong table and broken down Hammersmith & Sons piano, reverberating out the steel-mesh covered jalousie windows and into the summer afternoon.

"Atta boy."

CHAPTER SEVEN

"What language, Judas?"

Now this was surreal. I stood in the desert night, face-to-face with Jesus Christ, the Messiah, the Lamb of God, trying to explain what "English" meant.

"Years from now, these people called the Anglos are going to run into some other folks called the Saxons, and they'll bastardize languages from Latin to Slavic. Their posterity will sail off to the other side of the world, practically, and then they'll bastardize it even more. That's what you heard me singing. If you can call it that."

My face must have been a mass of confusion even as I tried to make sense of this for him. I mean, I grew up with priests and nuns beating me over the head with the idea that Christ *was* God. Not just some aspect or piece of the Creator, mind you, but the literal personification of the One True God. How demoralizing it would have been for Father Goodman or Sister Dacherman, I thought, that if they could travel back in time somehow and have no way to communicate with this man they presumed to be all-knowing. It was obvious that even the term Latin would fall on uncomprehending ears.

"Anyhow, it's a song by this guy who called himself Sting. He was one of my Grandmother's favorites."

"The council said you were something of a lateral thinker…"

"They have no idea."

"Well, I just thought I'd see how you were managing. I wanted to make sure you're acclimating okay. I was surprised to see you separated from the group."

We continued to stroll as we conversed, mostly by my direction. I just couldn't stand and look at this man eye-to-eye. First of all, he was charismatically stunning. His eyes had the fiery conviction of Muhammad Ali, Malcolm X and Patton rolled in together. Looking into those eyes convinced you that he could win…anything. But there was a tenderness to them as well. I found myself staring ahead when I spoke to him. I couldn't look into those eyes and say everything I needed to say.

"The group and I had a parting of the ways. Or John and I did at any rate."

"Well, I'm sure it's nothing that can't be mended. We're on a mission here, and the focus of that mission is to lead these people to a new age. Now, I understand things were difficult for you back home…"

"Jesus, I *am* home."

I told him everything then, starting with Times Square. The journey to Hell and Lucifer's offer, reincarnation on that torturous planet, being blasted across the galaxies, right up to him materializing out of nowhere just moments previous; everything. We were approaching a large dune about the time I finished. I turned and sat down at the base of the hill in a frustrated heap. Jesus sat down beside me.

"Well, that's quite a journey. But you're here now, and I'm glad to have a person with such varied experiences on my team. Right now there are certain goals we're expected to achieve on this planet and it's going to take some focus on your part to make sure we achieve them."

"What?" I was incredulous. "That's it? Sorry about the whole tearing-your-life-a-new-one thing, but we've got to move on? This sucks!"

I looked at those eyes again. They were neither surprised nor insulted by my outburst. But they didn't display an ounce of sympathy either. It was the first I'd clued into the fact that his demeanor was going to be pretty much consistent regardless of the circumstance. I felt a chill.

"There's nothing I can do to rectify everything that's happened to you recently…"

"Recently," I chuckled. "You mean after the 20 years on your planet? The 2000 years I've lost on this one? Define 'recently' for me."

"But, as I've said, you're here now," he continued, unabated by my sarcasm. "We have an agenda which, once it is met, will set this planet back on the correct course of spiritual healing."

"That's the problem, Mr. Christ, sir. I'm not convinced it will." I faced him then, taking the chance that his overwhelming congeniality wouldn't sway me from these convictions. I needed for him to really listen to me and take me seriously.

"What we're about to do is to create a new system of elitism. An alarming amount of people who follow your teachings will become very intolerant of any opposing, or even slightly dissimilar views. People will become so convinced that yours is the only true path, they will convert others by any means, including torture. And that's only if they don't kill them outright. It will happen again and again for 2000 years, and probably long after that. Now, I understand that you only have my word to go on this, since you're not nearly as omniscient as your followers will believe, but I know this for a fact. I just don't know if I can be a party to it."

"I have no doubt that what you're saying is true. I can only hope you'll trust me when I say that it's necessary." He said this with the same unflustered, casual expression he'd carried since I was downloaded to this God-forsaken place.

"I don't think I could ever believe that," I began, trying to keep from becoming emotional. "I don't have exact figures, I doubt they even exist. But I'm confident when I say that the numbers are probably around the tens of millions. Tens of millions of people beaten, raped, slaughtered or worse. Yes, worse. The Inquisition alone brought a new, fresh Hell to Earth in your name. And you're okay with that? Why?"

"Growth will always involve a certain amount of attrition."

"Attrition? We're talking about living, breathing people! Not some stats in a corporate spreadsheet!"

"It's all part of a process. We went through the same manner of grow-ing pains on our planet. Every developed society we've studied pro-gressed in almost the exact same fashion. This species is no different. There will come a time when they will advance enough to know the error in killing for an unsubstantiated belief. But they have to make the journey alone. We just set them in the right direction."

"What if you don't?"

"I don't understand."

"What if you don't set them in the 'right direction?' What if, just for shits and giggles, you leave well enough alone? What's the harm in that? It's not like you're promoting anything too novel. Do onto others as you'd have them do unto you, right? We could probably figure that out for ourselves."

"Do onto others is the golden rule. We're trying to improve on that foundation by the time we take our message to the people. Something more like 'Look the other way…'"

"You mean, 'Turn the other cheek?'"

"There you go! Now you're thinking!" It was the most enthusiastic he'd been during the whole discussion.

"Oy." I put my head in my hands. "*You* said that! I'm just quoting *you*, for Christ's sake! And, y'know what? No one turns the other cheek! If you do, you're a sucker for giving some asshole another chance to tag you."

"Really? *I* said you should turn the other cheek? Hm. I wonder if I came up with it or it was one of the staff. Turn the other cheek. Sounds like me!" He beamed a smile at me, full of modest pride. I think he was having fun with me at that point. I looked at his smile and looked back at the sand and rocks.

"They're going to kill you, y'know. And I'm supposed to ensure that it happens."

Jesus was still smiling as he got up and stretched.

"We've all got our parts to play, Judas. Tell you what: why don't you rejoin the group and spend some time with the people of this world.

According to your story, you've been gone awhile. I'd be interested to see how you feel things will proceed without some kind of guidance. I'll make sure John won't give you too much of a problem. Then, if you still feel that teaching people about love and understanding will bring more harm than good, we should discuss it. Agreed?"

He stretched out his hand, both as a symbol of truce and to help me to my feet.

"Well," I began as I allowed him to help me up. "It's obvious you're not going to take anything I say to heart right here and now. And, frankly, I'm a little too tired to continue the debate. I think I'll stay in Nain tonight. I'll meet up with them tomorrow."

"Whatever you think is best."

It didn't dawn on me until I reached the top of the dune that Jesus wasn't following me. To be honest, I was lost in thought right up until I crested the top and saw that I was within a half-mile or so of a town.

I looked back to say something astoundingly intelligent like, "Hey! We're right outside a city!" when I finally realized he was gone. Looking back toward the meager light of the town entrance, I noticed a small group of men making their way toward the gates. Somehow we were right outside Nazareth.

"Showoff." I made my way down the dune, wondering what exactly I should tell the rest of the apostles once I caught up with them.

●

"We're taking back what's ours. The day of Christ is at hand."

Tom wasn't in the mood to banter with Don anymore. In the offices outside the studio, people were obviously panicked. He had eleven minutes before his next scheduled break, but it was better to cut bait and float than to get dragged down with the chum.

"Going to let you go now, Don. And of course you know the quickest way to Jersey…" With the push of two buttons Don was disconnected and a flushing toilet sound bite rushed over the airwaves. "Now that

Don's safely tucked back in, we'll be right back to the Tom Green Radio Hour after this dribble." Clicking off his mike, Tom signaled his producer. "Wake up, Billy! I need some commercials here!"

Jackson was almost in the production booth before the On Air sign blinked off.

"What's the story, Danny?"

Danny and Billy where both glued to the computer monitor in the far corner of the booth.

"This is pretty fucked up right here, Jacks," Danny started. "It looks amazingly well organized too. Anybody with a Darwin fish or anti-Christian sentiment on their car or person is just getting hammered. Arrests are into the dozens. And they just started with the book burnings."

"Are you kidding me? What year *is* this?" Jackson turned away from the monitor and looked out into the offices. "It's pandemonium out there. Where are the cops?"

"There's up to a thousand people in the street out front," Danny noted. "And it's not like they're allowed to carry guns in the city anymore. It could take them awhile to push through."

Someone began screaming in the station's reception area, loud enough to be heard inside the soundproof booth.

"Now what?" Tom was treating this more like an annoyance than anything else. "Dude, I have to recommend that you conduct interviews from your house from now on."

"Better your house than George Carlin's," Danny commented, still surfing the news sites. "They're burning that place to the ground as we speak."

"For the love of Christ." Carlin was one of Tom's first guests when the radio show began in 2004.

"I think that's supposed to be the idea," Jackson said as he opened the door to the outer offices.

"They're inside the building! They're tearing the place apart!"

People ran back and forth through the cubicles and halls. Panic ruled supreme. Jackson quietly stepped back into the booth, closed the door and lit a cigarette.

"Just when you think there are no surprises left in this town," he said.

Billy looked at Cross as if the writer had just gone insane. "You can't light up in here!"

"Shut up, Billy," barked Tom. He then reached into his shirt pocket and pulled out his own pack of smokes. "Make yourself useful and see if you can get the security camera feed on that thing."

"I guess that was kind of stupid," Billy admitted, sheepishly. Pulling up the KFX2 Intranet site, he quickly entered a password and pulled up camera options. "Looks like they're pretty much contained in the lobby. They won't be able to get to the stairs or elevators without a passkey."

While he spoke, two men on camera picked up a long coffee table from the sitting area, marched passed the (presumably) abandoned receptionist desk and flung it through the plate-glass doors which were designed to separate the building's reception from the elevator banks.

"Holy shit." This came from Jackson, Danny, Tom and Billy in unison. Gaping at the computer, they watched the silent, horrific footage of dozens of righteous men and women crawling, pushing and shoving over broken glass.

"Isn't there some procedure for something like this," asked Billy, trying to sound less petrified than he really was.

"For *what*, Billy?" Tom retorted. "Could *you* have foreseen an instance where a raging mob would storm the building? What kind of 'procedure' could they possibly have planned?"

It was that moment when, simultaneously, the computer blinked off, the control panel went dead, the lights flashed out and the air conditioning stopped.

"Son-of-a-bitch. Maybe they *did* have a plan."

"I don't think so, Tom," Cross disagreed. "It could be that they wanted to kill the power to keep looters out of the elevators, or it could be that the freaks downstairs want to limit *our* options."

"Either way," commented Danny. "I'm kinda glad we're thirty floors up."

"How many floors in this place?"

"Sixty-five, Mr. Cross," Billy eagerly responded.

"May as well not lose our head start. Who feels like hiking some stairs?"

The four men cautiously stepped from the booth. The offices were dark and empty. Emergency floodlights only contributed to the siege-like atmosphere of the vacant floor.

Billy took the lead.

"We should go to the southeast stairwell. It's furthest away from the elevators."

"Wait a sec. I want to get our stuff from the green room." Danny broke away from the group and started to jog back in the direction of the lounge. Upon turning the corner, his face ran directly into the chest of someone who appeared to be Secret Service: black suit, black shades, earpiece and crew cut.

"Jackson Cross," the giant inquired. Another, identically dressed man moved up behind the first, and glared down at Danny.

"Oh shit. A little help here?!"

Jacks, Tom and Billy were behind Danny within seconds.

"Who the hell are *you*?" demanded Tom, trying to sound like he had some kind of authority over the situation.

"Jackson Cross?"

"Who's asking, jar head?"

"Tom?" This came from behind the two grim goliaths.

"Stu?"

Stu Petermen, the station manager, delicately stepped out from behind the two large men in the hall. He came up to about their waists.

Sweat was pouring across his receding hairline and the few hairs he had managed to comb over looked like seaweed at low tide.

"Mr. Cross? I think it's best if you went with these gentlemen."

Giant Number One (being the only one who spoke up to that point) followed the direction of Stu's eyes as he addressed the group. He immediately locked in on Jackson. "We have been charged with getting you to an appointment, Mr. Cross. It's time to go."

"Now just a damn minute!" Tom stepped between Jackson and Giant Number One and was summarily shoved against the wall. Each of the gargantuans took one of Jackson's arms and marched him toward the nearest stairwell.

"Watch the threads, man!"

"That's the main stairwell," Billy called out after them. "They'll be coming up that way for sure!"

"Maybe that's why they're taking him that way," Tom noted from a crumpled position on the hall floor. He watched helplessly as Danny tried to keep pace with the grim captors. "They're going to fuckin' execute him."

"They're not part of the riot," Stu confided as he squatted down next to his radio personality. "They work for the Chairman."

"You're not serious."

Stu silently nodded.

Tom looked around and found his still-smoldering cigarette on the floor. As he returned it to his lips and dragged, he heard the stairwell door close behind the four men. He looked up, shaken and confused, at his producer and station manager. Each of them looked as if they'd just been through a war.

"What the hell is going on?"

The apes shoved/carried Jackson up almost 20 flights of stairs before he could finally wrangle free. Even as they lost grip on his arms, they were scratching at him to get him back under control.

"Hey, hey, hey! Hang on a sec!" Jacks waved his arms about, funky-chicken style, to stay out of reach. "Somebody's gonna tell me what the fuck's going on around here!"

Giant Number One was actually a bit winded. "Sir, we truthfully don't want to hurt you, but we have our orders." He said all this in a calm, rational tone before frantically trying to grab at Jackson again, who was backing up the steps and slapping all four of the grabbing hands.

"Danny? Little help here!"

A good flight-and-a-half down, the raspy, exhausted response came, "Right there with ya, Jacks." Deep, agonizing breath, "Gonna carve those guys new assholes." Then, a barely audible, "Oh god." Jackson presumed the next sound he heard was that of his best friend collapsing on unforgiving stairs.

"Shit."

The pair of hulks rushed him and took hold again.

"Goddammit! What's going on?!"

Jackson heard a door open some floors below. "Who's that? What's he doing in here? Get him!"

Cross tensed up in the muscle-men's grip. "'Get him?' Oh, fuck." He turned to meet the face of Giant Number One. "You gotta help him. You guys gotta!"

With his pleas proving to be ineffectual, Jackson began to panic. He envisioned Epstein greeting a batch of rushing lunatics in the stairwell, "Get Off The Cross" emblazoned on his chest.

"Danny! Take off the shirt! Take off the fucking T-shirt, Danny! I'm not kidding!"

He began to kick and wail, but the monstrous bastards had thoroughly unsympathetic grips at this point. They were even doing double-time. Jackson couldn't distinguish the stamping of their feet over the rising chorus of the mobs rushing steps. He thought he heard someone say, "He's one of Cross' people!" God help him, it sounded like Beth, the publicist.

"Well FUCK YOU TOO, Danny! I never want to see your face again, you fuck! You hear me? We are not now, NOR EVER WERE FRIENDS, MOTHERFUCKER!"

They still had ten flights to go.

Upon the approach of the final landing, Moe and Curly were barely keeping themselves up. Of course, Jacks wasn't making it any easier for them. They had to drag his feet up each step while he remained perfectly limp and listless in their arms.

"If anything's happened to him, I'll pay someone to fuck the two of you up. You got me, you emotionless pricks? I know *I'm* no threat, but I'll find somebody who is, and I'll meet his price."

Their expressions never revealed even a moment's reaction to his tirade. Upon reaching the top landing, a carpeted area with glass doors leading to the outside, they let go of his arms and urged him forward. Both men desperately tried to remain cool as they continued their assignment, obviously in a great deal of pain. With choreography rarely seen off Broadway, the two reached into their coats and pulled out large, impressive looking guns.

"Hey, now. Shit. You coulda shot me downstairs and saved us all the trip!" Jackson raised his hands defensively and started to back up toward the roof exit.

"You're appointment is waiting for you outside, Mr. Cross," said Giant Number One in-between short, wheezing breaths. They turned then, and faced the descending stairs, weapons held out offensively.

Speechless, Jackson backed up through the glass doors.

Shit! We never got our coats!

Frigid, February winds ripped across the roof and through Jackson. An already deadly experience, made considerably worse with the presence of a helicopter, idling on a landing pad.

Jackson glanced behind him, weighed his chances of rushing through the gorilla roadblock (let alone surviving the oncoming mob), recalled the fact that the person in that helicopter was ultimately responsible for whatever just happened to Dippy, and jogged to the whirling machine.

The cabin door slid open. This was a sleek vehicle; all black and shiny. A hand reached out from the plush interior. The hand possessed two rings, a Rolex and an arm which escaped the wind into an Armani sleeve. It wasn't until Jackson was just a few feet away that he could focus through the wind enough to see who was extending the invitation.

What the hell? It's a kid!

The skinny, gangly young man offering a hand-up appeared to be fourteen at the outside. Befuddled, pissed and cold, Jacks accepted his hand.

The boy yelled above the howling blades, "Jackson! Welcome aboard! My name's Frank! You can call me Mr. Sinatra!"

The door shut, and Jackson was swept away into the magnificent Manhattan morning.

CHAPTER EIGHT

When we pulled into Nazareth, I was feeling about half-past dead.

I stayed out of sight and behind the group as they entered the gate. I was just hoping that whoever allowed them entrance would recognize me as one of their party when I strolled in a few minutes behind them. Luckily, I assumed correctly.

"Hey, Judas!" This came from one of the turrets.

I waved agreeably. I hoped whoever called out wouldn't continue pursuing a conversation, in light of the fact that I didn't want to draw any attention to myself and I didn't have the foggiest notion who any of these guys were.

"Still hanging out with the fishermen, Judas? Or did your senses return and you've come to ask Pilate for your tax collecting job back?"

Thankfully, this came from one of the guards on the ground. A quick glance confirmed that the other apostles were too caught up in their own conversation to hear any of this ruckus behind them.

"We'll see, my friend," I said, trying to sound amiable. Then a thought struck. "Pilate's in Nazareth, then?"

"Just till tomorrow night, like every other month. All that praying in the desert warped your head?" This was followed with some healthy laughter from the group.

"Maybe," was my only response. I picked up my pace so as not to lose sight of Jesus' men.

"Maybe Pilate will just have you all locked up instead of crucifying the lot of ya'!"

More laughter. I considered responding with, "It must be nice having Pilate's dick out of your mouth long enough for you to make stupid fucking jokes," but thought better of it. It was their world, at this point. I let them have their fun.

So Pilate was in town, I thought. *So what?*

So maybe a few well chosen words could put the kibosh on this whole deal and you won't have to spend the next three years following these dinks around.

Maybe, I realized, *but I doubt it.*

I caught sight of the guys going into a tavern-like establishment. Drunken men and ugly women were having a raucous time both inside and out. As inconspicuously as possible, I circled the outside, keeping an eye on them as best as I could.

My plan was to get James' attention. I figured he'd know the best place to keep out of John's way for the night. I was pretty sure Jesus was going to download a dream to John, possibly even visit him outright, and get him off my back. I just wanted to give him the time to do it. I hadn't quite managed to catch James' eye, when one of the women making rounds with the men inside saw me looking in. She smiled, gave me a quizzical look and then dashed for the door.

Shit. I'm spotted.

Running would have garnered more attention, especially if this chick would start calling out after me, so I just leaned against the wall and waited for her to circle around and approach.

She wasn't very tall and had some weight to her, but wasn't even close to being unattractive. From the rest of the women I'd seen, she was definitely the cream of the crop. She wore a flowing outfit reminiscent of a toga. Her long dark hair bounced in time with her unencumbered breasts as she jogged up to me in the alleyway. The put-upon feeling I had when she initially grabbed my eye was quickly becoming something more anxious and aroused.

"Judas!" I was torn between hiding from her and shutting her mouth with a kiss. She made the decision for me, pressing her lips forcibly against mine. I looked over her head and back through the window. No one inside seemed to notice her outburst, so I gave in to the comfort of her touch.

She was laughing easily, possibly drunk. "Why are we hiding out here, Judas? Everyone inside's been asking for you." She held my gaze while she spoke, running her hands up my tunic and working down the shorts underneath. "I'm not complaining, or anything. We haven't spent time in the alley forever."

My mind was a flurry of questions. Was this my wife? Could we get in trouble for this? Was I expected to pay, maybe? Did any of that matter since it had been twenty years since I had sex?

"Who was asking about me?"

"Oh, y'know, everybody. Once James and them showed up…" She had my (well, Judas') penis out and partially erect within seconds. Then, while still expertly massaging me, she began hiking up the flowing material that covered her legs. "John was trying to get me to go out back with him, but I told him you and I were supposed to get together when you got back. And he was like, 'What's so great about Judas, Mary?' and I was like, 'It's nothing personal, John. We just have an understanding.' But, to be honest, he kind of scares me. Ooh, there you go."

And, indeed, there I went. She was up against the wall and I was a good five inches inside of her when I stopped.

"Mary," I said, mid-stroke. "Magdalene?"

"Judas," she responded, with a smile. "Iscariot?" She giggled. Her giggle turned into a sigh as she locked her legs around my back and pulled me in deeper. The ample lubrication and lingering musky scent indicated that, John notwithstanding, I wasn't her first companion of the evening. Ask me if I cared.

This was Mary Magdalene, for Christ's sake! Whore to prophets and gods! I mean, if Cleopatra, Mata Hari or that Babylon chick were nowhere to be found, this was about as good as it gets. I began thrusting in earnest.

"That's it, Judas. That's it."

Who's your betrayer? I thought. Then the second thought came, *I wonder if she's doing Jesus.*

My mind immediately flashed to a bumper sticker I remembered seeing on the interstate back in the future. It was on this really small compact with a really large black woman behind the wheel. The sticker read: Don't Nobody Do You Like Jesus.

I stifled a laugh.

Does it matter?

Nope, I decided. *Not in the least.*

I braced myself a little better against the wall, dug into the dirt alleyway and lost myself (or whoever) in the moment. Tomorrow's troubles could wait till tomorrow.

●

Don was furiously scanning the Web for confirmation of Jackson Cross' death.

It was about 3:00 in the afternoon, and he'd not left the Motel 6 for more than the ten minutes it took to get McDonald's take out.

There were over thirty disciples of Minister Max scattered in rooms just like Don's through-out the tri-state area. Over thirty people dedicated to getting on Tom Green's Radio Hour that morning and declaring "a call to arms." Max had been confident that at least one of his people would get on the air. Don was so excited to be the One, the harbinger (as Max put it), that he could barely contain himself. It was one of the most significant moments in his entire life.

The previous four years led up to that single event. Getting off the drugs, studying the Book (as best he could), helping Max with more recruits and with planning the big day was all preparation for that morning.

Admittedly, they hadn't planned something of this scale until Max had been introduced to Cross' *Judas Conspiracy*. Before that, it was all just some broad ideas of how and when they were going to make an impact for Jesus.

Cross brought it on himself by writing that piece of trash. Not that Don, Max or anyone else in the church had read it, mind you. But they knew enough to know that this book was the key to bringing down the Wrath of God. Someone would just have to save the heretics from themselves!

Max taught Don enough about the Internet so that he could surf certain kinds of religious sites and chat with some of the people out there who may have had similar inclinations. Dozens of contacts became hundreds of disciples, all ready to help teach the lost and pathetic souls the evil of reducing Jesus' work to some fictional alien plot. They were all sick and tired of having their faith dismissed as superstition by liberals and Suits alike.

Some (like Don) were also compelled to expand the race agenda, but Max wanted to take the fight one stage at a time.

"Strength in numbers, Donny, m'boy," Max would tell him. "We're not going to turn anyone away if they're willing to fight the good fight. Once we've established a healthy fear of Our Lord back into the nation's conscience, we'll take a look at everything else from race to homosexuality, I promise!"

Max had also promised to pick Don up from his motel room sometime after the initial demonstration. Don wished he had been more specific about the time.

Windows featuring news groups jockeyed for position with Religious Right chat rooms on Don's notebook screen. He never once questioned where Max got the money for this campaign. He never even considered it.

The day had been a monumental success! Over 100 atheists and heretics had been hospitalized. None had been killed, and that was important. The only sanctioned death had been that of Cross, but the cowardly bastard went missing in the middle of the broadcast. Most of the email Don received, when it wasn't praising him for his stellar performance on the Jew's radio program, was wanting to know where they were hiding Cross. Don's only response was a cryptic, "He'll get his," before moving on to the next correspondence.

He was reading yet another piece of fan mail when the door to his room opened, allowing the afternoon sunlight and bitter cold to sweep in.

"Don! How's my hero?"

"Max?" Don shielded his eyes from the light. He was prepared to grab the notebook and throw it into the bathtub should it have been an authority of some kind.

"Of course, Max! Who were you expecting?"

Max moved toward Don without bothering to close the door.

"Stellar job this morning, Don. Just stellar."

"Did you hear me? Was I alright?"

"Alright? Do you see what we've done today? We're taking back the faith, Don! People shouldn't be frightened of being Christian. They should be scared of the alternative!"

A dark, massive shadow moved in behind the minister then. This new person closed the door, keeping his hands behind his back the entire time. Don's eyes took a second to adjust. He had to catch himself before his bladder released.

"What's *he* doing here?"

"Hm? Oh, I'm sorry. Manners. Have you met my new bodyguard? This is Nailz. Nailz, this is Don, speaker for the people. Harbinger of faith!"

"I know this cracker," replied Nailz.

"That's right, you two were in Stark together. Nailz here just got his parole last month. We were lucky to be able to pick up a man of his caliber."

"What do we need him for?"

Max straightened out his long coat and sat down on one of the beds, keeping some distance between himself and his disciple. Nailz remained behind the preacher, looking disdainfully at Don all the while.

"Well, Don, as nice of a job as you did for us this morning, there's one more position which needs filling to make this movement truly unstoppable. It's going to take the talents of yourself and Nailz combined to fulfill this need."

"We don't need him, Max. Whatever you want, I can take care of myself." As he spoke, he kept a nervous gaze on Nailz.

"Afraid not Don. If the good Book taught us anything, it's that it takes two to martyr."

Don dropped his eyes to Max's face, looking for some kind of sign that this was a terrible joke. The minister was checking his manicure. Don looked back up to Nailz, but really only focussed on the silencer which sparkled keenly on the end of the .44.

"But…" was all Don could get out before the part of his brain that controlled speech was hurled against the scenic picture on the wall to his back.

Max removed a pair of surgical gloves and a CD from his coat. Being careful not to trample on any evidence, he inserted the disk into Don's bloody laptop.

"Now, this release is programmed to be distributed across the AP and to all Christian and Right Wing groups. Someone's bound to be pissed that Don's been given the old heave-ho. It's just good luck for us that the New Atheists are taking responsibility, eh?."

"What about that Cross guy?"

"He'll turn up. It'll be worse for him now, I'll guarantee you that. Ready to go?"

"Hey! I've got some business with this fuck!"

Max looked back at Don's crumpled form with the perpetual look of betrayal on his face. "No, no. Don's been through enough. And even *I* wouldn't believe that the liberals would be driven to murder *and* rape."

"C'mon," Max patted the large man on the back and led him toward the door. "I'll buy you a Happy Meal."

Don's body slipped from its chair several moments after his guests left, like an old, neglected rag doll.

CHAPTER NINE

Darlene Tyler made her way through Grand Central station with a pinched look on her face.

What was I thinking?

The thirty-five year old executive pushed through the rush-hour crowd in an attempt to make the Metro North glider before 6:30. It would already be close to an hour before she'd be home; she didn't want to extend the frustration by being trapped with this woman for another twenty minutes waiting for the next magnerail.

"I still can't believe you've never read the book! How is it even possible?"

The younger woman trying to engage Darlene in conversation followed her down to the Harlem line.

"It's just a different mentality, I guess," the young girl continued. She would trip over herself every few steps, dropping papers from her portfolio. The fact that Darlene never slowed her pace while papers were being retrieved, or appeared to be interested in talking to her, made no impression whatsoever.

"If someone wrote a character about me, I know I'd be thrilled! You couldn't stop me from reading it if you tried!"

The two women paraded down the final flight of stairs and onto the platform. Darlene was grateful that the hum of the magnetic generator, along with the constant drone of people walking and carrying on their own tedious conversations, drowned out her companion. They dashed through the doors and into the crowded tube, pushing past prodding umbrellas and wet winter coats and slickers, desperate for some kind of personal space.

Standing in front of a businessman who looked at least as annoyed with humanity as Darlene felt, she freed her Pocket-Mac™ and checked to see if she had received any messages since leaving the office. Her companion was obviously unaccustomed to life in the City. She practically clung onto Darlene while giving terrified glances toward almost every other passenger on the glider. But she was being quiet, so Darlene was satisfied.

●

The annoyed-looking businessman disembarked (surprisingly enough) at 125th Street. Darlene slid into the available seat with the fluid motion of a practiced commuter. The girl to her back was nearly panicked upon turning around and discovering Darlene was gone. It took several seconds before she realized that Darlene was still right there, merely sitting.

"Geeze. I thought we got separated!"

Darlene looked up and felt a pang of guilt. "Do you want this seat, Nicki?"

"No. I should be getting used to standing, I guess."

True enough, Darlene thought. *Guilt assuaged.*

People came and went and the doors closed with a hydraulic rush. Darlene began typing herself notes. The sense that she was being stared at became more powerful the further they traveled from the 125th Street magnestop. Darlene slowly raised her head from her work, her eyes almost immediately drawn to the mascara-ridden gaze of the lithe, petite blond standing directly over her.

"Did you know he was writing about you? I mean, did you at least see, like, rough drafts or something?"

Darlene sighed and set the PM firmly on her lap. She drew in what was meant to be a cleansing breath before responding to this new line of questioning.

"I know this is a big deal for you, sweety. That's why I invited you back to our place to watch Jacks' show…"

"I can't believe you call him 'Jacks!' Doesn't it make you just want to die?!"

Darlene shook her head. "Not really. I call him asshole more than anything. He's a close, personal friend who happened to loosely base a character on me…"

"Loosely? Loosely she says. Look here…" Nicki reached into her already-ransacked folio and produced a thick, dog-eared paperback. She speedily flipped through the pages, skimming various paragraphs until finding the appropriate passage.

"Darlene was a walking contradiction. Fiery-red hair created the impression of someone given to impulsive emotions when in fact she was the most even-tempered, apathetic New Yorker I knew, and that's saying a lot. Partly, she didn't give a shit about anything outside her career or immediate family. Mostly, she had no stomach for confrontation. Now, even this was a contradiction since she chose Public Relations to make her living; a profession wrought with pushing and shoving and manipulating whole corporations (not to mention the media) in the best interest of the client.

"She didn't smoke or drink, but spent little to no time on personal physical improvement. She rarely gave away a smile but, when she did, it was the kind of smile you'd like to wrap around yourself. Her smile could change your life, and she didn't even know it."

Nicki stopped reading and looked at Darlene for a reaction.

"It happens that I have a tremendous temper and exercise twice a week." She looked back down at the leather case between her boots, decided not to do more work and, instead, rested her head back and closed her eyes.

"I just don't understand it," Nicki continued, unabated by Darlene's obvious attempt to distance herself from the conversation.

"You don't have to," Darlene commented, eyes still closed.

"What are you doing waving that book around?" This came from a man standing to the left and behind Nicki. His shirt was buttoned to the top, but he had no tie. The windbreaker he wore, besides being woefully inadequate for the time of year, looked to have spent the better part of its existence being repeatedly run over with farm equipment. His trousers were cuffed above his ankles. It was obvious from the quickest of glances that the bible he clutched in his right hand was the only possession for which he cared deeply.

"What? *This* book?"

Darlene opened her eyes to see Nicki naively holding up her book. "Don't make conversation," she tried to warn her young companion in as loud of a whisper as she deemed safe. "Put the book away."

"You're going to get yourself killed, girl!" The unkept man snatched Nicki's paperback from her outstretched hand.

"Hey!" People already began giving a wide berth for the conflict, turning their backs so as not to be involved, but listening intently to know when there might be bloodshed.

The high-waters man managed to tuck his bible safely into his belt before furiously ripping out pages of *Conspiracy*.

"Stop that! That's mine!"

Darlene reached up and grabbed a hold of Nicki's coat just as the blond was preparing to charge the man who was destroying her property. She got up from her seat while forcibly pulling Nicki down into the vacated space. Then she positioned herself with her back to the crazy man who was still shredding the novel.

"Do not *say* or *do* anything else," Darlene scolded. "Hear me?"

"But...he's..." Tears of frustration and surprise welled up, immediately glistening over the black mascara.

"I'll get you another copy." Darlene was standing erect now, not talking to Nicki directly. "Just don't look at him, don't talk to him, don't respond in any way."

The seeming madman finished tearing out pages of the book. Then he kneeled down and began ripping apart the loose pieces on the ground.

"We don't have to put up with this anymore!" He wasn't addressing anyone in particular. He appeared to be talking directly to the paper he was so intent on destroying. "We're not here for your amusement! Our Lord is no joke!"

Darlene looked out the window of the magnecar. Nicki was quietly sobbing to herself.

"Don't tell me you didn't hear about today's riots," Darlene seemed to be asking the window above Nicki's head. "Crap like this is happening all over the country because of that book."

"Wasn't that just terrible?" A middle-aged, Asian woman with boxes wrapped in brown paper sitting at her feet looked excitedly at Darlene. "All those people hurt because someone didn't like what someone else wrote."

Please shut up, Darlene thought. *I wasn't talking to you.*

"Like it's that simple!" A young black man dressed in a suit and tie directed his comments from across the car, on the other side of the maniac. "I'm sorry about your book, but we're tired of our faith being ridiculed. And I'm not saying I condone the riots…"

"That's what I'm hearing," said a portly man in construction clothes.

"But *I am* saying people need to take this seriously."

"Or what?"

"Or we will make you take us seriously!" The man on the floor held up two fistfuls of shredded paper as proof.

"Fuck you, ya' fruitcake!"

"See! It's okay to stand up for niggers or queers, but don't try to be proud of your religion now-a-days!" Darlene wasn't sure from where this opinion came, as she was too busy trying to calculate how much further it would be before Mount Vernon West.

Should have taken the local. More stops. Who knew?

"We will lay down no longer! Don will be avenged!" The high-waters man came to his feet. Tears were beginning to well up in *his* eyes. "A Christian was killed today. Killed by the people who read this garbage! But we say no more! Don will be avenged!"

He began chanting, and he wasn't alone.

"Don will be avenged! Don will be avenged!"

The buttoned-up man made his way back toward Nicki. "Don will be avenged!"

"Leave her alone, asshole!" The construction worker got up. He didn't motion forward, but he could have been on top of the chanting man in less then a second.

Darlene tried to keep her tone conversational, and continued to speak above Nicki's head instead of addressing her directly.

"You need to get up and step in front of me. We're moving to the next car. Now."

Without a word, the Asian woman sitting next to Nicki picked up her boxes before standing in front of Darlene.

Darlene glared at the woman.

Once again, I wasn't talking to you!

The older woman looked sheepishly at Darlene. "I'd like to go too. Please?"

Darlene shrugged. Nicki stood between Darlene and the stranger and the three women moved through the crowd, which was fast-becoming unruly.

"Don will be avenged! Don will be avenged!"

"Shut the fuck up!"

The three moved quickly through the separating doors, glad to put the chaos behind them.

A large, dark-skinned man with dreadlocks caught Nicki's eyes as they looked for a place to sit and regroup. "What happened back there?"

Nicki looked back at Darlene before fixing her eyes ahead and to the floor.

Now you're learning.

The dreadlocked man shrugged as he returned to reading his paper.

●

Darlene and Nicki stepped through the doors and onto the platform at Bronxville. They waited until the doors closed, the glider pulled away and all the other disembarking passengers were gone before leaving the relative safety of the well-lit magnestop. They hadn't spoken since the incident over two stops previous.

"Who's Don?"

Darlene shook her head as they moved to the stairs taking them under the magnetic field.

"Do you have any idea what happened this morning?"

"What?"

Darlene felt some anxiety as they approached the dark part of the tunnel that would take them to the south side of the platform. When they turned the corner and no one was there, she felt comfortable enough to begin talking again.

"You're supposed to be a big fan of Jacks, right?"

"His book changed my life! I read parts of it every night!"

"But you didn't hear anything about the whole Tom Green thing?"

"Who's Tom Green?"

"Tell me you're kidding. The radio guy?"

"I don't listen to the radio. I don't watch TV or surf the Web or any of that. I read books and go to the movies. And hike. And rockclimb."

"Ok, ok. Jackson was on this radio show this morning…"

"Really? See, now *that* I would have liked to have heard. I'm just really lucky that you heard me talking up his book so much in the office that you invited me to watch his HBO show on your monitor at home. If you hadn't mentioned it, I would have never known he was doing something like that!"

Darlene imagined a tremendously intricate device. It provided her with a pulley that, once tugged, put the contraption through an elaborate series of maneuvers, resulting in an old-fashioned rubber boot striking her hard on the ass.

"Don't mention it. Anyway, while Jackson was on the air, some people claiming to be religious began attacking people who were openly atheist. That, or people who were openly fans of Jacks."

"Bummer."

"Totally. So this guy, Don? He's the one who called up the radio show and laid it all on Jacks. Said they were doing this cause of the book and Jacks making fun of Christ and all…"

"But, that's not the point of the book!"

"Regardless. Once this guy gets hung up on, a mob tears into the radio station and disrupts the broadcast."

"Oh my God! Why didn't you tell me this before?"

They left the steps of the tunnel exit and followed the sidewalk alongside a brick apartment house.

"To be honest? All you've done is grill me on his book since someone at the office finally clued you into the fact that I'm in it. I usually like my rides home to be kind of chit-chat free."

Nicki was hurt. Darlene had no idea.

"Is he okay?"

"Jacks? Couldn't say. Don, however, the guy who got hung up on and who might have been in charge of the whole thing, was reportedly found dead this afternoon."

"Whoa."

"To say the least."

Nicki walked quietly behind the executive. They followed the sidewalk to the front of the building and then Darlene turned toward the entrance.

"You live this close to the magnestop?"

"Yup," she confirmed while unlocking the building's entranceway. "One of the apartment's selling features, let me tell you."

They walked down a small, dimly-lit hall toward an elevator. Abruptly, Darlene turned and headed up a staircase. "…'Spent little to no time on personal physical improvement' my ass. C'mon, we're up on three."

"Ms. Tyler?" Nicki inquired, not even climbing the first step. "Do you want me to go?"

Dalrene looked down on her from the first landing.

"Why? Don't you want to see the show?"

"Well, I'm sure you're worried about him. And, I mean, you didn't really even know who I was when you invited me. You were just being nice."

"You're right. But I like 'just being nice' sometimes. And, as for being worried…" Darlene grabbed the rail and sat down on steps several feet above her young protégéé. "Let me tell you a story.

"A few years ago, back when he and I were working together in San Diego, Jackson took some time off in October to go to New York. He arrived on a Friday, and immediately set camp outside FAO Schwartz. Literally. He brought a tent, a chair, some dry goods and reading material and camped out in front of the store. When the manager asked him what was going on, Jackson said he wanted to be the first person in line to get this new 'interactive viewer' coming out that Monday morning. He claimed that it was his right as a consumer to ensure his purchase by any means not considered a health violation, or some such.

"Well, the cops didn't see any reason to move him. People camp out for stuff all the time. It just happened that Jackson was the only person who felt the need to camp out for this particular product. And that's what started to pique people's interest.

"See, this 'interactive viewer,' which turned out to be one of the first all-inclusive environment simulators, had never been advertised. There was not a single piece of marketing available. No one knew what it was and they certainly had no idea when it was coming out.

"But, over the next few days, the media began to take notice of Jackson's little sit-in. Stories about his vigil were run across cable and the 'net. In one interview, he asked Stone Philips to take his place in line so he could go to the bathroom. By Monday morning, toy stores all across the country had kids and techno-geeks clamoring to get through the doors.

"So, now picture this, they open the doors at FAO Schwartz and it's practically a press conference as Jackson Cross, non-famous, obscure citizen, calmly walks over to the display, picks up one of the boxes and marches to a cashier. He stops midway through the stanchion and begins to look at the packaging. He studies it intensely for several minutes, puts it down, says to the cashier, 'I'm sorry. Changed my mind,' and starts to walk out of the store.

"Well, one of the reporters present has the wherewithal to ask him what the hell he's doing. After three days of waiting, he wasn't even going to buy it?

"Jackson looks directly at the camera while the morning sun projects something like a halo behind him. He smiles and says, 'That machine right there might need to be outlawed. If it does what it says, it'll be the most addictive entertainment ever devised. To quote Dennis Miller, 'It'll make crack look like fucking Sanka,' and I just don't like the idea of technology providing that much pleasure in my life. Maybe it's me, but I don't need some escape that's so real I won't want to go back to reality. Do you?'

"It was amazing. There was a second's pause before the store almost exploded as people began buying three, four, five of the things at a time. EpTech's Interactive was sold out across the country before the end of business the next day without spending so much as a nickel on advertising.

"You want to know if I'm worried about Jacks? Of course I am. But I also know him better than the reporters who've been all but reciting his obituary today.

"For instance, I'm one of the few people who know that Danny Epstein, Jackson's best friend, owned EpTech Interactive. I'm also one of the few who know that Danny positioned his IPO the week following the viewers in-home date. And I may be one of only four or five people who know that Jackson took no stock in EpTech, before or after the stunt. He could have made millions.

"Worried? I wouldn't be surprised if Jacks and Danny aren't behind the whole thing. Now, c'mon. Let's get upstairs."

●

"Is your husband home already?"

Darlene was fishing the keys from her leather case as they stepped up to the third floor landing. "Scott and I aren't married, hon. And anyway, he's not due home for at least half an hour."

"So that's not your door that's cracked open?"

Darlene froze where she stood. She looked down the hall both ways before focussing once again on her own apartment.

We're on the right floor. This is *my place. Damn.*

"Stay right behind me."

"Not a problem."

The two women inched their way into the foyer. Darlene delicately placed her case next to the hall table and picked up an umbrella from the adjoining stand.

Movement in the kitchen. A voice.

"I hear what you're saying, Lisa. But I'm not hearing anything about postponement or rescheduling. You guys are just cutting me off here."

"Son of a bitch." Darlene dropped her umbrella and marched into the kitchen.

"Darlene!" Nicki whispered as loud as she could. "What are you doing?"

Nicki stood stock-still in the hallway, confused and scared. Darlene disappeared into the kitchen.

"Asshole! Asshole, asshole, asshole! I should have never given you that key!" Nicki listened both to Darlene's tirade and the smacking sounds that accompanied it. Whoever the invader was, he was being thrashed.

"Cut it out, Darlene," the intruder half-chuckled, half-admonished. "I'm on the phone here."

"Nicki? It's okay. You can come in."

Nicki slowly approached the kitchen entrance from the hall. An average-sized man dressed in black was leaning on the counter at the far end. He had his back to her, but would occasionally turn as he spoke into the cordless receiver. She found his hair and his profile strikingly familiar.

"Nicki Sims, Jackson Cross."

Jackson looked over and gave a little wave. "I told you I understood, Lisa—Hiya, Nicki, pleased to meetcha—but I'm just not feeling very reassured at this point."

Nicki stopped breathing. She felt as if her heart had stopped and her stomach was caving in on itself. Jackson winked and turned his attention back to the call.

"Right…" "Ok…" "Alright…" "Fine." "What else can I say? I guess we'll just hope for the best. Thanks Lisa." "I know it's not your fault."

Cross clicked the phone off. He rubbed his eyes for a second before turning to Darlene.

"Y'know, it's fine that you guys don't smoke, but the courteous thing would be to have a few loose joints around for guests, know what I'm saying?"

"C'mere shithead."

The two hugged warmly by the kitchen table.

"I was worried about you."

"I'm still worried about Danny. We got separated at the radio station. I've been calling hospitals and the cops trying to nail down where he is. And, on top of that, that was Lisa at HBO. They've cancelled tonight's show."

"Oh no!" Nicki immediately covered her mouth. Her outburst genuinely surprised her as much as anyone.

Darlene smirked. "Nicki here is a fan."

"Oh yeah?"

"Well, I think the term fan has poor connotations these days," Nicki defended. "I mean, I'm not like a stalker or anything. I mean, I didn't even know you were going to be here. I mean, it's soooo cool that you *are* here, but it wasn't something I planned. Obviously. I mean, it's probably *not* something you planned either, but…"

"Do you think you could do me a favor, Nicki," Jacks asked, barely hiding his impatience. "I mean, since fate seems to have given us this chance to meet?"

"Of course! Whatever you need!"

Jacks reached for his wallet and pulled out a twenty.

"There's a general store on the other side of the magnestop. Do you think you could pick up one pack of filterless joints and two packs of Light 100 cigarettes? Brands aren't too important."

"I'll be back in two minutes. Two minutes!"

She grabbed the cash and was out the door before Cross had his wallet back in his pocket. Darlene looked at him reproachfully.

"What? She *wanted* to go!" The two laughed.

"So, how did you manage to get out of the radio station anyhow?"

"It's a long story that I can't get into right now. How's Scott?"

"Scott's fine. He's due in any time. He's still pissed at you."

Jackson made his way to the living room and flopped down on the pit-group.

"Why be mad at me? I made him quasi-famous. I'll bet Nicki would fucking love to be mentioned in a book of some kind."

Darlene sat down on her coffee table, facing her friend.

"Not for nothin' but, Scott has no interest in having attention drawn to himself. Neither do I, for that matter. It would have been nice if you asked."

"Asked? I told you! I told both of you! Remember? We were having a get-together of everyone from Titanic Entertainment back in San Diego. We were hanging out at Dick's Last Resort, and I gave you two an entire plot outline."

"Jackson, that was one book out of dozens that you had been threatening to write for years. How were we supposed to know that you'd actually finish one?"

"Did you ever read it?"

Darlene looked back toward the kitchen. "Don't you still need to find out what happened to Epstein?"

Jackson laughed. "Bad form, Tyler! It's bad enough that you don't read my work, but you attempt to derail me with faux concern for my friend? Shame I say."

Cross did get up, though. He returned to the kitchen, retrieved the phone from the counter and fished for his wallet again. Extracting a business card, he began to dial.

"You're not off the hook, you know," he commented while punching numbers. "It just happens that I really am concerned…Tom! It's Cross." "I'm fine, I'm fine. Listen, have you guys heard from Dippy?" "Shot in the dark anyway." "Huh?" "No, the show's been canceled. Too much concern that what happened at KFX2 will happen at the Neil Simon Theater. It's not that big of a deal. I probably would have bombed. Can I give you a number where I'm at?" "If you hear anything, a rumor, an AP bullet, anything about Danny, give me a call?"

The front door to the apartment opened with the sound of men conversing.

"We're home!"

Darlene moved from the coffee table to the hall. "Who's 'we?' Oh, geeze. Call off the guard, Jacks."

"Just a sec, Tom" Jackson stuck his head out of the kitchen. "What's…Oh you bastard! Tom? We got him. I'll give you a call when you guys have the station repaired. We'll have to do this again real soon!" He hung up in the middle of Tom's reasons why Jackson would never be on his show again.

Jacks and Danny stood in the foyer like reunited veterans. "We were on the same glider but didn't know it until we got off," Scott explained.

Jackson hugged his friend. "Man, I thought they were gonna kill you for sure!" He stepped back and opened Danny's coat to reveal bare skin. "You took off the shirt?"

"Well, yeah! It seemed important to you. Scott's going to loan me something."

Jackson and Scott shook hands. "How're we doing, Mr. Lloyd?"

"I'm alright, Jackson. Seems like you've had a busy day."

"That's the rumor."

"I'll get Daniel that shirt." Scott made his way down the hall toward the bedroom.

"Thanks, man. Hey Darlene, is it okay to turn on your monitor? I've got to check the market."

"Be my guest." Darlene smiled a bemused little smile as Danny, practically back from the dead, bounded into her living room. She looked at Cross. "Business as usual?"

"What can I say? We're a hearty breed."

Jacks moved into the kitchen and poured himself a glass of water. "So, what happened to you exactly, Dippy?"

"Well," Danny began, eyes glued to the ticker at the bottom of the 45" screen. "It wasn't like you were fooling anyone, yelling and carrying on like that. But you did get their attention, and they wanted you bad. They pretty much just ran over me while chasing your voice. However, not to sound egotistical, I figured someone would be happy enough to hand me my ass if they thought they weren't going to reach you. So I stripped while being trampled on. Once the first wave of storm troopers passed, I slipped out of the stairwell and into one of the offices. I eventually made my way downstairs and got my coat."

"Why didn't you get help from Tom, or that guy Stu?"

"By the time I got back to the thirtieth floor, the cops were grilling all the employees. It wasn't my scene, man. I figured you'd be here eventually, so here I came. So, what happened to you?"

"I'll tell you in a bit. You ever been to Colorado?"

Scott was coming in from the bedroom. "I've got this flannel shirt. It's a little big on me…"

The intercom buzzed. Darlene answered. "Yes."

Heavy breathing. "It's Nicki! I've got the stuff!" Darlene buzzed her in.

Jackson grabbed the phone. "Well, sorry we can't stay. I just needed a safe house to hunt down Dippy. We'll get out of your hair."

Darlene jumped up. "You just got here! Since your show's been canceled…"

"Your show's been canceled?" Danny asked while pulling the flannel over his head.

"I thought we'd have dinner. We haven't seen each other for so long." Scott tried to look noncommittal. "Well, honey, if they have to go…"

"Shut up, Scott." Darlene grabbed Jackson's hand just as he finished dialing. "I've missed you."

"Yeah? I've missed you too. But I've got a new boss, of sorts." He listened to the receiver. "This is Cross. Ready to be picked up. We'll be at the Blue Line magnestop in Bronxville. Five minutes." He clicked off the phone and replaced it in its cradle. "All ready, Dippy?"

"To meet your new boss? Always!"

The two reached the door with Scott and Darlene flanking them. They opened it to sounds of footfalls racing up the steps.

"I'm here! I've got the stuff!" Nicki's mascara streaked like black icicles. Her cheeks burned like streetlights.

"Thanks very much, Nicki. This is Danny. Danny, this is Nicki."

"Well met, Miss Nicki." Danny leaned over and kissed Nicki's cold, trembling hand.

"You're…I mean he's…" She shook her head violently to clear the thoughts. "Um. I got Red Apple brand," she finally settled on. "I hope that's okay."

"You did great." Jacks took the sack from her. "You got a pen, Darlene?"

Darlene produced one from a bowl on her hall table. Jacks emptied the bag, turned it over and began writing. He recited as he went.

"To Nicki, Thanks for that incredible, magical night. I'll always treasure your memory, Jackson Cross"

He handed the bag to Nicki (who was stunned to silence), hugged Darlene and palmed her the pen.

"I love you, you know," he said as they parted the embrace.

"Yeah? I love you too."

"Take care of yourself, Scott. Let's go, Dippy."

Nicki, Scott and Darlene watched as Danny and Jackson descended the stairs.

"Staying for dinner, Nicki?"

"Are you kidding? Do you think I'd leave now?"

Scott sighed as he led them back into the apartment. "What's this fresh hell?" He asked Darlene.

"Be nice," Darlene insisted. "How many times in your life will you have an honest-to-goodness fan over for dinner." She looked down at the pen before depositing it in the bowl. "Damn."

"What's wrong?"

She held up the pen for the other two to see. A house key dangled from the pocket clip.

"You told him you wanted it back," Nicki pointed out.

"I was just kidding. Why do I feel like we'll never see him again?"

"We should be so lucky," Scott joked as he closed the door behind them.

Book Two

"And now for something completely different…"

A friend of mine spent six years going to veterinary school. True story. She finally graduated and got a job working for a zoo. She gets to work with pedigree animals. Now, this sounds cool, right? But the thing is, these animals aren't allowed to mate. Apparently they don't have the funds to raise and care for additional pedigrees. But the animals have needs, dig? It's dangerous for them if they aren't allowed to find some kind of release. So, who gets to help "relieve" these animals of their pent-up tensions. That's right. My friend spent something like 100 Gs on her veterinary degree just so she could masturbate exotic animals. Her parents are extremely proud.

But, you know, forget about the parents. What about her boyfriend? She comes home after spending the afternoon trying to whack the pud of some 600 pound gorilla—with both hands, and an assistant!—and she's got to contend with some delusional white-bread idiot waving the equivalent of a cocktail wienie in her face. How can he compete with like, literally, a Clydesdale? How exciting could sex be for her after a day of stepping in elephant spunk?

My question is whether or not woman's lib has reached the Serengeti. Chicks have needs too, know what I'm saying? I just have this image of her getting ready to leave work when her supervisor comes out:

"Sally? Are you clocking out?"

"Yes."

"Did you eat out the orangutan?"

[Sighs] "No."

"Well? It's not like she can do it herself!"

Jackson Cross
2011 Young Comedians Special
Turner Comedy Channel

CHAPTER TEN

Lyle was checking his heart rate at the tail-end of his morning run when his headset vibrated. He stopped pressing his wrist and tapped his earpiece.

"Good morning, Jennifer. You're early this morning."

"Calling for Status."

It certainly wasn't Jennifer's voice, and no one outside his family, partner and secretary was supposed to have his private number. He continued jogging in place on the side of the road, approximately two blocks from his Georgian home. He immediately changed to his business tone.

"This is Lyle Status of Status & Sons. With whom am I speaking?"

"I was told your agency handles…discretionary investigations?"

"If I don't know who you are and how you acquired this number in the next five seconds, I will disconnect the line, trace it and have a cease and desist order personally handed to you, wherever you are, before I finish my first cup of morning tea. Care to start over?" He returned to checking his heart rate.

"My name is Charles Fleishman. I represent someone who wishes to remain anonymous at this time. I'd like to meet you for lunch today, if that's convenient."

"You haven't given me any reason to alter my current schedule, Mr. Fleishman." 72 bpm. Not terrible. He resumed his run.

"Your secretary will be receiving an overnight package this morning. Enclosed will be a bankbook for an overseas account established in the name of your agency with $2000. You will receive the access codes during our meeting, regardless of whether you accept the assignment. I believe this is a considerable increase from your standard consultation fee."

Lyle turned into his circular drive.

"Pretty cloak and dagger, Mr. Fleishman. I assume there's a point to all this coverture?"

"I'm afraid any further discussion will have to be conducted over lunch. Say 11:30?"

"Where did you intend to meet?" Lyle stood in front of his house. He wanted to get this taken care of before going inside.

"There will be a limo in front of your Atlanta office at 11:30 this morning. Are you interested?"

"I'll think it over. If I get in the car, I guess you'll know."

Lyle clicked off his headset and opened his door.

"Katy? You ready for school?"

"In here, Daddy!"

Lyle spotted his seven year-old daughter sitting at the kitchen table, dressed and eating cereal. She was engrossed in the morning news coming across the wall monitor.

"I don't want you watching that kind of thing, honey. The world's an ugly place. Aren't there cartoons on or something?" Lyle poured himself a cup of hot water and laid a tea bag in the cup.

"Not sure. Why would somebody steal a dead body?" She inquired with a half-full mouth of corn flakes.

"Alright. Enough of that." Lyle picked up the wireless mouse, turned off the news site and clicked on "Katy's Music." Puff the Magic Dragon wafted through the kitchen. "There'll be plenty of time for that when you're older."

"Lorena's mom let's her watch the news. She gets to drink coffee, too."

"Honey, even I'm not old enough to drink coffee. Besides, isn't Lorena's mom on her fourth husband?"

"She *is*?"

"Ok, that's not something to be repeated," he attempted to correct. "All I'm saying is that Lorena's mom isn't the litmus test for good parenting." He moved to the refrigerator to get some fruit. Instead of an orange, he extracted a stuffed penguin. "Katy? Why is Mr. Tuxedo in the 'fridge?"

"Miss Wiley told us yesterday that penguins live in the ant-artic where it's cold all the time. I figured he'd like it better in there."

Lyle took a second to consider this. "Seems logical," he admitted. He set Mr. Tuxedo back on top of the sour cream container and fished out an orange. A car horn beeped out front.

"That's Lorena. Remember, try not to mention the divorce thing. You'll just upset Lorena *and* her mom, and we don't want to do that, right?"

"Right. Have a nice day, Daddy."

She pecked her father on the cheek and was half-way to the door before he stopped her.

"Katy? What's 'litmus test' mean?"

She huffed her frustration, swinging her book bag around her legs as she turned around with a jerk.

"I don't know," she responded testily.

"Well, what are you supposed to do when I say things you don't understand?"

She scrunched up her face as she pondered this. The car horn sounded again.

"Well?"

"What's a 'list-mus test,' Daddy." He was amazed at how she could speak and sigh at the same time, and after only seven years.

"A litmus test is when you have one example and use it as the standard. Do you understand?"

"I guess so…y'know, Lorena's mom's waiting!"

"Ok, good enough. Have a fun day at school. I love…" The door closed.

Lyle sipped his tea and watched his daughter get into the minivan parked in the street. He waived to Mrs. McCormick, contemplating,

"How much you want to bet the first thing she asks her is how many husbands she's had," not quite under his breath.

He watched the car pool pull away, then he headed up the stairs to shower and change for work.

●

The headset vibrated again as he was driving.

"Status," he barked after tapping the receiver on.

"Good morning to you too, boss," replied his secretary.

"Sorry, Jennifer. Somebody got hold of this number this morning. Speaking of which, is there a package waiting for me at the office?"

"Overnight delivery? It's here. I didn't know we were expecting anything."

"We weren't. How's my schedule around lunch today?"

"Well, you have an appointment with the Board of Directors from Atlanta's Municipal Hospital at 1:00. Seems some of their more expensive equipment is missing and they want to get your thoughts on security. Other than that, you've got a ton of skip tracing work for the Nations group, and Collene is coming in to discuss her trip to Seattle."

"Do me a favor. Push the Board back until 3:00, send any of the skip claims under $50,000 out to Peachtree Financial…"

"Nation's won't like that."

"Did I say you should tell them? And ask Collene if she's free for lunch. I think I'd like some backup."

"So you've got a lunch meeting then? Is this on the books?"

"No. Best to not put this on my schedule. Or Collene's for that matter. Anything else happening?"

"Not really. I've got your papers and faxes waiting on your desk. Is there anything else you'd like me to do before you get in?"

"Now that you mention it; my daughter said something this morning about a dead body coming up missing."

"Katy's watching the news?"

"Only until I caught her. See what there is to that. Download whatever information you can find. She might have heard wrong, but I'd like to know more about it."

"Will do. Anything else?"

"Yeah. Let's get this line changed. I'm not too happy about any Tom, Dick or Fleishman being able to reach me here."

"Will do. See you in a bit."

●

Lyle strolled into his agency, which consisted of a reception area, two offices and a conference room. Jennifer was holding out a stack of papers supported by an overnight delivery envelope. As she was on the phone, she just waved hello.

Taking the stack, he went into his office and closed the door.

He had barely sat down before his partner stepped inside.

"I heard you come in. Is this a bad time to get together?"

"Not at all. How's Seattle?"

Collene flopped down into a chair across from his desk. The brunette draped her legs over one arm of the seat.

"Seattle sucks. I don't know how people can live in such a damp, oppressive environment."

"What about our client?"

"Oh, he's fine. Dumb as a post, but fine. Believe it or not, nearly his entire staff was ripping him off. They were selling off proprietary information in pieces, each person making a drop. It was kind of cool. I'm pretty sure the Senior VP was the ringleader, but he arranged it so, knowingly or not, every single designer and developer in the company was implicated. I laid it all out for the boss, and he was stuck. If he had to fire everyone involved, he'd be left with a handful of secretaries and the janitorial staff, and I'm not even convinced *they're* all entirely clean. I swear, how do morons become so rich?"

"Morons keep us afloat, you know. So what's he going to do?"

"Who knows? I provided enough evidence for him to bring the VP up on charges. The rest is up to him. We're getting paid either way."

"Excellent. Well, *I* got a strange call this morning on my private line. Someone wants to meet for lunch. Whoever they are, they like to play it hush-hush, but I'm not terribly comfortable with the way they're conducting themselves. Think you could tag along?"

"Safety in numbers?"

"Something like that. What else do you have to work on today?"

"Not much. I've got a meeting with a trucking union today. They think their foreman might be skimming."

"Ouch. Be careful with that. Here…" Lyle threw a folder onto her lap. "In your spare time, you want to root around and see what you can dig up about this missing corpse."

"I don't remember Jennifer saying we got a call about this."

"Indulge me. The body was stolen from a morgue in Jersey. If it happens we can assist the case, it could make for some important friends."

Collene looked over the file. "I don't know, Lyle. Cops get pretty ticked about this kind of thing."

"I'm not saying we need to go to Jersey and stir stuff up. Consider it a test. Let's see how far we can get before the cops find the body. Look at it this way, according to this list Jennifer gave me, we sent about 2,500 skip traces to Peachtree Financial. Why?"

"Because the guy at Peachtree Financial owes you a favor?"

"Exactly. So, you could be in charge of a bunch of boring old skips, or you could do some juicy investigating into the disappearance of a corpse and maybe garner us a favor from the Jersey D.A. Which would you prefer?"

"What time's lunch?"

"11:30. *And* we even get to ride in a limo!"

"Well la-dee-freakin'-da," Collene returned the sarcasm in kind. "I'll see you in a couple of hours."

●

The portly gentleman in the back of the limousine was visibly shaken when two people crawled in at the curb.

"I'm sorry, my driver was instructed to pick up a Lyle Status."

"I'm Status," the thin, gangly man confirmed. "This is my partner, Collene Sons. Are you Fleishman?"

"Um, yes. Yes I am. So, Status & Sons…?"

"Consists of myself and Ms. Sons. You probably expected a group of older gentlemen?"

"He expected me to be a boy," Collene said with a grin. "It's my father all over again."

"Actually, I was under the impression this meeting would be private."

"Well, I was under the impression that you wanted to do business with my agency. Ms. Sons may be assisting me in whatever it is you'd like me to do, so I thought it would be best if she attended as well."

"Don't worry," Collene chipped in with a smile. "I'm a light eater."

"If you'd prefer us to go, we'll just take that account code you were discussing, say thank you very much and go have lunch at Chuck's Steak House."

"Ooh, I love Chuck's. I haven't been there forever!"

Fleishman followed their banter like a tennis match. "No, no. It's fine." He leaned out to signal the driver, who was still holding the door open, unsure as to whether or not he let in the right people. "It's fine. We can go."

The driver closed the door once Lyle and Collene settled in the seat facing his employer. Within moments they were fighting downtown Atlanta traffic. Fleishman put up the privacy screen.

"Once again, this is very private…"

"And you want to talk about it in the back seat of a rented limo? Hang on." Collene reached into her bag and produced what appeared to be a radar detector. Once turned on, it began producing a high pitched static. She set it on the floor in between them.

"It takes a bit to get used to a jammer, but you'll forget it's there. Go on."

Fleishman was noticeably disturbed by the white noise, but continued.

"I work for a law firm out of Los Angeles. We have a client by the name of Perry Ashland. He owns a chain of funeral homes. Perhaps you've heard of Ashland Funeral Directors?"

He paused for a response, received none and moved along.

"It's a family business, and Mr. Ashland has been in charge since the late '70s. In that time, he has acquired a rather unusual collection of…memorabilia, let's say."

He paused again. Status and the woman waited for him to continue.

"Something's come up missing."

"With all due respect, Mr. Fleishman, you can stop the pregnant pauses and dramatic narrative. We do this for a living. It takes quite a bit to shock us, so could we just get to the point?"

Fleishman considered this for a moment. He straightened the line of his trousers. He opened the mini fridge and took a sip of bottled water. Finally he looked soberly at the two private detectives.

"We need you to retrieve the blood of Timothy Leary."

I was at the concert for Melissa Etheridge's 50th birthday recently. Any other guys there? No? Well, it was mathematically improbable anyway. As far as I know there were five of us, men I mean, in the auditorium. Two roadies, a T-shirt vendor, and some other confused soul who had made the trip from Switzerland after having had a penis attached earlier that week. Apparently, since he/she couldn't carry Melissa's first two kids, he/she wanted to be the father of the next one. Skippy's getting his/her own spotlight next month on a very special Rosie O'Donnell & Kids.

So, other than that, it was essentially 15,000 lesbians…and me. I call that a good night. The only problem being that, within an hour or so, the line to the ladies' room actually wrapped around the arena. Twice. So, naturally, there was spillover into the men's room. Have you been in the men's room at the Gardens? They've got those banana shaped urinals that jut out from the wall like a giant athletic supporter. Here I am, trying to figure out if I need to straddle this thing, or go head to lip or what, when this leggy blond in a leather skirt steps up next to me, throws one leg over her urinal and just releases.

"How'ya doin'?" She says, giving me a wink. What do you say? "Just hanging out?" No reason to state the obvious, so I just gave her a little wave.

CHAPTER ELEVEN

Lyle and Collene were laughing hysterically as they poured through the doors and into their reception area just before 2:00.

"Somebody had fun at lunch," the receptionist observed from behind her desk.

"Jennifer, put the phones on auto-pilot and come into the conference room with Collene and me. Have we got a story for you!"

"Sure thing."

The two partners were still giggling furiously as they found chairs around the conference table. The receptionist came in a few seconds later. Jennifer was somewhere in her early fifties and quite reserved. Lyle knew that she wouldn't enjoy the story nearly as much as he and Collene, but he had to tell it to someone out loud, if only to convince himself that it actually happened.

"Ok, you've got my attention," she said, finding her own seat.

"Get this," Collene started. "Some big uppity-up funeral director in California got ripped off. You'll never guess what they want us to track down..."

"Hang on," interjected Lyle. "You've got to start from the beginning. What the guy looked like and all that."

"Oh, you're right. Ok, ok. So we get in the limo with this fat, sweaty, weasely guy..."

"He wasn't *that* bad. You're just upset because he didn't want you to be there."

"Whatever. Although," she considered, putting a hand in front of her mouth to hide a grin. "He did look like he was going to drop a load when I got in the limo. It was probably the closest he'd been to a woman out of court. I think he thought I was a pro."

"Easy now. Anyway, Jennifer, this guy works for a law firm out west who has the funeral director as a client. Apparently, he's a pretty significant client too, because they're going above and beyond to take care of this for him."

"You're not kidding. They're paying us a bundle."

"Well, it *is* patently illegal—what we're doing."

"Very true."

"Please," Jennifer interrupted. "Could just one of you tell the story? I'm getting dizzy."

"Sorry," Lyle offered. "So this funeral director…"

"Perry Ashland," Collene inserted before motioning that she was locking her lips.

"Perry Ashland," Lyle agreed. "He's been in charge of the business for over thirty years. And it seems in that time he has amassed quite an interesting collection of…memorabilia."

"That's a direct quote. 'Memorabilia.'"

"Being out in Los Angeles, he's had access to more than a few famous corpses."

"He's got John Wayne's eyes!"

"You mean his eyes resemble John Wayne's," Jennifer interpreted hopefully. "Like someone having Bette Davis eyes?"

"No," Lyle emphasized. "Supposedly he has John Wayne's actual eyeballs in a jar. He has also acquired a pound of flesh each from John Belushi, John Candy and Chris Farley. He's said to have the heart of Phil Hartman with an actual bullet hole in it. And that's just his Saturday Night Live collection."

"This is morbid. You talked about this over lunch?"

"Well, Collene and I talked about it over lunch…"

"We had the entire interview in the limo. Fleishman, the lawyer, had himself dropped off at the airport. He arranged for our lunch at the Hilton, and then the limo dropped us off here. Great lunch!"

"Fantastic lunch. Jennifer, I'm sorry you couldn't have joined us."

"I doubt I would have had much of an appetite after the whole body parts discussion."

"It was hysterical!" Collene laughed as she said it. "The lawyer guy was so flustered about what he had to tell us! He was positively mortified!"

"Half the fun was watching him squirm." Lyle pointed to Collene. "And you! This one kept asking for more and more details, just to watch him blush!"

"So, what did this all have to do with the job?"

"Well," Lyle continued, trying to be more serious. "It seems he has one particularly obscure collection of…"

"Memorabilia?" Jennifer offered with a hint of disgust.

"Exactly. This one collection is from the famous Lennon-Oko bed-in back in the early seventies. He has Lennon's tongue, Arlo Guthrie's hair, a bunch of other stuff from people Fleishman had never heard of…"

"Wait a second," Jennifer interrupted. "I was twenty when John was killed. He was in New York, walking into his apartment building. How did he…?"

"Oh, he trades with other funeral directors," Collene noted. "Apparently, there's a whole underground that shares this obsession."

"Lovely." Jennifer blanched.

"Anyhow," Lyle continued. "One of the pieces from that collection— and, again, these people not only participated in the bed-in, they per- formed background vocals on 'Give Peace A Chance'—one of the 'memorabilia' has turned up missing."

"I'm not sure if I want to know."

"Timothy Leary's blood."

"What?"

"You heard me right," Lyle confirmed. "There was a big rumor about how Leary was having his head frozen in case they find some way of bringing him back. Fleishman says it's true. But even cryogenically frozen…people, I guess, need to be embalmed in some fashion."

"The blood won't keep," Collene added.

"Exactly. So, when this service was performed, his blood was kept in a series of vials, distributed throughout the funeral community, as it were."

"And his vial was stolen?" Jennifer deduced.

"Bingo!" Collene and Lyle confirmed in unison.

"And he won't go to the police…"

"Because having this collection is illegal, not to mention unethical and immoral. Exactly."

"What are you supposed to be doing for him?"

"Find out who took it and steal it back." Lyle smiled as he said it, taking joy in Jennifer's look of stunned disbelief.

"Tell me you turned him down."

"For that kind of money," Collene commented. "I'd get him Leary's blood if the acid freak was alive today!"

"You can't be serious. You'd be risking everything."

"I'm not sure that's true. The person who stole it certainly won't be calling the police if it's missing. And, provided we adhere to our confidentiality—employees notwithstanding—we have what appears to be an impressively large law firm willing to protect us should things go awry. Which they won't."

"You almost sound delighted about the whole thing."

"Oh, I'm stoked!" Lyle agreed and high-fived Collene, a first in the three years Jennifer had worked for the firm.

"It makes me feel like a real private dick," Collene contributed.

Lyle sighed. "This has to be the best I've felt since Tammy took off on us last year. It's the most excited I've been about work in close to ten years. It's pretty cool."

"It's gruesome."

"But in a really cool way," Collene corrected.

"Well, you two do what you want, but I'd prefer not to have anything to do with this."

"No problem. This job won't be showing up on any of the books. We will be needing your help with redistributing some of our cases, though."

"So you two will be leaving for Los Angeles?"

"Not quite yet. We're waiting to get the employee records faxed in. They want to send it from a third party. They want no connection to our agency from either the funeral home or the law firm unless absolutely necessary."

"Keeping you out of jail, as an example. And even that will be up to their interpretation of what's 'absolutely necessary,' right?"

"Jennifer's worried about us, Lyle," the senior partner observed with a grin.

"Well, that's very sweet. But we've been adults and in this business for a while. I'm confident that the risk is negligible when compared to the rewards."

Jennifer chose not to meet her bosses gaze. She began taking notes instead.

"You'll need your tickets, hotel reservations…It sounds as if you're both determined to go, so these reservations are for two?"

"I think Collene would shoot me otherwise."

"Damned straight."

"Will you be meeting your scheduled appointments today?"

Lyle settled back. "We'll be good for today. But we're on a freeze for any more business until further notice. Feel free to refer any of our steady customers over to Miller & Adams. They'll do a competent job, but their attitudes are so contemptible we should have no fear of losing future contracts. We should change the Website to read 'On Assignment,' and cancel any links for the next month or so.

"And if you could do me one more favor," Lyle added as Jennifer got up from the table. "My housekeeper should be at my place right now. Could you let her know that I'll need her to stay a few extra hours tonight? I want to clean up my current workload as much as possible."

"Anything I can do for you, Collene?"

"Not right now. I'm going to be leaving soon for my Union meeting, anyway."

Collene and Lyle watched silently as Jennifer left the conference room without saying another word.

"She's pissed," Collene observed.

"She's a trooper. She'll get over it. Listen, we didn't get a chance to review what you found out about that missing body."

Collene unhooked the PDA from her folio. "The stiff was a guy named Don Owens. Execution-style murder. Shot to the head at close proximity. He was discovered yesterday, late afternoon. About thirty million people were listening to him nationwide when he was on the Tom Green show earlier that morning. Some think he masterminded the whole riots thing. There's allegedly a counter-group calling itself the New Atheists Movement, which took credit for the hit, but no one's ever heard of these guys or know how to reach them. The body was taken from the morgue sometime between the hours of 11:00 PM last night and 4:00 this morning."

"Wow. Good stuff. I envy the Jersey police."

"We're not going to get into this thing, right?"

"No, no. Not anymore. This Leary case should be enough to satisfy my work-a-day blues."

"Not to mention the fact that we're getting paid for it."

"An outstandingly solid point, Ms. Sons. Shall we get back to it?"

The two pushed their chairs back and rose from the conference table.

"Can you believe all that hoopla yesterday over some stupid book?"

"Not hardly," Lyle agreed. "Did you ever read *The Judas Conspiracy*?"

"I tried a couple of different times. I just couldn't get into the style."

"You didn't miss much. It's all plot twists and constant dialogue trying to masquerade as provocative literary technique. Even if you can disregard the lack of any real story, what killed me was the way scenes just cut one into the other, sometimes in the middle of exposition. It was dead annoying."

Now, the oddest thing about standing and urinating next to a woman who's also standing and urinating was how genuinely arousing it was. I moved in so as not to be showy, and the next thing I know, my dick's brushing up against porcelain that had been used by thousands of drunken rednecks at monster truck rallies and killer death wrestling matches.

So I'm at the sink, washing him off...What? It's disgusting! So I'm washing him off, and these other two girls walk in, look at me washing the Winkster and start laughing. And I'm thinking, Is that necessary? *I mean, they've made their decision and don't want anything to do with the penis, but that doesn't mean they can make fun!*

Anyhow. Eventually I got back out to my seat, and Melissa start's playing a real nice slow song. And my girlfriend, she starts feeling...frisky. She starts grooving and rubbing and dirty dancing real slow. And I finally had to make her stop.

"I'm really sorry, honey," I said. "But there's two AMAZINGLY HOT women making out about three rows down. Now, if you could just let me concentrate on them, it'll pay off for both of us later on. Promise!

CHAPTER TWELVE

"Olga? I'm home!"

Katy dropped her book bag in front of the hall closet. She heard the housekeeper's voice coming from the laundry. She was out of her sneakers and half way to the family room before the woman in the utility area responded to Katy's presence.

"I don't know if she's ever coming back. She just left last…Oh! Katy! I'm on the phone with my sister, dear. Your daddy says he'll be a few hours late, but you should get your homework done and he's taking you out somewhere nice to eat. Ok?"

"Whatever. I'll go start my homework now."

Olga smiled too broadly. It made Katy uncomfortable.

"That's a good girl! I'll fix you a snack as soon as I'm off the phone!" The middle-aged woman turned back into the utility room. "She's such a sweet girl. I feel so sorry for her…"

Katy looked over at her book bag leaning against the closet, looked back at the utility room door as it closed, and made a beeline to the family room.

The seven-year old dragged a cushion off the couch as she passed it, and flopped it down on the floor. Then she grabbed the remote from the coffee table and, keeping it firmly in her grasp, flopped herself down on the cushion.

She put the control on the carpet and placed her fingers on the keypad. Then she looked very deliberately at the 60" monitor. She began testing herself in this manner only a few days before. She knew the sequence by heart.

Monitor, Power, Cable, Power, Home CPU, Connection, Modem, Connection, Menu, Password, By-Pass Channel Lock, 012905 (her birthday), Find News

She finished tapping the sequence and had several seconds to watch the display catch up to her commands. When the stone serious face of the Trump News anchorman blinked into place, Katy giggled at her own abilities.

"...no further rioting or demonstrations have been reported since yesterday," the chiseled, well-manicured man announced. "Surprisingly, no Trump properties were effected. The focus of the activities, writer/comedian Jackson Cross, has not been available for comment since surfacing at the Sinatra estate in Colorado. When questioned about the events, The Donald, who also owns property in Colorado, had this to say..."

The picture cut to a frazzled looking real estate barren.

"What? Who? I don't know where he is. I was sleeping with a 23-year old supermodel last night. What do I care?"

"More from that interview with The Donald later in the program."

"Donald," Katy repeated, shaking her head disdainfully without really knowing why. She clicked the Next icon. A talking head nearly identical with that of the Trump reporter blinked onto the screen. An out-of-focus view of some mountains surrounding a mansion hovered over his shoulder.

"...nt Brockman reporting for UBBN. We're now getting footage from the Sinatra complex in Colorado. A press release was issued earlier this afternoon from, and I must state again that the existence of this organization has not been confirmed, the American Clone Association, demanding the emancipation and naturalization of all clones engineered in the United States. Most surprising is the existence of this so-called ACA. In a counter release issued by a group identifying itself as the Nevada Entertainment Conglomerate, allegations of Grand Theft have been issued against writer/comedian Jackson Cross. This release accompanied numerous legal documents attesting to the fact that biological organisms created by the

Nevada Entertainment Conglomerate for the express purpose of entertainment will be the sole property of the NEC. We're going live now to Frank Mellows in the heart of the New York Stock Exchange. Frank?"

"Thanks, Kent," came the reply from another grim newsman. "Things are at a bit of a stand-still here with regards to trading of both the biological sciences and the various Nevada Entertainment properties. We think people are waiting to see what the extent of breakthroughs have been accomplished by the heretofore unmentioned American Clone Association, and why this Nevada Entertainment Conglomerate is taking this so personally. We'll be here, live at the exchange, until there's some kind of reaction, either way. Reporting live for United Bank Business Network, I'm Frank…"

"Boring." Katy clicked Next. Even as a glamorous pair of newscasters within a high-tech set blinked into view, she was browsing toy sites on various smaller windows on the monitor.

"*Entertainment This Very Second* has Jorge Dominique at the Sinatra Complex. Jorge?"

"Thanks, Julie. I'm standing at the gates of the Sinatra Compound in Grand Ravine, Colorado where writer/comedian Jackson Cross is approaching the crowd apparently with something to say. We're running this live and I believe…yes! Mr. Cross is at the gates. He is accompanied by two young men, I would have to guess pre-teen, and is addressing the crowd."

The audio continued piping through, although Katy was mostly preoccupied with screens featuring Tubular Girl accessories.

"How's everyone doing today? A funny thing happened on the way to my crucifixion. We just wanted to let you know that we'll be having an official press conference in a couple of days to explain all this. I can tell you right now that I've been commissioned by these folks to represent their cause as a spokesperson. I haven't stolen or, more accurately, kidnapped anyone's property. Did I kidnap you, Sammy?"

"Hell no! Anyone with two good eyes can tell that we're the ones who dragged you out here, baby! Dino?"

"Who let all you people into my room?"

"Anyhow, let all your fellow newshounds know, we'll make formal statements on Monday. Now, if you don't mind, I'm freezing my ass off out here!"

"Mr. Cross! What about the murder of Don Owens?" "Do you accept any responsibility for what happened yesterday?" "Have you been threatened by any known Mob enforcers?" "Any plans to clone Ethel Mermon? Well? She was an amazing talent!"

Katy got up from the floor and padded into the kitchen. She was fishing through the trash when the housekeeper exited the utility room.

"Your father's on the phone," she whispered while holding the receiver. "Don't hang up, my sister's still on the other line. Long distance." Then, as she held it out for the little girl, she blurted out loud, "What are you doing in the trash?"

Katy took the phone with a huff.

"Yes, daddy."

"What *are* you doing in the trash? You're not trying to find one of my credit card receipts again, are you?"

"No, daddy."

"Good. Because I shred them now, you know. Did you have a good day at school?"

"I guess."

"Did you get your homework done?"

Katy looked over at her book bag leaning on the hall closet.

"Yup. All done."

"Katy?"

"Well, I'm almost done."

"You're not watching the news, are you?"

"Where are we going to eat?"

"Wherever you like."

"Sushi?"

"How can you…? No, no. That's fine. I'll have teriyaki something or other. If you want fish, you'll get fish."

"Cool. Can I go now?"

"Please just turn off the news?"

"Ok, daddy. Bye-bye."

"I love…" The phone was disconnected and on the counter. Olga came out of the laundry with a basket of clothes.

"Oh, honey! You didn't hang up, did you?"

"M'sorry. Forgot. Do we have any tape?"

"I think there's some in your father's desk. Why?"

"He shredded my homework by mistake. I'll get it!"

"I'm sure he wouldn't have shredded…" But Katy was already bounding up the stairs. "The poor girl," Olga sympathized as she picked up the receiver and pushed redial.

Frankly, I'm a big fan of Melissa Etheridge. David Crosby's sperm aside, I think she's tremendously talented. But I found that the giant screens on either side of the stage were just creepy. Huge pictures of her girlfriend and kids...it just seemed kind of—I don't know—intrusive, maybe?

Then we went to the Hard Rock café for a late dinner after the concert. Talk about intrusive!

In the middle of the meal, my girlfriend asks, "Why is there a turkey baster mounted alongside a gold record edition of Yes I Am?"

"I'm not sure, but this Santa Fe chicken is very salty...

"And suddenly I'm in the mood for fish."

CHAPTER THIRTEEN

"Hey Sons, check this out."

Collene put her coffee down in the rental car's cup holder and turned around to look at her partner in the back seat. They'd driven to this San Fernando Valley residence directly from the airport, and he'd been playing with a package the whole time. Lyle had the open box in his lap, foam packaging splayed out across the seat and floor. He was holding what appeared to be a tricorder from that old sci-fi series.

"This is a pretty nice piece of equipment right here."

"Well? You've been promising to tell me what it does since we picked it up on the way to the airport yesterday. Give it up, already."

Lyle moved up in the seat so his partner had a better view of the display.

"This is going to sound a little far-fetched, but…see those orange lines?"

Lyle pointed the gizmo at the bungalow directly across from the alley in which they were parked.

"It's all orange lines."

"It takes a bit to get used to. Those lines represent electrical current. The bigger ones display power running through the house.

"The smaller, less defined lines represent components within electronic equipment. See how fuzzy some of those shapes are?"

"I guess."

"The thing is, electrical currents attract dust particles. Those really fuzzy images are older appliances; that's probably his toaster, there's his microwave…and so on."

"Static electricity?"

"Exactly! The longer you have an appliance, the more static electricity. Now, these shapes here show pretty intense currents with little-to-no static occurrence. Meaning…?"

"New electronic components."

"Bingo. Our boy here's been on something of a shopping spree over the last few weeks. I'd guess that's a new disk relay; that over there's probably a stereo…and that, if I'm not mistaken, is a brand new wall monitor. Not bad for a floral delivery driver making about ten bucks an hour."

"Well, that all follows the massive deposits he's been making into his account. What are those bunch of yellowish wavy lines bouncing around over there."

"Hmm. A fringe benefit. I guess it reads either heat or personal electrical impulses. Apparently he's got company."

"Active company at that. When's the last time you had sex like that at 7:30 in the morning?"

Lyle moved the display around so that the electric eye was facing his partner.

"No readings here. Makes sense. You have to have a brain to register electric current."

"Yeah, I'm sorry. You haven't had a date since Tammy took off, have you?"

"Katy's not ready for that. Hell, I'm not ready for that. She had her reasons for leaving. Who's to say she wasn't right? I'm in no hurry for another woman to get sick of me."

"And who wouldn't? You don't smoke, you don't drink, you're in great shape, you own your own business and you never lose your temper. I don't know why it took her six years to dump your sorry ass in the first place."

"Harpy."

"Oh yeah! And you don't swear either! Man, what an asshole."

"I have my vices. Speaking of which," he noted, turning the machine's attention back toward the house. "It looks like somebody's in the shower."

Collene took a sip of her coffee.

"It's a cool gadget, and all, but I'm glad our entire case doesn't rely on some wavy lines."

"What case," Lyle questioned, his attention riveted to a series of impulses apparently rubbing itself dry. "We're not on any case. No case, no rules. That's the appeal here."

"Y'know, we've worked together for nearly five years. I'm still not always sure what you're talking about."

"See? You and Tammy *did* have stuff in common."

The two partners sat in silence for a few moments; her with her coffee, he with hot tea. A woman exited the bungalow while still drying her long, red hair.

"Check this out," Collene invited.

The tall, rail-thin girl stopped drying her hair and dropped the towel onto the folding chair on the small porch. She looked around quickly before lifting her halter-top and exposing herself to the neighborhood.

"Hey now," Lyle lifted his eyes from the electronic wave reader. "What's that about?"

Within a matter of seconds, the girl had a strapless, push-up bra on and her halter back into place. Her pumps were tied together, and she flung the shoes over her shoulder along with her purse. She strolled away from the house barefoot.

"Stripper?" Lyle inquired.

"Definitely." Collene confirmed.

"The boy does like to spend his money."

Lyle watched the small screen of his new toy for a few moments longer.

"Looks like he spent more than just his money," Lyle continued his train of thought. "He's out cold. Alright then. I'm going in."

Lyle began packing up the equipment and prepared to leave. Collene stared in disbelief.

"What the hell are you talking about? You're not going in there while he's in the house! Don't be stupid…"

Lyle snapped his gaze at his partner like a rattlesnake.

"I'm not playing around here, Collene. We've had a great relationship over the past five years primarily because we don't step on each other's toes. But the rules are a little different here, so I'm going to have to ask you to trust me."

"I should come with."

"No. You should stay in the car in case there are any problems," Lyle said, putting on surgical gloves as he spoke. "I'll have the headset on, set to our private number. Vibrate me if something happens out here. As for what happens in there? Don't worry about it. I'll be back…ten minutes. Tops."

Collene was staring at her partner as if she'd never seen him before. Lyle quickly and quietly exited the car and crossed the road.

Gary Marsh was enjoying a deep, post-orgasmic sleep, when he had the odd feeling that his arms were being manipulated. It was fast becoming uncomfortable, forcing him to swim out from the cozy darkness of dream and into a harsh, staggering reality.

He came-to while still in bed. His arms where fastened behind him with some kind of cord. Someone was sitting on his back, their knees grinding into his elbows.

"Candy? What're you doin'?"

A hard, metal cylinder pressed up against his temple. The click of a gun hammer was unmistakable in the small bedroom. The voice was absolutely not Candy's.

"Morning, fuckstick. Time to pay the piper."

Unfortunately for Gary, his first instinct was to thrash around against his captivity. The man on his back responded by pushing Gary's head forcibly into the pillow, ensuring that he couldn't breathe. After several seconds of exerting energy without taking oxygen, Gary stopped and tried to regroup.

"Hmp-ooh-uu-unt?"

The man eased up on pressing his head.

"What was that, cum sucker?"

"What do you want?"

Without a response, the man let go of his head. In seconds, Gary was blindfolded and turned around. The man continued sitting on his torso. The prisoner's arms were rapidly starting to fatigue.

"What do I want," asked the man from the darkness. "What do I want?" Gary's head snapped from a hard slap. "What do you think I want, you ignorant fucking piece of garbage? Huh?" Another hard slap.

"I don't have it! I swear I don't!"

The stranger grabbed Gary under an armpit, hoisted him off the bed and sent him, naked and blind, flying into the wall.

"Do you want to continue insulting my intelligence? Is that what you want you fucking cunt?"

"Dude," Gary pleaded, crumpled on the floor, trying to spit out his own blood. "I swear to fucking God I don't have it!"

Gary had no way to prepare for the kick to his stomach.

"Who am I, dipshit?"

"What?" Hard slap to the face.

"Who am I, you little puke? Do you think I'm fucking around here?"

"I have no goddamned idea who you are!"

"Exactly. You don't know who I am or what I look like. You fuck with me now and you won't see me coming the next time either. Now, where is it?"

"I don't know!" Hard punch to his naked testicles. "Oh, Jesus! C'mon!" Gary rolled into a fetal ball. He started coughing violently. His assailant lifted him back into a sitting position.

"Let's start over. Who contacted you?"

"Some guy…I don't know!" Hard metal crashed against his jaw. Gary felt one of his teeth loosen.

"If I don't start feeling like you're going to be fucking cooperative, I will end this right now." Gary felt the cold cylinder press against his temple again.

"Shit! I'm telling the truth, man! This guy came up to me when I was on a break at the sandwich shop. He told me about the blood! I didn't know the old man was doing anything like that!"

"So I'm supposed to believe some ignorant fuck like you pulled this off with no direction?"

"Hey, fuck you!" The stranger punched his forehead. "Ow!"

"Don't talk back to the man with the gun, numbnuts. To continue, you got the blood. Then what?"

"I gave it to him. He paid me." Gary felt what could only be a shoe stepping delicately on his genitals. "Hey! C'mon!"

"Don't move, fuckhead. This next part will be very important to your future wife and kids. How did this 'guy' know when you were ready to trade?"

"Phone number! He gave me a phone number! It's on a card in my wallet!" Gary sighed and fell back over as he felt the shoe remove itself and heard the stranger walk away from him.

"Ok, let's see. In the pants we have a blade. Tough boy, eh? Cigarettes, pills…no end to your bad habits. Where's…ahh. The nighstand!"

Gary tensed up as he heard his captor move toward and across his body to get to the bed table.

"Damn, you've got a lot of cash in here! What is this, like $1,500? And you slept while that whore was packing her shit? You're more lucky than smart."

"Candy's not a whore," he replied in barely more than a whisper.

"She ain't fucking you for your attributes, needledick. Driver's license—terrible picture, Gary—bowling card, I assume this picture came with the wallet. Here we go…"

The stranger huffed his disapproval. Gary tensed up. "What?"

"Kobayashi? The name above the phone number says Kobayashi."

"Yeah? So? That's what he told me!" Even blindfolded, Gary knew that the assailant was shaking his head. "What?"

"Nothing. When did you make the drop?"

"Last Wednesday."

There was a nerve-wracking pause as the invader considered his options. When he finally spoke again, Gary twitched uncontrollably.

"Here's how it's going to work, asshole. I've got your switchblade…"

"Yeah?" His voice cracked. Gary was so nervous he started to tear up.

"I'm going to put it on your kitchen counter on my way out. You'll eventually find it and cut yourself out. If I'm not satisfied with this number, I'll be back. You got that, bugfucker?"

"I swear to you! That's everything I know!"

"Somehow, I don't doubt it. But, before I go, I need to make sure you're not peeking out the window…"

"I won't! I won't! I'll count to a thousand! A million!"

As he pleaded, the intruder grabbed Gary under his armpit once more and unceremoniously dumped him into the closet.

"Don't lock me in here! I can't see!"

"That's the idea, dick-for-brains."

There was a rattling of the latch, footfalls, and then the sound of the front door closing.

Lyle crossed the street and hopped into the rental, looking no different than when he left.

"Everything alright?"

"Fine. I've got a lead. We should go."

Collene backed out of the alley and began driving down a suburban road, blocks away from Gary's bungalow.

"I've changed my mind about a few things while you were gone."

"Oh?"

She leaned over and picked up the electronic wave reader from the floor at Lyle's feet.

"Firstly, this thing is not bad. When you need to see what's happening behind closed doors, it does the job very well."

Lyle's face held no reaction. "And secondly?"

"Secondly? Maybe you do have some vices after all."

Lyle smiled at this.

"Ms. Sons," he began. "We've barely scratched the surface." With that, Lyle reached into his pocket and pulled out a wad of bills. "Let's find someplace nice for lunch. This job had a bonus."

I was born and raised Catholic, although I think that's a pretty specious thing to say. No one is born Catholic. They recruit you before you know any better. I think it was Pope I'm-A-Self-Riotous-Bastard IV who decreed that babies should be baptized into the faith before they can say their first word.

"Let's get them right out of the box," *was the official papal edict, I think.*

It's just dumb. They made me say my first confession when I was something like seven. Seven years old! How much real, honest-to-Christ sinning do you do before puberty? And we had to go every week. These nuns would stand over us, all grim and hairy, making us go into a little closet to tell a priest how bad we were. It's deplorable.

I ran out of sins pretty quickly. So I had to start making shit up. Do you see the irony there? I had to lie, which is a sin, about sinning that I didn't do because otherwise I was going to hell. What a racket.

"Forgive me Father, for I have sinned. My last confession was…about nine hours ago! I've been sleeping! How bad could I have been?"

"Did you have any impure thoughts in your sleep, my son?"

Fucking perverts. They really only want the juice. 'Round about the time I was twelve, I found my dad's Penthouse collection. Then my confessions got a little more interesting.

"Well Father, I've always heard about these kinds of stories…I mean sins, but I never thought I'd be…confessing one. [I'm twelve now, remember?] See, I was out of town on business

and staying at this hotel. It happened that a circus was in town, and the performers were also staying there. I was down at the bar having a drink when the sword swallower and her sister, the bearded lady, invited me up to their room..."

It didn't take long before the priest caught on. It got to the point where I'd be kneeling in the confessional and he'd be like:

"Before we begin, what month and year did you sin this time, my son?"

I'd check out the cover of my dad's Penthouse. "Um, June of '92?"

There'd be some magazine shuffling and some pages flipping from his side of the confessional.

"Please continue my son! That was a great month for sin!"

Chapter Fourteen

Salvator Vega (or Sally, if you were made) sat at his bar and stared into a glass of club soda.

He usually enjoyed these quiet moments in the club. Club? One bar, three pool tables, a juke box and a couple of dart boards hardly constituted a club. But his grandfather bought the place in the '50s, and Sally wouldn't trade it for all the cigars in Havana. Artie was hauling boxes from the back room and refilling the cooler.

"What's the matter, boss?"

"Turn on the tube, will ya' Artie? The press conference is getting ready to start."

"Sure, boss." Artie grabbed the wireless from next to the cash register, turned on the monitor and logged on. "I figured you'd want to watch this at the office. Y'know, with all the lawyers an' all."

"This was my grandfather's office, Artie. He'd want me to be right here, on this stool, taking it like a lady. Besides, those lawyers don't know dick about this kind of thing. It's betrayal, Artie. Pure and simple."

The AOL News Network logo hovered in place. A status bar clicked down the time until the live feed would begin.

"It's a new world, Artie," Sal stated as the bartender covered bottles with ice. "Roberto must be doing the funky chicken in his grave."

"Your grandfather would be very proud of you Sally."

Sal turned to see his Uncle Vince standing in the doorway of the dark bar.

"I knew you'd be here, watching this crap."

Sal slid off his barstool to hug and kiss his uncle.

"Why's Frankie doing this, Uncle Vinny? Didn't we give him the life?"

"People go their own way, Sally. The world turns."

Vinny pulled up a stool next to his nephew. "Scotch please, Arthur."

"Now, Mr. Vega, it's 9:30 in the morning. Your wife would have my balls if she knew I was serving you this early."

"Fuck my wife, Artie. Please." The three men chuckled as the drink was prepared.

A slightly pixilated image of an attractive young black woman appeared on the monitor.

"Here we go," Sal announced, steeling himself for what was to come.

"Good morning! I'm April Givens reporting live for the AOL News Network!"

Her image improved considerably as a wave of pixels refined the picture.

"We're here at the gates of the Sinatra Compound in Grand Ravine, Colorado. The current residents of the estate have refused to allow anyone entrance, claiming fear for their well-being, and that much is understandable. Accompanying dozens of reporters here to cover the press conference, protesters have been arriving steadily over the last few days. Some are pro-clone rights, some dispute the idea of cloning entirely, while others still are here in general protest of the group's spokesperson, Jackson Cross. The police are constantly moving through and around the crowd trying to administer a modicum of order to these proceedings. On the opposite side of the gates is a dais with microphones, where it is assumed the people who called this press conference will be giving their statements."

"Enough with the cooze and the blow-by-blow," Sal growled. "Get the fuck on with it."

"There is some movement up at the house...yes! I believe the residents are coming down to address the crowd. Jackson Cross is leading the small group of men and one young woman down to the staging area at the gates. They appear to be in good spirits. Most of the group appears to be in their early teens or younger. Some of the more somber gentlemen in the group would almost have to be bodyguards. There are a couple of older men accompanying them. These may or may not be attorneys representing the group. I suppose we'll find out when they begin speaking. They're taking their seats at the table…"

"Jesus Christ! We can fucking see, you stupid bitch! Shut up already!"

"Easy, Sally. You'll blow a gasket."

"And it appears they are ready to begin…"

●

"Well, I guess the first thing would be to thank everyone for coming out here today."

"Cross is the Anti-Christ! Open your eyes!"

"That didn't take long. Don't panic, everybody. The police are taking care of the problem."

"Take your hands off me! I have a Christian duty…!"

"If we could just say what we came out here to say, then we can go back inside where it's warm while the rest of you can hang out here in the snow and heckle us to your heart's delight.

"Ahem. Towards the end of the 20th Century, biological engineering had progressed to the point that cloning was not only possible, it was fashionable. Sheep, monkeys, chickens. You name it. It seemed to be a fantastic breakthrough to solve a tremendous amount hunger and medicinal problems. But with the advent of the Internet, all the pertinent information regarding this scientific miracle was available to anyone with a modem.

"It was about this time that a group of business men envisioned the entertainment potential of this amazing science. Imagine a stable of the greatest talent of our times, manufactured, owned and controlled by a consortium. Think 'Olsen Twins,' to the ninth. So this group, since labeling themselves the Nevada Entertainment Conglomerate, engineered the showcase of the next millennia, from the DNA of the last one. I'd like to take the time to introduce the people sitting with me here today. To my far left…He may look like he's ready to start little league, but he is in fact crooner/comedian Dean Martin."

"Thank you, Mr. Spokesman. I'd also like to thank the academy…"

"That thing's not Dean Martin! It's not even really alive! It has no soul!"

"But I do have manners, pally. Maybe that's why the police are hauling you out of here instead of me. Don't worry, though. Everybody spends some time in the poky sometime."

"Directly to my left is a man who spent most of his first life tearing down racial barriers and building bridges of tolerance with tremendous talent and patience. Mr. Sammy Davis, Jr."

"Thank you for that, baby. You're a mensch, I don't care what they say about you. Is it cool to say I love you? Because I do man. From the bottom. Right here."

"Over to the far right of the table is a talent too incredible to be contained in one lifetime; Liberace. Lee?"

"I'm very cold. Can we go back inside, please?"

"Just a couple more minutes, Lee. The gracious young woman trying to warm up our fragile friend here, is none other than the versatile and lovely Judy Garland."

"Hello everyone! I've missed you all so much!"

"And finally, no introduction will suffice. I can only repeat was has been said thousands, if not millions of times before. Ladies and gentlemen, Mr. Frank Sinatra."

"Very nice. Nice job, kid. Hey! Where's that Connie Chung, babe? How come she ain't here?"

"I think she's retired, Frank."

"That's a shame. How 'bout you, honey? That's right, you with the microphone. Listen, toots, I got 100 years of experience and I'll be hitting puberty any day. You need to climb on board before this train leaves the station. And what did I tell you about addressing me?"

"Beg your pardon, Mr. Sinatra. Moving on, these young people were raised in a lab by folks who claimed to own them. They were told, from the moment they were old enough to comprehend anything, that they were property, created to expand the bottom line. Legal slave entertainment.

"It wasn't a terrible life, I'm told. Once they were old enough to begin training, they were provided with reasonably nice accommodations and an almost limitless expense account. But, for all the guild, the fact remained that they were someone else's property. And that did not sit well with them. They figured out a way to escape, contacted the Sinatra family and have been granted asylum on this property. They merely wish to be recognized as free people, now and forever.

"I'd now like to turn this over to a friend of mine. Since hearing about the plight of these entertainers, he has committed himself, as I have, to bringing their story to the masses. May I introduce the Director and Chairman of the American Clone Association, Mr. Daniel Epstein."

"Thank you Mr. Cross. Loved your book, by the way."

"Boo!"

"Alright, settle down. What we've done is create an organization to act as cowcatcher for the movement. The idea that these kids are anyone's property should be abhorred by anyone with even a hint of a conscience. We'll be hiring additional lawyers, people far more familiar with legislation and the law than either myself or Jackson could pretend to be.

"Our worry is that their story might not be so unique. First of all, there is the possibility that the NEC may have even more kids in captivity. If they've been born then, and you must believe us on this, they are living, feeling, individual people who are entitled to all the rights the rest of us take for granted. And if anyone knows of other incidents such as these, please contact us through our web site."

"Thank you, Mr. Epstein. And now, we'll entertain a few polite questions before moving back into the comfort of indoors. Ok, you."

"David Kroft from WNGT in Chicago."

"I know you, David. I used to watch your work when I lived in Ft. Wayne."

"Um, thanks. At any rate, Mr. Cross, why you? Why were you sought out by this group?"

"Good question. I think the answer comes down to exposure and philosophy. Like it or not, I'm currently a magnet for the spotlight. And people who share my beliefs regarding tolerance need to be aware that this is happening now. These kids don't want to live like slaves for the ten years it takes to change the laws. They need our help right this minute. Next? Go ahead."

"Alishia Gertler from the Vegas Gazette. Are your clients willing to testify against their…creators, as it were?"

"I know, I know. Everyone's thinking that the mob's behind this whole thing, and they may be right. But the whole idea of the mob and their influence is pretty archaic in this day and age, don't you think? I'll guarantee you that this is more corporate business than family business. The mob just doesn't have the influence it used to…"

"Um, Jackson?"

"Just a second, Sammy. We're not here because we're afraid of some hit going down."

"Jackson?"

"Hold on, Dean. We're here because the law has not evolved enough to protect everyone it needs to protect. Not because we're afraid of a group of over-the-hill gangsters who forgot what century it is."

"Hey! Kid! Shut the hell up!"

●

The image of young Frank Sinatra wrestling a microphone away from his newly appointed spokesperson remained on a few of the shards of the monitor's screen, even after the Scotch bottle shattered inside its casing.

Artie and Vince kept silent, ready to duck away from the next projectile.

"You two need to go."

The uncle and the bartender looked at each other. Artie opened his mouth to say something (something reasonable and sympathetic, from the look on his face), but Vince waved him off.

"You know where we are if you need us," Vince said as he stepped off his bar stool. "C'mon, Arthur."

"But I need to get the gear ready for the boys coming in this afternoon," Artie whispered to Vince as he exited from behind the bar.

"People bitch about a warm beer in here, you tell them to come talk to me," Vince reassured him as the two made their way to the door.

Sal was quiet and courteous as he let the two out into the cool Las Vegas morning. Vince and Artie shielded their eyes from the brilliant light.

"If it wasn't for being so bright, I'd swear you were kicking out for closing time, Sally."

"I just need to be alone for a while. Come back in about an hour to finish stocking, Artie. Uncle Sal? I'll call you."

The door closed and locked behind them.

Sal leaned against the door and listened to the two men grouse before he finally took his master key ring and walked away. He turned, marched through the dim, dank club, through the kitchen and into the stockroom. He made sure the back door to the alleyway was locked before going into his office. Using the same key ring, he unlocked the bottom drawer of his desk and removed an old-fashioned medicine bag. He inspected the contents of the bag. Satisfied, he then returned to the kitchen and walked over to the deep freeze. Once the door to the freezer was closed securely behind him, Sal turned his attention to the metal floor. He moved two giant bags of frozen meatballs and uncovered the latch. The floor opened up like a trap door. The decrepit stairs leading down may have lead to a wine cellar at a previous time in the club's history. Medicine bag in hand, Sal descended the stairs and lowered the door behind him.

At the bottom of the rickety steps was a large door with a polished-steel surface. He punched a code into the keypad to the right of the entranceway and the door unlatched with a hydraulic rush of air. The brutish man with a doctor's bag stepped through with a sigh.

The little entranceway had a ceiling and floor comprised of metal mesh. Another keypad on the opposite side of the small room blinked a constant message that read "Initiating Decontamination." Sally crossed the room and punched the Cancel button just as a fine mist was enveloping him. The alarm sounded immediately. Another code into the keypad silenced the noise and opened the next door.

People in full lab regalia were racing to investigate the alarm when Sally stepped through.

"Mr. Vega!" Even underneath the skullcap, facemask, gloves and booties, the man who addressed his boss emanated fear. "We weren't expecting a visit this morning. Not that anything should be wrong. Um, we really should get you decontaminated."

Sally held up a dismissive hand. "How many people are working down here this morning?"

"Well, the night crew's mostly left. I guess between the engineers and nursery attendants...about thirteen of us?"

"Let's get everybody together."

The underground facility ran approximately half a square block. The main entrance connected to what seemed to be a standard medical technician lab around the corner from Sal's Italian-American Club. The group on staff that day gathered in the breakroom.

Sal looked around. Everyone here was on his payroll. He alone was responsible.

"I'm going to make this as short and painless as possible. Everyone is going to have to clear out of here in the next five minutes. These jobs are no longer available."

"What? What did we...?"

"The particulars are not available for discussion. However, no one here is unemployed. Just report in to the lab upstairs tomorrow morning and there'll be new assignments available for everyone. For now, let's just consider this a paid day off. Ready to go?"

"But, what about the nursery?" This, fortunately, came from a nurse. If one of the tech poindexters had questioned him like that, Sally might have killed him where he stood.

"Everything here is being transported today. People are on their way as we speak to take care of the subjects. Now let's go."

The small group of people were approaching the elevator that would take them up to the main lab when someone blurted out, "My pictures! I've got to get the stuff from my desk!"

The lab tech wasn't completely turned around before Sally's beefy paw had clamped onto the back of his neck.

"Your personal items will be waiting for you upstairs tomorrow. Now, I've never been big on diplomacy, so it breaks down to this: Whoever isn't on this elevator in the next thirty seconds, or whoever opens their mouths for that matter, will be terminated from my employment. Permanently."

The technician, wincing and rubbing his neck, remained docile as everyone quietly stepped into the elevator. No one dared to question why Mr. Vega wasn't going up with them.

When the elevator reached the ground floor, Sally found the key on his ring that locked it in place. He walked down the empty corridors and into someone's office. Sitting back in their cheap Managerial chair, he punched the speakerphone option and dialed three numbers.

"Dolce Vita Travel. How may I direct your call?"

"Erma? It's Sal."

"Mr. Vega! How can I be of assistance?"

"I need to be connected to the Attorney General now."

"Right away, sir!"

Sal sniffed at the coffee in a mug left on the tech's desk. He grimaced. "Fucking pansies."

A few moments later, a harried voice came on the line.

"What can I do for you, Mr. Vega?"

"What can you do for me? Why don't you take a fucking guess!"

"I assume we're discussing the current incident in Colorado?"

"Don't fucking tapdance around with me, Cooper! You know goddamn well I mean Colorado! You need to fix this!"

"I'm not entirely sure what you think I can do. The United States government neither condoned nor had any prior knowledge of the interests of the Nevada Entertainment Conglomerate…"

"Jesus Christ! Your spin-doctors spend all weekend working up that line? Every fucking piece of equipment I got down here is only two steps away from the FDA's sign-off. I can't take a shit in here and not wipe my ass with federally funded toilet paper. This gets messy, I'll not only have documentation of your involvement, I'll be able to prove that growing these little fucks was a personal favor to you AND President Dickhead to perform at his daughter's debutante-fucking-ball!"

"Even if that were true, what is it you expect of me?"

"Are you kidding? You need me to spell it out for you? I want you to wipe them the fuck out! Go Waco on their asses, for Christ's sake!"

"I don't think I'm hearing you right…"

"Did I stutter, cocksucker?"

"Even if it were feasible, and I'm not anywhere near saying that it is, what possible motive would we have?"

"I can have whatever paperwork you need to show that Frank was stockpiling weapons in that house back when he was really alive. And they've made threats to take out as many people as they can to keep from going back to the lab…"

"I've never heard…"

"Don't be fucking ignorant! Do you have any doubts how hard I can step on your dick? Do you? Cause you just let me know."

"I'm not doubting your capabilities as much as mine."

"I don't give a fuck about your capabilities. You just make it happen." The phone casing shattered as he slammed the receiver home. Sally took a couple of cleansing breaths and left the office.

A few doors down was the main lab. Sally didn't have a clue as to what ninety-percent of the equipment was designed to accomplish. He walked along the machines and tables, randomly pressing buttons and fidgeting with dials. Three large vials on the end contained what could only be human fetuses, floating in a pink liquid with a plastic tube sticking from their belly buttons. These three were labeled with bar codes and stickers. Handwritten on the stickers were the words "G. Burns," "R. Clooney" and "H. Belefonte."

Sally leaned his head against an empty glass jar.

"I still can't believe how much money we spent exhuming Graceland. Where did that bastard go?"

He shrugged and stepped back away from the tanks. He opened his doctor's case and withdrew a semi-automatic scatter gun—a gift from his nephew in Chicago.

"The simple solutions are always best," he rationalized to himself before opening fire on the lab. Glass exploded while sparks flew from computers and other equipment. He razed the room to the full extent of the clip. The constant click of the auto trigger brought him back from his revelry. He dropped the empty cartridge on the floor amongst the scattered liquids, glass and plastic. Pulling a new cartridge from the bag, he reloaded, placed the gun back inside and carried it out of the room.

"Uncle Sal!"

The nursery resembled a typical high school band room with a piano and stage area. The padded walls prevented the half-dozen residents of the nursery from hearing Sally's progression through the underground complex up to that point.

The children swarmed to him. Their ages ranged from four to seven years old.

"Easy Joel. Watch your hands Carol. Settle down everyone!"

The kids straightened up immediately.

"I know you're all excited. It's been a while since I've been down here. But now we're going to play a game."

"Yeah!"

"Ok, you ready? Bobby? You ready?"

"Ready Uncle Sal!"

"Alright. Everybody line up over there, facing the wall."

The young clones scrambled to get into position. For a brief moment, Sal felt ashamed. Their desire to both please him and to play had to be amplified by the fact that they were allowed so little recreation time. The nursery staff was to maintain a strict regiment of practice and rehearsal for their performances. This was the life Frankie and the others were fighting so hard to escape. Maybe they could have done things differently, but Sally determined it was too late now.

He quietly removed the gun again from the medicine bag.

"Now, everybody close your eyes."

He opened fire before finishing the last command. The scatter gun ripped through the children like paper dolls. He continued firing even after they were all prostrate. He didn't want to hear any screaming. He didn't want them to suffer. He took no joy from the act. This wasn't sport or even some vendetta. This was destruction of compromising evidence, pure and simple.

When the clip was empty, he slowly walked over to inspect the damage. All the small bodies were still. Gunpowder and wall padding fluttered down in the eerie silence. Then, just when he was preparing to leave, the dark haired girl on the end drew in a strangled breath.

He reloaded the gun and approached her. The child looked up just as Sally was taking a bead on the back of her head.

"Why," she mouthed.

"The same reason God does, Liza. Because I can."

Sally emptied the third and final clip he would use that day.

I was nearly excommunicated at a surprisingly young age, I'm proud to say. In my own defense, they pretty much brought it on themselves.

This nun I had in 7th grade tried to convince us that acne was the physical manifestation of the evils of masturbation.

Look at my face. No pock marks, no scarring. I was one of the fortunate few who grew up without even the hint of acne, and I was ready to kill myself.

For months this nun had me convinced that I was fucking up jerking off.

How do you screw up jerking off? The rules seemed simple enough. If I came, I won! But, without pimples, I became completely neurotic about my self-indulgences. I began keeping a chart, tracking my time, technique and duration of orgasm. No matter what variables I introduced into the equation, still no pimples!

Then I talked with this friend of mine who's face looked like a lunar topographical map. I finally had to ask, "What am I doing wrong?"

"What do you mean?"

"Well, I mean, look at your face, man! You must have a wrist like a piston! How can you possibly jerk off so much? Do you sleep on a fur bedspread?"

"What the hell are you talking about?"

"Sister Payne (no shit. Real name) says you get acne from masturbation, and I haven't gotten a single fucking zit. While you? You could fry eggs from the grease on your face!"

So, the first thing he says is, "Dude, you're starting to piss me off." Which was understandable. I tend to get overzealous. "And, I hate to tell you this but, I've never jerked off in my life."

"You're lying to me! I mean..." By then all I could do was point, for fear of pissing him off even more and never hearing the secret to proper Rocks Off-ology.

"Even if I am lying, and I'm not, do you believe everything a nun tells you?"

And so began the descent.

CHAPTER FIFTEEN

Lyle and Collene strolled into the reception area of DEE Pharmaceuticals, impeccably dressed and emanating power and control.

The receptionist had two delivery persons (one for pick-up of a package that wasn't at the desk, one for an unscheduled drop-off of a box containing hazardous material), a disheveled sales rep (who had been waiting for well over the promised "few minutes") and a lit switchboard to contend with just as the two detectives arrived.

"We're looking for Clark Carpinelli. Is he in?"

Linda (per her nameplate) looked up. She carefully evaluated the crisp suites, sunglasses and attitudes of this new intrusion, and promptly beamed a warm, inviting smile.

"Good morning! Is Mr. Carpinelli expecting you?"

"I would be surprised if he was," Lyle commented. The partners reached into their coats and presented official-looking IDs. "I'm Federal Agent Singer, this is my partner, Agent Spacey. Is Mr. Carpinelli available?"

"I'll check."

The badges caused everyone else swarming around the desk to take a pause from their own concerns and allow Linda to focus on this new development.

"Lori?" "Hi, it's Linda. I have a couple of federal agents here who are asking to speak with Mr. Carpinelli." "Uh-huh." "Uh-huh." "Okey-doke." She disconnected the line. "If you agents could please take a seat, Mr. Carpinelli will be out in just a few moments."

"Don't believe it," grumbled the sales rep before shuffling over to the reception couches.

"That will be fine," said Collene. The two left Linda to her struggles and found their own seats on the couches. The deliverymen watched the (supposed) agents sit down before resuming their barrage of questions on the lone receptionist.

Collene opened her leather case and produced what appeared to be a small clipboard. The keypad on the board was paper-thin. She typed for a few seconds before turning the object over on her lap and devoting her attention back to the reception desk.

Less than a minute after she finished her pecking at the board on her lap, Lyle's headset (which was resting around his neck, under his jacket) began to vibrate. He gave Collene a curious glance, but her attention was focussed on the front desk. Lyle moved the earphones into place and clicked the on button. He was very careful to listen before speaking.

The voice coming out of his headset was Collene's, only computerized.

"Check this out. I type stuff in here and you hear it over there. I love this thing."

"I'm very happy that you're happy," Lyle commented, seemingly to no one.

Collene, appearing independent of the conversation Lyle was having with himself, turned the board over and typed some more.

"What is wrong with you today?"

Lyle looked around casually. "It's Katy. We'll talk later."

The salesman got off his seat in a huff and approached the viewer on the far wall.

"Is it okay if I turn this thing up?" He inquired of the entire room. No one responded before he pushed the volume button and increased the sound.

The image on the viewer showed trucks and tanks winding along mountain roads. The voiceover was commenting: "It is still unclear why the ATF feels the need to bring in so much artillery, and no one at the Sinatra estate has been available for comment since the press conference yesterday."

"Sir?" Linda was cupping her headset microphone with one hand, and lowering the monitor volume via the remote control in her other. "Please don't adjust the settings? Thank you!"

"I asked!" But Linda's attention was back on her call. The salesman turned and sat down next to Lyle. "Is it so much to ask to be treated like a human being?"

Lyle stared straight ahead behind his sunglasses. Collene was typing next to him.

Collene's electronic voice piped through his headphones. "Want me to put a cap in his ass?"

Lyle shook his head subtly. The salesman reacted to this as a response to his rhetorical question.

"This is what I'm saying! You know. You guys are Feds, right? You're probably on the road all the time, getting the run around by the likes of her. We're not so different, am I right? I mean, in the final analysis."

More typing. "Seriously. At least let me break his thumbs."

Lyle was careful not to respond to this voice message, but the salesman was already feeling a kinship to Lyle, whether he met his gaze or not.

"See, I'm like that. My company's got me traveling all over the place, trying to get their medical packaging picked up by all these pharmaceutical places. But they don't want to see me. They just want to order off the web. They don't want samples or lunches or any human interaction at all, y'know what I'm saying? But that's what it's all about. It's about people. They're making a living, I'm making a living, you're making a living. It's all the same, y'know? In the final analysis."

Lyle continued staring straight ahead. A Suit came out from the doors behind Linda. He leaned over the receptionist's desk while quickly and awkwardly slipping on a coat. Lyle and Collene looked at each other before looking back at the desk in unison. The nervous executive left Linda's desk, eyes darting at and away from the detectives, and half-walked, half-ran for the office's entrance.

Collene typed. "Shall I?"

"Be my guest," offered Lyle.

Collene silently rose and followed the harried-looking man out into the hall.

"Mr. Carpinelli will be right with you!" Linda bellowed, still with a smile.

"Just getting some air," Collene commented sweetly on her way out.

The salesman glanced around slyly before looking back at Lyle. He lowered his head and whispered, "So, anything happening around here that honest business people should be wary of?"

"Well, sir, I'd be happy to tell you why we're here. But then…"

The salesman laughed. "Don't tell me. You'd tell me, but then you'd have to kill me. Right?"

Lyle still watched the receptionist as he spoke.

"Kill you? Not on your life. If you're important enough to be privy to confidential information, potentially involving national security, you'd obviously be invaluable to the Bureau. We'd find a safe house for you, but then we'd have to eliminate all existing family members—being that they're too expensive to maintain, and too high a security risk. We would need to destroy your employment records and possibly the entire company you work for, eliminate all credit history, accounts, birth and school records, and systematically dispose of anyone you've been in contact with your entire life."

Lyle lowered his shades enough to finally meet the salesman's gaze.

"Killing you would be a snap. Making sure that, for all intents and purposes, you've never existed? That's the tricky part. In the final analysis."

Lyle pushed his sunglasses back against his forehead. The salesman chuckled uneasily before getting up.

"Any idea how much longer I'm going to be left out here?" He directed the question towards Linda, but merely moved to a seat closer to the desk without pushing for a response or even looking at anyone, especially Lyle.

●

Collene and the Suit waited together at the elevator banks.

Collene tried to engage the executive. "Got to love Los Angeles in February, eh?" The Suit responded by pushing the call button again. "Yeah, that should help bring it up quicker." The Suit stared blankly ahead. "Say! Do you work at that place we just came out of?" The Suit looked at her sheepishly, nodded and then looked back at the closed elevator doors. "See, I wasn't sure because I couldn't see your ID badge." A succession of button pushes. "Those badges are great. Y'know what I like best about them? Those pictures they take are digital. They keep them on a database. Did you know that?"

The doors to the elevator opened. The Suit rushed in and pushed the lobby button.

"I left mine at home," he commented, practically under his breath.

Collene stepped into the doorway, preventing the elevator from closing. She opened her leather case. "That's a shame. I might have something here to help you out." She withdrew a piece of paper with a color copy of a DEE Pharmaceuticals ID badge. The picture on her copy was that of the Suit in the elevator. She held it up, compared and examined his face to that of the print out and whistled.

"You must have been having a better day when this picture was taken, Mr. Carpinelli. Why don't you just come back into your office where you, my partner and I can sit down and discuss everything?"

"I really don't have anything to say without my lawyer."

"Okay. Maybe we can talk with Mr. Kobayashi instead?"

Mr. Carpinelli walked off the elevator and back into the office.

●

"I'm finding it hard to believe that Ashland contacted the FBI. He must be at least as culpable as we are for having his little collection in the first place."

Lyle and Collene sat comfortably in the leather guest chairs across from Carpinelli's desk. The Suit closed the door to his office, adjusted the blinds to obscure the LA view, and sat down in his executive chair.

"So, what are we talking about here? An inquest of some kind?"

"Nothing so elaborate," Lyle insisted. "It depends on how willing you or your company would be to return the property."

"How did you find me?"

"Mr. Carpinelli," Collene pointed out. "We're not in the habit of telling criminals what mistakes they've made so they can streamline their efforts in the future."

"I will tell you," Lyle added. "The whole Kobayashi thing was dead irritating. If there's one thing I can't stand, it's lack of imagination."

"That's what I get for trying to be cute. You have my apologies, Agent...?"

"Spacey. Agent Spacey."

"But...isn't that?"

"Coincidence is all."

Carpinelli considered the likelihood of this coincidence.

"You guys aren't really Feds, are you?"

"If we were in fact federal agents, chances are we'd be closing this place down right now. We'd physically remove everyone from these offices before they'd have the chance to tamper with any potential evidence, and spend the next six weeks to three months pouring through your files. Which means your company makes no money while it accumulates astronomical lawyer fees in an effort to keep any new evidence of illegal propriety out of court. And it's been my experience that companies dallying in operations such as the Leary sample has whole warehouses full of skeletons. Is that what you'd prefer?"

"You'll have to forgive my partner," Collene requested with a smile. "He just loves to play God."

"But, just so we're clear on this, you two *aren't* federal agents?"

"Consider us doormen for the FBI," Lyle said while taking out the phone pad attached to his headset. "They can be here in ten to fifteen minutes. Hang on, I've got them on speed dial."

Carpinelli wasn't scared so much as pleased. "I don't think anyone here really wants that. But if you've done your homework you know that I'm merely a Senior VP here at DEE Pharm."

"We know you set up the drop," Collene pressured.

"I'm not denying that, seeing as you're not really police or anything. But I do have to make one phone call before simply turning the package over. You understand."

Collene looked a bit anxiously in the direction of her partner, but Lyle was staring straight ahead at Carpinelli.

"I've never been one to trust Suits, so you keep this in mind: Any leaks to the police or the press will be far more detrimental to both your career and this company than it will be to either ourselves or Mr. Ashland. You have my word on that. So you go ahead and sit behind your desk and make your call, and Agent Singer and I will sit right here and wait for you to finish."

"Fair enough." Carpinelli picked up the phone and dialed his secretary. "Lori, I need you to do a couple of things for me ASAP. First of all, I need you to get the president on the phone for me." "No, I'm not kidding. There's an emergency number in my electronic rolodex. Second of all, once I'm on the phone with DEE, I need you to call the lab and have them bring up—are you writing this?" "Good—Sample TLA13, and it needs to be ready to transport. Got that?" "Thanks." Carpinelli cupped the receiver while waiting for the connection of his call. "Singer, eh? Wasn't that the name of the director…?"

Lyle smiled for the first time that morning. "The world is chock-full of coincidences, Mr. Kobayashi."

Carpinelli chuckled. "Ain't that the truth…yes, hello sir! It's Carpinelli." Listening intently. Chagrin. "No, I understand you're *extremely* busy right now, and I wouldn't have called except…" More listening. "No, I do understand. But I have some people here asking me for the Leary sample." "No, they're not police." "If I had to guess," the Suit eyed the partners carefully. "I'd say Ashland hired some very good private detectives." "Well, they're not very forthcoming, as you might expect." "Well, no I haven't…" "If you insist."

Covering the receiver once again, he addressed the two. "I'm being told to ask if you two are private detectives."

"Who the hell is this guy?" Collene asked incredulously.

"They're not going to say, sir." "Oh, we've done all we need to do with it." "No, no. It's really no problem." "I see. I see." Looking them over again. "I'm not sure." "Of course I'll try." "I understand. Will do." "Yes sir, I apologize again…" The line was disconnected.

"He's very busy right at the second."

"We gathered," Collene confirmed. "So now what?"

A rap at the door preceded a petite woman in a lab coat coming into the office and delicately placing a steel container on Carpinelli's desk. She left encapsulated in the same silence with which she entered.

The Suit took the box and removed the top. It appeared so seamless as to be almost startling to even have a top half. The executive turned the box, revealing to the detectives a lone vial resting firmly in a contoured bed of foam.

"Here's Ashland's item. He'll find less than 10% missing, but there'll be no retrieving that. You'll have to take my word."

Lyle leaned forward. "What did your people do with five c.c.s of Timothy Leary's blood, Mr. Carpinelli?"

"I'm afraid that's not open for discussion right this second, Mr. *Spacey*," came the reply as he refastened the lid of the box. "The point of discussion right now is a certain missing corpse. Are you familiar with the Don Owens case in New Jersey?"

"I've read a thing or two about it," Collene calmly noted.

"My employer would like to become your employer."

"He wants us to find the missing body?" Lyle's eyes lit up. He would later be embarrassed by the sudden flood of expression.

"No, sir. It isn't our concern where the body is. We, or rather he, would very much like you to find the killer. The rest will take care of itself."

Lyle and Collene looked at each other. They looked back at Carpinelli in unison.

"We're going to have to meet with your boss."

"He anticipated this. How quickly can you be in Colorado?"

So I sat down and wrote this amazingly romantic love letter and gave it to Sister Payne.

But I signed another nun's name to it.

Now, the two are living quite happily together in San Francisco to this day, but this REALLY pissed off the church. Apparently, weaning a nun out of the convent is like snatching a really profitable whore out of some pimp's stable. It's simply not done.

I was living in fear for my soul, dig? What's THAT about? Who has that kind of power? Who SHOULD have that kind of power?

You know what I'm talking about! Why do we believe in God? Because it's safe, it's comfortable, it prevents us from having to pose the REAL questions…and because we're going to go to Hell if we don't!

And it's not just the Catholics and the Baptists and the Jehovah's Witnesses and the Pentecostals. It's not just the Christians. It's the Jews and the Muslims and every other cocksucker who holds a deity over our heads and says, "Obey or pay the consequences for an Eternity!"

An Eternity!

"You mean the shit I do for sixty or seventy years determines my comfort for all time?"

That sucks! That's like a parent who beats you, hard, your entire life—sixty to seventy years, let's say—because you shit your pants coming home from the maternity ward.

But this is the logic they use to keep you in line. "Oh, you've got free will. Just make sure you use it like we tell ya'!"

And even most of that's common sense! "Thou Shalt Not Kill" No shit. The vast majority of us are aware that we shouldn't be killing each other. All the others have some kind of manufacturer's default and should be recalled. Forcibly, if need be.

Believe in yourself first. If you're incapable of conceiving of all this…this world, this universe, Cameron Diaz—if you can't grasp any that without the help of God, what can I say?

It's the religions I'm really after. Those that teach us to distrust or dislike others who don't believe like us. Those that dictate what we should do, based on what we do already.

Tell you what! I'm going to start my own religion tonight, and you're going to help me. I'm going to command you to leave this club tonight, something you were going to do anyway. But, because I've told you to, and you do, you will officially be a part of this new religion. The Crosstians. Ready?

Be sure to tip your waitresses.

Leave now! I command it!

Goodnight.

Jackson Cross
2011 Young Comedians Special
Turner Comedy Channel

CHAPTER SIXTEEN

Collene navigated the treacherous route through the mountains toward Grand Ravine. Lyle sat in the back seat of the rental and tried to catch up on his email.

"Colorado in February," she commented. "Whose bright idea was this? My nipples are so hard they're going to set off the airbags."

Status grunted in reply. His autocrypt was dreadfully slow that morning. Every correspondence was taking 2-3 minutes to boot up, and he wasn't exactly in a patient mood.

Collene looked back at her partner through the rear view mirror before blindly reaching over and into her leather case. She was paying as close attention to the snowdrifts as she could while fumbling with her notebook on the passenger seat.

Lyle was waiting for another letter to file through the encryption process when his headset vibrated. He looked up to see Collene, both hands on the wheel, focussed on the slippery road ahead. He clicked the speak button.

"You've got Status."

"Why so glum, dum-dum?"

"Do you mind?" Lyle clicked the phones off so hard that he was bound to have a mark when he removed them from his head. "Just about the last thing I need right this second is your comgen voice coming through this thing. It's possible I could be getting a real call some time. Did you ever consider that?"

"Geeze. Excuse me for trying to hold a conversation. But, I understand. I'm just the hired help around here. Let me jez shut mah mouth and drives the boss where's he needs to go."

"Ah for love of...You don't even *like* my driving! You're the one who always insists on taking the wheel when we're on the road."

"Well, I've always felt that the person with the least amount of complications in life should be the pilot."

"So your father's come to terms with the whole lesbian thing, eh?"

"No, but I've come to terms with him not coming to terms, you prick. Why don't you stop being hostile and let me know what's going on?"

"My mom's been taking care of Katy while we've been on the road this week."

"Yeah."

"Tammy picked Monday to come back. She's ranting and raving and my mom's got the cops keeping her away from the house. It's ugly."

"Holy shit. You've had this going on and you didn't say anything?"

"What were you going to do, Collene?"

"Take over the fucking case for one thing! What's wrong with you? You should be home, fighting for your daughter!"

"I told my mom to let Tammy have her."

"What?"

"She doesn't want to be with me. She resents the hell out of me since Tammy took off. I think it would be for the best. My mom's the only one fighting this. I've sent a certified letter to Atlanta, turning custody over to Tammy. This is the strangest case I've ever worked on, and it's all I have keeping my head on straight, so I have no intention of going home now. Anything else you wish to discuss?"

Lyle lowered his head and continued catching up on his files. Collene drove in silence.

●

"Well? Now what, pale face?"

Lyle looked up from the back seat to see a full-scale military block in the road up ahead. Outside the hastily constructed gate were dozens of protesters braving the sub-zero temperatures.

"Cloning is against God!" One proclaimed.

"Cross is the Anti-Christ!" Yelled another.

They railed against the powers as the detectives drove through. No one touched the car, but signs and fists crowded the windows as Collene maneuvered the human maze.

"Slow down a little. Let me get my paperwork ready."

"Sure thing. Always a good idea to give a mob more time to piss and moan."

Collene slowed to a crawl, which annoyed the MP at the gate considerably. He raised each hand, still clasping his rifle, to blow warm air on them. It was obvious he wanted to be back inside the makeshift guardhouse.

As the car pulled up beside him, Collene lowered her window bare inches to keep the warmth inside the car.

"State your business, ma'am!"

Lyle leaned up from the backseat. "We've been sent here as representatives of the American Clone Association. I was told we'd be expected."

The guard took Lyle's papers through the slit in Collene's window, flipped through them briefly and passed them back.

"I'm supposed to keep out anyone without official business here. I'm inclined to let you through, but I wouldn't expect to get up to the house if that's where you're going. No one's allowed on or off of the property right now."

"We'll take our chances," Collene beamed as sincere a smile as she could muster in the freezing temperatures.

"Fine by me." The soldier hustled back into the guard shack and raised the blockade.

"What are we going to do once we get there?" Collene asked as she maneuvered the single lane path that was covered in snow and ice.

"Sure, *now* you just want to be the driver. You could come up with a plan just as easy as I could, y'know."

"Oh, you bastard! You're all mister 'take-charge' guy when it suits you, but you wait until we're in a real jam before you…"

The explosion of sound that erupted some distance ahead of the car derailed Collene's outburst.

"What the hell…?"

Before Status could focus on what may have happened up ahead, a gunshot went off behind the car. The detectives turned around and watched as the lone guard at the station was wrestled to the ground. Apparently he'd only gotten off a warning shot before being swarmed with protesters. Those not piled on top of the MP were starting their trucks and Winnebegos. One four-wheeler was breaking through the gate while Collene and Lyle watched.

"Step on it, Sons."

"What? And race headlong into the really big explosion up ahead?"

"I'll take my chances with that before I sit here and let them roll over us."

"Good point." The tires raced fruitlessly for several seconds before catching and sending the two further into the forest.

●

"Jesus Christ, what a circus."

Lyle sat in silent agreement of Collene's assessment as the road they traveled opened up onto a clearing. It was odd for both of them to be part of this scene that had been displayed and replayed across all the news networks for the better part of that week. Military personnel had camps and equipment spread over an acre in front of the property's gates. A large transport battering ram (the source of the previous explosion of sound) was gearing up for another assault on the stone and reinforced steel barrier. The next hit was sure to crush the entranceway.

On the right side of the troops was a caravan of vans and cars. More protesters.

"How did they get in here with the guard out front?"

"Take a close look, Collene. These people have been here for days. The military probably put up the guard station to keep any more idiots from getting in here."

On top of one of the vans was a man with a megaphone. He led the several dozen protesters around his camp to a chant of "Retribution! Today!"

The side of the van was decorated with a lovely sunrise over some mountains. The words "Church of the Modern Light" were painted in awful Day-Glo colors across the top.

"Modern Light my Ass."

"Hey, check out the news crews." Collene followed Lyle's direction to the left of the military. The reporters and cameramen weren't quite as well organized as the ATF, but they were just as busy. News vans jockeyed about with one another, trying to attain the perfect, unobstructed view of the pandemonium. Lyle watched as a fistfight broke out in the media camp. Over what he could only guess.

The trucks and campers which broke through the check point caught up and overtook the detective's rental car. They roared up to the protestor's camp before screeching to a slippery halt, bumping a few fenders in the process.

"Welcome, my brothers and sisters!" The man with the megaphone greeted these new participants. "Join me! Together we'll see retribution! Today!"

Lyle and Collene sat in their parked car, engine and heat still running, and watched the show.

The new group of protesters all-but leapt from their vehicles. Collene estimated at least forty people, all jumping up and down and shaking signs and (this almost had to be a first) cheering the soldiers on. Some

of the news people unable to find a very good vantage point for the
gates or mansion, turned their attention to this new wrinkle.

A black man, conspicuous for being out in the snow with merely a
dinner jacket on more than anything else, jumped onto the top of the van
with the megaphone instigator. He began chanting, "Max! Max! Max!" It
wasn't long before the rest of the demonstrators followed in chorus.

"What's *that* about?" Collene wondered out loud.

"What's *any* of this about?" Returned Lyle. He opened his notebook
and began typing notes.

"Aren't we going to…" She thought about what she could possibly
propose. Upon reflection, she realized there was nothing for them to do.

"Max! Max! Max!"

"This isn't about me!" The man with the megaphone was attempting
to drown out the crowd. "This is about Don! He spoke the truth, and
they killed him for it! These soldiers are doing Don's work!"

"For Don! For Don!"

"Are they talking about who I think they're talking about?"

"Seems to be the way my life's working right now," Lyle confirmed. "I
know the ATF can't address the civilians directly, but are you looking at
their faces? I bet a good portion of those guys would love to be able to
pick off some of these idiots. Just once."

It was true that the person seemingly in charge (General, Major,
Captain—Lyle was too far away to tell) appeared to be extremely annoyed
by the constant activity of "Max" and his demonstrators, but forced himself to ignore them as much as possible. Once the ram was back into position, he spoke what could have only been two to three words tops into his
squalker. The carrier plowed back into the gates with another deafening
clamor. Lyle's earlier assessment of the entranceway's condition proved
accurate. A cheer rose up from the crowd as the gates caved like tin.

Immediately, before the battering transport even had an opportunity
to back up, protestors began racing toward the broken gates.

"Maybe they'll get the chance to shoot somebody after all," Collene noticed.

With trained efficiency, a line of soldiers moved in front of the demonstrators and pushed them back into the snowdrifts on the perimeter fence.

"Let the military do their job," commanded Max—after, Lyle noticed, it became unavoidably clear that his group wouldn't be able to sidestep the army.

The engines of tanks and trucks all kicked into gear as the better part of the division present prepared to mobilize.

"This is going to get ugly fast," Lyle noted as he zipped up his mylar jacket.

"Where are you going?"

"We're not going to find out anything huddled in this car," he said before opening the back door and jumping out into the bitter cold.

"Goddammit," Collene grumbled as she buttoned herself up. "Five minutes ago he didn't even have a fucking plan. Now the plan's apparently hypothermia or military execution." Opening up her door to sludge and snow, she carefully stepped out and followed her partner into the elements.

CHAPTER SEVENTEEN

Max was in his glory.

The troops poured into the grounds of the Sinatra complex, cheered on by the minister's own makeshift army. He knew full well that the ATF wasn't there on his say-so, but it didn't stop the empowering feeling that swelled within him as he watched them march up to the mansion.

It was so much better this way! If Cross had been killed by the preacher or any number of his followers, it opened the door to martyr-dom. But here, in this frozen purgatory, his death in the midst of defiance to the government helped define him as pure evil in the eyes of most of the country. Or at least that would be the spin Max would put on it in sermons for all the foreseeable future. Sermons to be performed in his chain of churches that will be erected throughout the continental U.S., and maybe even abroad.

"We're not here to kill, my brothers and sisters! But we will be the witnesses to His Judgement and Execution! God's Will flows through these good men and women of service! Can I hear an Amen?"

"Amen!" The crowd responded in unison.

"We are witnessing the fall of the Anti-Christ, through his own evil machinations and devices! Can I hear an Amen?"

"Amen, brother!"

The wind whipped through his hair and blazer, but Max was oblivious to the cold and snow. Everything was coming together better than he could have hoped.

"And together with our brothers and sisters of the armed forces, along with God's Divine Influence, we will avenge Don!"

"Do it for Don!" Nailz began to chant.

"For Don!" The congregation exalted.

"Excuse me!"

Max tore his attention away from the mobilizing force and looked down to see a lone man standing a few feet away from the van.

"Sorry to interrupt," he shouted above the still chanting crowd. "Could we have a word?"

"For Don!" The crowd continued, unabated by the sudden intrusion on their shepherd. Max looked over at Nailz and motioned toward the stranger. Nailz let himself down from the top of the van. "For Don!" Max shouted into the megaphone and resumed monitoring the chaos.

Nailz meandered up to the tall, unassuming man wearing an odd looking headset.

"Can I help you with somethin'?"

"Maybe you can," the gentleman agreed. He looked back over toward the media camp. Nailz followed his gaze and noticed a striking young woman walking toward the news vans. "My partner and I have been sent here on behalf of the ACA. The American Clone Association?"

"I know what it is. How come you're over here while she's hanging out with those dumb-ass reporters?"

"Lucky me? Anyhow, we were just wondering: Was Don Owens a member of your congregation?"

"Now, why the hell would the ACA need to know that?"

"Listen to yourselves. 'For Don! For Don!' It is Don Owens your group is going on about, am I right?"

"We fight for the same cause, is all. We respect what he was trying to lay down."

"Really? Because, as far as we've been able to determine, he held no public platform previous to the bit he did on the Tom Green radio show. And that was hardly enough to start a movement, am I right? You guys have been out here freezing yourselves nearly to death over…" The man opened up his pocket notebook. "'You're going to die you kike bastard.' Is that the focus of this movement? Because that's a direct quote."

Nailz stood there for several seconds, processing what this man was saying to him.

"You asked me if he was a part of our group. I told you no. Any other questions, you go ahead and send that pretty little thing over here to ask. Other than that, you might just want to move along."

This time it was the stranger who was momentarily silent. Not because he was searching for something to say, Nailz knew, but because he was sizing up the bodyguard.

"How long you been out, son?"

Nailz leaned in close.

"The fuck you say to me, cracker?"

"Well, the scarring tattoos aside, you got the smell of the joint all over you. You taking these rubes for a ride? Or did they sponsor your parole so you could do their heavy work?"

"I'll show you some fucking heavy work."

Nailz moved toward the man, but stopped short of assault when the man began shouting, "For Don! For Don!"

"For Don!" The congregation echoed.

The stranger moved in close to the ex con and spoke in low tones. "How happy would your benefactors be if you started beating up a supporter in front of all the news cameras in the world, huh? Big guy?"

Nailz smiled a broad, welcoming smile before leaning in and embracing the man.

"We're all brothers here! Why don't you and I take a walk over here to…discuss this further?"

"Why not?"

The two men maneuvered around to the opposite (and considerably less photographed) side of the van.

●

"I need more snow in here!"

David Kroft was sitting inside his news van, nursing a swollen eye.

Tara Bankcroft, his segment producer, opened the door, reached outside, scraped a ball of frozen slush from the top of the vehicle and handed it to the reporter.

"I told you drop it. Didn't I tell you to drop it?"

"Screw that Rivera pussy!" Kroft winced as he applied the ice ball to his puffy face. "We've been here all week! He and his crew come waltzing in here at the last minute and expect us to just roll over!"

"Pull yourself together, David! Everything's going down and I need you on camera like now!" Tara clicked her two-way. "What's happening Craig?"

"Looks like they're just getting themselves lined up in front of the house," was the reply that came from the cameraman in the crow's nest on tope of the van. "I don't know if there's going to be a final warning or what."

"Right. We need some make-up in here." No response. "Hello? Andy? Cindy? Where's my makeup crew?" The radio remained silent. "Goddammit! Where the hell is everybody?"

Tara left her sulking reporter and dashed out the door of the van, slamming directly into a woman passing by outside. "Oh!" Neither woman stayed on their feet from the impact.

"Shit!" Tara felt the cold wetness seep through her wool skirt. "I'm sorry! Are you okay?"

"Um, I think so," the woman began. "I may have sprained…"

"Hel-lo!" Tara yelled as she pushed herself up from the ground. "Where the hell's makeup for Christ's sake?" She was on her feet and racing toward the media tent.

The leggy brunette brushed herself off and carefully stepped up into the news van.

"Hello?"

"In here! You'll need to work some magic so that this shiner won't show."

"Um, I'm not makeup. I just got blindsided by someone coming out of here. I twisted my ankle a little. Can I just sit down for a second?"

"Oh, sure!" The reporter got up and adjusted the passenger chair so that it swiveled around. "That was Tara, our producer. She's a little frazzled right now. You ok?"

"I think so," she confirmed while delicately rotating and stretching her ankle. "Place seems to be a war zone."

"You're not kidding," the reporter confirmed while extending a hand. "David Kroft, WNGT in Chicago."

"Collene Sons," the woman offered while shaking his hand. "I've been sent by the American Clone Association. I guess there's no way of getting into that house, eh?"

"Do you really want to? Ten to one that place is going to be cinders inside a couple of hours. What do you do for the ACA?"

"This and that. Listen, I've been traveling for a couple of days straight. What's the ATF want from these kids?"

"Supposedly, they've got evidence of weapons stockpiling based on receipts from over thirty years ago. The group inside has ignored repeated requests for a search of the premises, and there's even been talk of threats against anyone setting foot in there uninvited—which never sits well with Big Brother, constitutional rights against illegal search and seizure aside. Of course, we've yet to see any evidence of any of this, and threats contradict the attitudes they displayed during the press conference, so there's quite a bit of skepticism from the press corps. But, for right now, it's the ATF's show."

A cell phone rang. The reporter grabbed it in the middle of the second ring.

"This is Kroft. Who? Look, this isn't exactly the time for pranks, asshole."

Collene watched as David's eyes widened further than what should have been comfortable given the condition of his face.

"Hang on," was all he could say. He took a deep breath before grabbing one of the two-ways next to the monitor console. "Tara! Craig! Everybody! Get your asses back to the van now! We're changing positions!"

●

Max felt the van shift some and had to center himself for balance as the man Nailz was supposed to be speaking with climbed onto the roof.

"How're we doing?"

"Do I know you? Where's my…parishioner?"

The stranger looked back over the side of the van. "You mean the muscle you sent down? Funny that. He was trying to help me up here and slipped and fell against the runner. Hope he's ok."

Max shrugged and turned his attention back to the activity at the mansion. "I'm a bit busy right this second. If you're looking for an interview, you'll have to wait until my press conference when this is all over, just like everyone else."

"Actually, I'm with the ACA. I was hoping to ask you a few questions about Don Owens."

"A tragedy we're attempting to rectify. Now, if you don't mind, Mr…?"

"A personal tragedy? A community tragedy? How well did you know the victim?"

"We fight for the same cause. My church respects the values Don exemplified before his brutal slaying."

"That's about the same rhetoric I got from your cohort down there, albeit slightly more refined." The stranger was standing next to Max, watching the troops position themselves. "I just don't buy it."

"Well, I'm trying to understand exactly who you are and why I should care about what you think."

Just then, the stranger's headset vibrated.

"This better be important," he said after tapping the earpiece. "What?" The stranger looked over at the media camp and then looked back at the road leading into the grounds. "Are you serious?" "Ok, ok. I'll be right there."

Just as he disconnected the line, an amplified voice came from the military group.

"This is your last warning! Throw out all weapons and surrender immediately!"

●

Corporal Troy Reagan was picking up the pieces of his blockade. He had two of the civilians who had assaulted him in protective custody inside the shack. He would be reprimanded for allowing the mob to get through, that much was a given, but he would make damn sure these two would be prosecuted for his troubles.

He was trying to determine if it was worth reconstructing the gate when he heard the roar of an engine coming up the mountain. Taking his rifle off his shoulder, he stood in the path and waited as the sound grew louder and impossibly louder.

The truck that came into view may have been a sports utility vehicle at some point. The windows were tinted black and he could swear it was armored. The engine was deafening. It was doing at least fifty on the icy road, and wouldn't be slowing down. Corporal Reagan did the prudent thing. He stepped out of the way.

●

"What the hell is going on?"

Tara jumped into the news van as Craig was trying to move it out from the position it held in camp.

"Where do you think we're going?"

"Not far," David assured. "We just need to get turned around. You need to get some of the other crews to do the same thing."

"What are you talking about? In case you've got a concussion, they're about to storm the place! Why the hell should we be turned around?"

"Because they need the buffer, that's why! And they called us!"

"WHO?"

David was too busy guiding Craig into position. "That's it. Let's just pull next to that car over there. I'm not kidding, Tara! We need to make a barrier of these vans and I mean now!"

●

Lyle was about to jump off the preacher's van when a hand grabbed his ankle, tripping him up. He dove, head first, into the snow and ice. Before he could catch his breath or bearings, someone was on his back. He was pretty sure he knew who.

"I don't give a fuck who's watching! You fuckin' owe me!"

Vicious blows began to reign down on the back of his head. The ice worked in his favor though, as he was able to turn himself around while still pinned and fend off some of the hits.

"Nailz! Get up here!"

The attacker turned toward the van and Max, giving Lyle the chance to grab a chunk of ice and stone and rap the large man up the side of his head.

"Ow! Fuck! My ear! You cheatin'…!"

"Nailz! Something's happening! Get up here!"

Lyle grabbed more sludge and dirt and slapped it flush into his assailant's eyes. After that, it was nothing for him to slip out from his confinement.

"We ain't done, fucker!"

"Not by a long shot," Lyle agreed as he hobbled away toward his rental car and the commotion of the news crews. He heard the megaphone sound out from the small army in front of the house.

"You have five seconds to comply!"

●

Tara stormed back into the van.

"I've got four other affiliates moving to flank us now, Kroft. That cost me some favors, let me assure you. This better be good."

"Oh, it's good! They'll be owing you big after this, trust me. Any second now."

"Are you sure the call was authentic?" Collene asked this as she watched her partner scramble to get their rental out of the road.

"Who are you?"

"Tara, this is Collene. She's the nice young lady you collided with a few minutes ago."

"Ok. Well, I'm sorry about that, but you'll have to go."

"Forget her right now. Craig! Is that digital set-up wired and ready?"

"Sure! It's been all set for days."

"Great! Get your ass topside and keep the main camera on the mansion. Tara will handle the close-ups with the digital piece. Move!"

Craig pushed past his confused producer. "Hey! Watch it! I'm doing *what* now?"

"Listen…" David instructed. Everyone did. The sound of an engine gained in intensity, rising over the sounds of the vans positioning themselves around the main road, drowning out the chanting of the religious demonstrators.

Everything stopped as the suped-up SUV broke out from the trees and into the clearing. It braked frantically, sliding to a stop mere feet in front of the horseshoe barricade of news vehicles.

"Who's this now," Tara asked as she aimed the digital camera through the front windshield and at the newest truck to join the caravan.

"Just wait," David teased, barely able to contain himself.

A sunroof opened on the top of the SUV. A man dressed in black maneuvered himself through. He had a microphone in his hand, presumably attached to the speakers on the roof of his truck.

"Ladies and gentleman," Kroft announced. "Jackson Cross."

"It's him!"

The murmur swept through the congregation around Max's van.

"What do you want to do, Max," Nailz inquired.

"What's he doing out here?" Max demanded. "What the hell is he playing at?"

"Do you want we should take him out?"

"In front of all the reporters in the country? Are you insane?"

Max jumped off the top of his van and stormed over toward the semi-circle of news vans.

"Stay away from the house!" Jackson's voice cracked with desperation over the speaker system. "For God's sake, don't go in there!"

But the armed forces were too far away to hear the warning. Three troopers with a battering ram were crossing the porch and closing in on the front door.

"Stop what you're doing," Jackson pleaded. "Please!"

The battering ram never touched the front door.

Every window was simultaneously blown out from the house. Multi-colored smoke began to billow and cascade out. Sparks and flames ignited at a fantastic rate.

"What did you do?" Jackson demanded. "What the fuck did you people do?"

The screams of children could be heard as far back as the front gates.

Tara was on the two-way. "Tell me you're getting this, Craig!"

"Every disturbing detail," the cameraman confirmed.

People gathered around Max, ping-ponging their attention from the mansion to the crying man in front of all the cameras.

"What do we do, Max?"

For the first time in the brief history of the Church of the Modern Light, the minister was stunned to silence.

The ATF soldiers backed away from the rapidly decaying mansion. Even the military was unprepared for the apparent carnage being displayed in front of them.

Cameras focussed on the troops that day would make out the quizzical, fearful looks of the hardened military as the scene was replayed countless times right through the Congressional investigation.

"There's no reason for this!" Jackson screamed. "They're just a bunch of kids!"

Within a minute of the ATF stepping foot on the front porch, the mansion gave forth a creaking moan and unceremoniously collapsed in on itself.

BOOK THREE

Cross Examined

CHAPTER EIGHTEEN

Katy's attention was immediately captured by the television in the psychologist's reception area. She let go of her mother's hand and sat cross-legged two feet in front of the old-style tube.

The man on the screen stood in front a pile of timber and rubble. Green pine and mountains provided a warm, expansive backdrop.

"It's been six month's since the events that have come to be known as the Grand Ravine Tragedy unfolded..."

Katy's mom spoke quietly to the doctor at the receptionist's window. "This is what she does. I've had custody for the last four months, and all she's done is stare at the monitor at home. I don't know what my ex-husband did to her, but I want my daughter back!"

"Attorney General Cooper resigned in the midst of Congressional hearings, and prosecutors are no closer to the answers they seek."

"Hang on a second. I didn't *abandon* her. I left her in her father's *care*."

"No evidence has been uncovered to give credence to the allegations of weapons stockpiling—the sole purpose of the ATF intrusion on this compound in Colorado."

"There's a fucking *huge* difference! Its not like I left her on some New York street and took off!" "Well, you *tell* her there's a difference! That's your *job!*"

"But the bigger questions remain about this tragedy's feature character. Six months after the debacle, and still no word from the man who allegedly orchestrated the entire event."

"C'mon, Katy! We're not getting any help here!"

"But I'm watching this!"

Katy remained focussed on the televised image even as she was taken forcibly from the doctor's office. She looked back as the door slowly closed and her mother led her back to the car. She watched until there was nothing left to see.

"Today we'll retrace the events of that tragic day and see if we can possibly unlock some of the mysteries that remain unresolved to this day. I'm Ben Dover, and you're watching Hollywood's True Unexplained Scandals: Whatever Became of Jackson Cross?"

# # #

Deana Brown pulled her '04 Surfer into her regular parking spot at the EA Business Center in downtown Indianapolis. She knew to sit in the car and wait for her friend Holly to pull into the spot next to her (she learned not to open her door too quickly last spring, when Holly nearly took the door off its hinges). Holly roared in on schedule. It was 7:53 A.M.

Deana gathered her folders into her attaché. It wasn't until she exited her own vehicle that she realized Holly was driving a brand new Vision. Holly remained seated, allowing Deana the full impact of seeing her friend in the new car.

"Hey! You did it! You actually bought this thing brand new!"

Satisfied with the reception, Holly slid out of her car. "Don'tcha just love it? Tell me you love it!"

"I love it! I love it! Now let's get inside already."

The two walked together into the campus of offices.

"I still don't know how you can afford that thing. I've been a supervisor in the telecenter for over a year, and I can still barely make my rent and web payments."

Holly shook her head. "I've been telling you how to get the extra cash."

"You're really doing that well in your marketing business?"

"Honey, you've known me for how long now? Do you think I'd extend myself like that if I wasn't going to able to pay for it?"

Deana walked up to the coffee station and made a cup each for herself and her co-worker. The phones in the banks of cubicles were ringing incessantly, but no one would answer before 8:00.

"I don't know. The whole idea of selling things door-to-door just gives me the heebies. No offense."

Holly laughed as she took the stark-white cup of coffee from her friend's dark skinned hand. "None taken. I won't even try to tell you how easy it is. But…y'know what?"

"What," Deana asked skeptically.

"Well, we're having a meeting tonight. You could come by…"

"Oh, I don't know, Holly."

"No pressure! Just think about it. We can even go together. I'll even let you drive my brand-spanking new Vision."

"Ooh!" Natalie stuck her head out from accounting. "You got a new Vision?"

"Want to see?"

Natalie stuck her head back inside her department. "Holly got a new Vision! Come see!"

Deana chuckled. "I'll talk to you later." She made her way back to her cubicle while her friend led a group of enthusiastic gawkers to the window to check out the new wheels.

●

Deana had to admit, the new electric vehicle handled like a dream. It was a gorgeous August night to be driving with the sunroof open and the windows down. Holly's hair was all over the place, while Deana's aunt had set her hair in rows that weekend, so the breeze zipped deliciously across her scalp.

The girls were still laughing as they pulled in front of a warehouse office in a commercial district near the airport. People were ambling about the front, talking and smoking. "Good," Holly commented. "They haven't started. He's rarely on time anyway."

"Who's he?" Deana inquired while stepping out from the car.

"Ezekiel Tree. Zeke for short. This is his place. He's got five different offices like this one all over the Midwest. He should be here tonight. Maybe you'll get to meet him."

Holly briefly chit-chatted with several of the attendants as the two made their way inside. Deana watched in quiet amusement as her friend shamelessly gladhanded and networked.

The reception office inside was pretty standard for a warehouse. Low ceilings and boxed walls made for a slightly claustrophobic environment.

A woman announced, "We're getting ready to start! Please step into the back!"

Deana noted the framed pictures of people on a stage, holding huge mock-checks in front of a cheering crowd. Such scenes peppered the walls of the extended hall leading to the back of the offices. The last picture before entering the warehouse section was of something that resembled a hi-tech phone booth.

Holly stopped to sign some kind of registry, then caught up to her.

"Is this the thing you have to sell?"

"That's it," Holly confirmed. "The IS-5000. Pictures don't do it justice. C'mon inside."

They crossed the threshold and into the warehouse, although the term warehouse was poor for the elaborate set-up. Instead of the bare rafters and I-beams common to the kind of distribution center Deana had envisioned, the ceiling was finished with modest chandeliers. Well over 100 padded folding chairs faced a moderate stage and, much to her surprise, they were nearly all full. Holly and Deana found seats just as the lights dimmed.

Deana covered her mouth with her hand. She didn't want Holly to be offended at just how ridiculous she found the presentation.

Dry-ice smoke began churning from under the stage. Multi-colored spotlights crossed and swirled through-out the mini-auditorium. Techno music pounded out from surrounding speakers, so loud they made her chair vibrate. Then, after close to minute of special effects, a voice called out over the sound system.

"Who's ready to get rich?"

A cheer rose up from the crowd.

"Who's ready to change the world?"

The cheer became even stronger. People clapped with the beat of the overpowering music. Deana stopped hiding her goofy grin. Everyone was smiling and laughing, including Holly. The difference was that Deana was the only one smiling in amusement. The rest of the crowd was totally into it.

"I want to bring up the following high octane performers on stage now," the bodiless voice announced. "These folks are the backbone of this company. Whose company?"

"My company!" The reply came in unison.

"That's right! Put your hands together for these superstars! Meg Chandler sold eleven units last week!"

The clapping intensified. A spotlight shone on a lone woman who leapt from her chair and raced to the stage.

"Way to go, Meg! Dorothy Truman sold ten units last week! Let's give it up for Dorothy!"

Meg and Dorothy hugged each other on stage before clasping hands and bowing in triumph.

"Holly Ferringer not only sold eight units, she signed a deal with Clancy's Bar & Grill to put an IS-5000 in every bar in the chain over the next six months. That's a contract for twelve additional pieces! Get up there, Holly!"

Holly turned to Deana. "Could be you," she said before leaping up to take her place on stage. "You know it!" Deana responded with faux enthusiasm.

The crowd was in a frenzy of delight.

"Now I want every person out there with five sales or more for the week to get up on stage! Give yourselves a hand!"

Close to half the audience got up from their chairs and rushed up to the platform. Deana started to feel conspicuous, sitting alone as she was.

"How does it feel to take charge of your destiny?!"

"Great!"

"How does it feel to be your own boss?!"

"Fantastic!"

"Who do you answer to?"

"No one!"

"Who's your boss?"

"I am!"

"Now you're talking!"

The music changed abruptly. It became more disco. Still very fast paced, with the verse "Taking Control" repeating over and over. A new voice came over the speakers.

"Ladies and Gentleman! The man who's faith in you has allowed you to take control and be your own bosses, the man who started it all…Mr. Ezekiel Tree!"

The curtains parted behind the sales people on stage. A man dressed in a black business suit and sneakers ran out and into the throng. His black hair was pulled back into a short ponytail, and his beard was bushy and unkempt. He high-fived each and every person on the raised platform. The applause was deafening.

Deana watched the man as he embraced everyone. There was something in his eyes. Something familiar.

●

The rest of the presentation was exactly what Deana imagined. Talks of sales goals and team leaders and pitches. How to overcome rejection. Why this wasn't solicitation as defined in the statutes outlawing door-to-door sales in '06. How this was the only way to empower themselves against the shackles of corporate employment. Ok, maybe it wasn't that strong, but that's what Deana took from it. Most of the time, she concentrated on

Ezekiel. His voice, his mannerisms, the way he carried himself. She understood why he held so many of the people in thrall. He was mesmerizing.

After the show, people began filing out of the warehouse, back through the front offices. Zeke was at the door, shaking everyone's hands as they left. Holly had joined Deana again, and the two were walking out together.

"So? What did you think?"

Deana considered the appropriate response while still smiling her goofy smile. "It was…different. I'll give you that."

"I know. I was a little skeptical at first too. Hey! Let me introduce you!"

"Oh, no, Holly. You don't have to…"

But her friend was already at the door, standing next to Zeke to make sure she'd capture his attention when Deana reached the door. A quick glance around confirmed that there were no other exits.

As Ezekiel shook the hand of the man directly in front of Deana, Holly whispered into the founder's ear. Zeke nodded, never losing eye contact with the gentleman he was saying goodbye to.

"And here she is," Holly gushed as her co-worker finally stepped up and took the hand that was offered. "I've been dying for her to come. Ezekiel Tree, please meet…"

"Deana Brown." The spokesman almost whispered her name. His face was a tangle of surprise and delight (and shame? Deana thought just maybe).

"You know her?" She looked at her friend with disbelief. "You know him?"

Deana felt flush. "We knew each other a long time ago." With no reason or forethought, the thirty-three year old black woman stretched up to kiss the man on the cheek.

"How have you been, Jacks?"

CHAPTER NINETEEN

"This is Alicia Marcone. How may I help you?"

"I was calling to speak with someone regarding your True Unexplained Scandals?"

"I'm a production assistant on Scandals. Do you have a story suggestion or a complaint?"

"Both, I guess. My name is Elizabeth Krumper. I was Jackson Cross' publicist for his HBO engagement?

"Uh-huh. How can we help you Ms. Krumper?"

"Well…how can I put this without sounding like a crank? Oh wait, I know! The cocksucker fucking ruined my life!"

"Uh-huh. In what way did Jackson Cross ruin your life exactly?"

"Well, six months ago when he was on the Tom Green show that last time, he asked me if it was ok if he played a little joke and bated me on air. He thought the audience would get a kick out of it. And I said it was alright, y'know? Give the client whatever he needs?

"Go on."

"Well, he gets on the air and plays so that we really hate each other and I storm off like I quit and stuff."

"I see. And then?"

"And then? Then the radio station gets taken over by a bunch of fucking Christian radicals, he pops up in Colorado and those kids get killed, and then he fucking disappears! And I'm left holding the bag!"

"What bag?"

"What…? It's a metaphor, you idiot!"

"Excuse me?"

"I'm sorry. Really. It's just been kind of bad for me over the last six months. Everybody and his cousin has a copy of that stupid fucking show. All they hear is us screaming at each other, and I come across as a raging c.u.n.t. It's tough, y'know? I've never had people question my professionalism—well, never like this anyway—and it's getting on my last fucking nerve, let me tell you!"

"I see. Well, Ms. Krumper, I'm not sure what we can do for you here at Scandals…"

"You just did a segment on Cross and the whole Colorado debacle. Couldn't you do another piece on the Tom Green interview? That'll give me a chance to give my side of the story and maybe people can see that I'm not out of my fucking mind."

"I'm so sorry, ma'am. The fact is we just did an entire hour on Jackson Cross…"

"Isn't that just what I said?"

"…and I tend to doubt we'll be doing another story in the very near future. Unless of course he shows up dead or something…but even then."

"But there's so much more you could be featuring besides the Colorado thing. Hell, besides the Tom Green show, for that matter. You could talk about the FAO Swartz thing, or what he did in high school…"

"Those incidents have been covered pretty extensively…"

"What about the cops having to remove that guy from Yuk-It-Ups?"

"I beg your pardon?"

"When Cross was on the circuit, he did a night at this club in New Jersey called Yuk-It-Ups. It's been run to death on Turner's Comedy Channel."

"Go on."

"Well, when they play his set on reruns, they always cut off about the last five minutes of the piece. He starts railing against religion and accuses people of being sheep."

"Uh-huh."

"So then, and I fucking begged him not to do this, he challenges the audience's free will by commanding them to leave the club at the end of his set."

"I don't think I understand."

"Neither did most of them. Nobody applauded after he was done. They just sat there looking stunned. Finally, at the manager's prodding, most of them left. But one guy refused to go. He said he was exercising his God-given right to free will by not leaving."

"So the club manager called the cops?"

"You're fucking-a right he called them. The asshole was getting belligerent. Demanded that Cross come back so he could prove that people control their own destinies. Then he got physical with the cops, had to be taken in, his wife refused to bail him out —he blamed Cross for the whole thing, and I don't fucking blame him!"

"Interesting, but I'm afraid we've got stories well through November. I mean, I'm looking at the schedule right now—Whatever Happened To Britney Spears, The Truth Behind The Howard Stern Auto-Erotic Strangulation Scandal, Michael Jackson's Fight With The Mob (being that they never tried to clone *him*), The John Tesh/Yanni Homosexual Scandal—and those aren't even the sweeps shows. I just can't imagine that Mr. Dover would be interested in another Jackson Cross story so soon."

"You don't understand! I'm having to do the publicity for Young Earnest Gets Shock Therapy! I can't live like this anymore! I need some kind of retraction!"

"Well, I'll make the suggestion at the next production meeting, ok? Now, I've got a conference call meeting with one of Robert Downey Jr.'s old cellmates. I'll have to let you go."

"See! This is what I'm talking about! You're blowing me off for some little bastard who used to blow Robert Downey for cigarettes, and my career's going down the fucking toilet!"

"Again, I'm very sorry. We'll call you if we decide to use your story. Have a nice day."

"Wait! Wait! You never took my number!"

"_____"

"Fuck."

#

Deana and Holly sat in the small warehouse office and waited.

"I can't believe you know him."

"It's just one of those things. It's no big deal. I'd really rather not talk about it."

"How long?"

"High school." She considered letting it go there, but decided the opportunity was too rich. "We dated."

"You what! Oh-My-God!"

Deana covered Holly's mouth. "Shhh! Don't make a big deal out of this, I'm begging you."

"Don't make a big deal," Holly whispered. "You dated Jackson Cross, the 21st Century J.D. Salinger, and it's no big deal?"

"I really don't want to talk about it. I really don't want to talk to him. If I'd driven my own piece-of-shit, ten-year old car, I'd be gone by now. And I wouldn't suggest that you go blabbing this to anybody either. Jackson isn't somebody you want to piss off. Believe me."

Jackson said his final goodbyes in the reception area, locked up and joined them.

"Sorry to keep you waiting, ladies," he said, taking a seat behind his desk and lighting up a cigarette.

"That's ok! I'm just thrilled to be here, Mr. Cross!" Holly looked chagrin. "Oh, I'm sorry. Should we still call you Ezekiel or Mr. Tree... or what?"

Cross smiled. "Jacks will do fine, Holly. So, how've you been, Deana?"

Deana glared at the man.

"Oh, she's fine. She's a supervisor at our office. EA Associates? We work in the telecenter."

"That's great," Jackson said, distracted by Deana's distance. "So what brought you here tonight?"

"Well," Holly enthusiastically began, oblivious to the fact that Jackson was talking with Deana. "I just got a new car with my IS income, and I was trying to convince Miss Skeptical here that she should give it a try."

"Really? Do you think you might be interested in this kind of marketing sales?"

"She doesn't know yet," Holly continued. "But I bet if we let her sleep on it…"

"Speaking of which," Deana interrupted, getting up from her chair. "It's getting kind of late. We should be going."

"What are you talking about? I was hoping we'd get a chance to talk."

"Yeah," Holly commented, looking at her watch. "It's barely 9:30!"

"I have to feed my cat," Deana argued, this time glaring at Holly.

Holly mouthed the words, "You don't have a cat." She then made an ugly face that only Deana could see, just to show her irritation right then.

"You haven't even seen what the IS-5000 can do. Tell you what, let me just give you a taste of this amazing technology, and you can judge for yourself."

"Oh, that's right! You've never been inside of one!"

Deana looked at their faces. She was feeling pressured. Trapped. "If I try this thing…once, then we can go?"

Jacks and Holly both nodded sincerely.

"Fine."

Jackson let the women into the now-empty warehouse. He maneuvered quickly to the back, behind the stage.

"You're going to love this," he called out as he began turning on the lights. "Some of Danny's people started working on the tube even before they released the first interactive viewer back in 2008."

"I assumed Epstein was involved in this somehow," Deana said as she and Holly joined Jackson in the back of the small auditorium. "How is Dippy, anyway?"

"Oh, you know: same old, same old." Jackson uncovered two pods resembling the phone booth Deana had seen in the picture in the office. "He's finally accumulated so many businesses that he has to act responsibly for a change. I haven't seen him more than a couple of times since Colorado."

"Wow," Holly reflected. "What happened *there*, anyway?"

Jackson stopped and looked first at Holly, then Deana. All he could do was smile and shake his head. Holly looked like she wanted to crawl into a hole.

"So," he finally continued. "Any idea what we're doing here?"

"D.K.D.C., Jacks. If you don't mind me being blunt."

"Wouldn't expect anything less. Holly?"

"Yes," she blurted, still reeling from her last apparent faux pas.

"Would you care to help me initiate Miss Brown…oh. Wait. That's a huge assumption. Is there a Mr…?"

"Ms. Brown is fine."

"Very good. Care to dazzle us with your presentation, Ms. Ferringer?"

"Sure!" Holly centered herself, mentally cueing her pitch. "Here we go.

"The IS-5000 was developed in 2011 by the researchers at EpTech International. It is the first all-encompassing, virtual simulation booth. Can't afford a trip to the Grand Canyon? Buy a program that let's the Grand Canyon come to you! You can visit Paris, Disneyworld or the moon! All without leaving the comfort of home. And the booths are interactive. Grandma can't make the trip for the holidays? Buy her an IS-5000 and she can visit each member of the family…"

"We're developing a larger booth that will allow several people in together," Jackson interjected. "But it's starting to get unwieldy. We want to keep the price point and portability accessible for just about everyone. Sorry, Holly! Go ahead."

"That's ok," the younger girl confirmed. She retraced her thoughts and got back into the pitch. "Each pod comes with four established environments, while additional programs are becoming available every day!"

"I'll bite," Deana said. "How much for this monstrocity?"

"An excellent question," Cross agreed. "Holly?"

"Um. The ticket price is $16,500…"

"What?! And you're selling these things door-to-door?"

"That does seem a little steep," Cross noted with a smirk.

"Well," Holly continued, unsure how to read her employers reaction. "If you sign up now, we have a payment program available. There's nothing down, and a very competitive interest rate, which brings the monthly payments to only $300 a month. But, before you answer, you may want to experience the magic of the IS-5000 for yourself!"

Jackson dropped his cigarette and stepped it out. "I think we're all warmed up here," he said while checking the control panels on the sides of the stations.

"Shall we?"

CHAPTER TWENTY

"What's so fucking important already?"

Sal looked around at the empty strip-club. *Fishnets* was an investment his uncle made a few years previous. Its back rooms had come in handy on numerous occasions. But something felt wrong about being in a titty-bar at 9:30 in the morning, even if he was part owner.

"Hey! Where the fuck *is* everybody?"

"Sally? Back here!"

"Uncle Vince? Tommy? You wanna stop with the fucking mystery already? I've got a lot of shit going down right now!"

Sal locked the door behind him and walked past the stage and DJ box before entering the "champagne room," where his uncle and one of his soldiers awaited him.

"This'll be worth your time this morning, Sally," his uncle promised. "Get in here and have a seat."

He looked at the vinyl couches and shot the other men a go-to-hell look. "I'm not sittin' on these fuckin' things. Are you crazy? Just tell me what the fuck you dragged me in here for!"

"You've got to feel it to believe it," Tommy said. Tommy had graduated from engineering school the previous summer. He was Sal's right-hand man for anything electronic.

"Fine," Sal acquiesced while taking a seat. "Let's just get this over with. Why am I here?"

"We got this package at the lab the other day," his uncle explained. "You won't fuckin' believe it. The note said it was 'compensation for lost revenue.' It also said, 'no hard feelings.' Like things just go away like that."

"Who sent this 'package.'"

"Some hebe jerk-off. Epstein. He was the prick standing up with that Cross asshole in Colorado."

"Jesus! You check it out yet?"

"We wouldn't have brought you down here if I hadn't had the fuckin' thing checked out, Sally," Tommy assured his boss. "Now, do us favor and fuckin' relax!"

"You're gettin' a fresh mouth on you, kid," Sal noted as he settled back into the couch. "Gonna get your ass into it someday."

"We'll see. You comfortable?"

"Much as I can be, what with all this secretive shit you're doin.'"

"Good. Kiki!"

The redhead stepped out from the dressing room next to the stage. The extent of her outfit was a heavy coat of mascara around piercing green eyes. The dancer floated into the back room and sashayed directly over to Sal.

"Hate to tell you guys, but Kiki's charms ain't exactly new to me. Ain't that right, doll?"

Kiki just smiled as she slowly straddled Sal on the couch. She let her hair flow down across his face and rubbed her breasts against his chest.

"Very nice, honey. But what am I really here for?"

Still no answer as she slipped one knee between his legs and began grinding up and down on his crotch.

"Don't start something I don't have the time to finish."

"Now you're getting the idea," Tommy hinted.

Kiki turned around on his lap and began to grind her bare ass across his zipper.

"How's the patient, darlin'?" Vince inquired.

"Just about ready," Kiki alerted.

Tommy bent down, opened up the leather case at his feet, and extracted a glove hooked up with wires to some kind of control box.

"What the hell is that?"

"Just relax, boss. Kiki?"

The nymphet carefully put on the glove, making sure not to tangle up the wiring. Then she turned around again to meet Sal's gaze.

"You ready?" She asked with a lascivious grin.

"I'm not sure," Sal replied with trepidation.

Kiki bent in and kissed Sal full on the mouth, thrusting her tongue inside. Simultaneously, she put her gloved hand down on Sal's clothed groin and squeezed.

"Hmph!" If Kiki's tongue hadn't been so far down his throat, he would've cried out loud.

Fire and electricity danced across his nether regions. His entire pelvis constricted and jumped outside of his control. Sal stood up so fast that he launched the naked girl from his lap.

"Ooh!" Kiki landed, sprawled across the worn, commercial carpeting of the lounge.

"Jesus Christ! I fucking came on myself!"

Vince and Tommy looked at each other and burst out laughing.

"This ain't fucking funny, you assholes!" Sal swayed a bit. "Jesus. I've got to sit back down."

He collapsed and remained seated with his eyes closed. Kiki moved back up to the couch, She stroked his receding hairline.

"You ok, Sally?"

"I think so," he said, still catching his breath. "You've had this thing apart, Tommy?"

"You bet. Fucking thing even came with an instruction manual and parts list. We can start mass production anytime you say."

Sally opened his eyes and concentrated on the wet stain on the front of his polyester digs. He looked up at his crew and smiled the broadest smile they'd seen from him in months.

"Boys," he commented while absently grabbing and squeezing Kiki's right breast. "This thing is worth fucking millions!"

# # #

Deana stood patiently in the dark booth. The floor and walls consisted of thousands of balls, like ball-bearings, that moved and rolled with her touch. Keeping her balance was a little tricky.

"Not too impressed so far."

"Hang on," Jacks requested from outside the tube. "I'm just getting Holly's equipment connected with your program. Remember how we always used to talk about going to Aspen for a ski trip?"

"We talked about a lot of things, Cross."

"Well, here's a promise kept from a long time ago."

The technology surrounding her began to click and hum. The base under her feet flashed bright enough to be momentarily blinding. It took a few seconds for her to realize that the stark white that remained actually represented snow.

The atmosphere clawed its way up the walls of the tube, about an inch at a time with a digitized jerk. She started to make out trees and bushes, some close by, others quite a distance away, as the environment moved up to her knees. Something brushed the back of her legs.

"Oh!"

"Yeah, sorry about that. The interior is set to conform to a seat if required. The only thing you can't do in there is lie down. Go ahead and sit back."

She did what was requested of her, and almost slid onto the floor. The seat was made of the same series of balls.

The digitized surroundings were up to her waist by then. The floor had a computerized representation of something resembling the footrest of a ski lift. Beneath that (or at least the illusion of beneath it) was what appeared to be a hill. About the time the environment reached her shoulders, the ground below was moving, receding. A perfect blue sky came into focus. It wasn't long before Deana was feeling the tilt-and-sway sensation that would accompany an actual lift.

A slight (but not-altogether cold) breeze blew into her face. More and more of the environment digitized into her surroundings.

"Hey up there!" Deana looked back to see Holly in the next car on the cable. "Not bad, eh?"

"Have to admit," Deana surprised herself by saying with a smile. "It's not too bad at all."

"It's still obviously computerized," Jackson's voice came from her right. "But it's becoming more refined every day."

Deana jumped, and then clung onto the seat for fear of falling.

"See? You're almost convinced that you're really there."

She looked over to see the somewhat blurred image of a fellow passenger in the seat next to her. It was doubly startling because, while she could distinctly make out Holly's face in the image behind her, this body had a more generic, computer-generated image of a head and body dressed in ski gear.

"Jacks?"

"Yep." She heard his voice, but the mouth didn't move. "I thought we'd be able to talk more privately this way."

"Who says I want to talk to you?"

"Who are you talking to?" Holly inquired from behind.

"She can't see me. I'm only jacked into your program."

"Just mumbling to myself!" Deana called back. "I wish," she whispered. "I'd appreciate if you'd just left me alone to do this thing and then I can leave."

"Look, Deana. I'm sorry about all the shit from before. But that's ancient history. We haven't seen each other in…what? Thirteen years?"

"Yeah. It's tragic to see such a solid record come undone. Let's see if we can hold out for the rest of our lives after this, ok? What do you say?"

"I say lift your feet. We're about to get off."

The skis materialized just as her feet were touching the illusional ground. She didn't feel the poles, but she could certainly see them. When she motioned as if to push off, the seat receded back into the wall and she was standing again. As she swung her arms, the vision of the ski poles touched the snow and propelled her on her way.

She noticed that Jackson stayed right with her.

"One trip down the hill and we're gone," she said to Holly, who hadn't quite made it off the lift yet.

The air blowing into her face picked up as she began coasting down hill. Jackson's image floated alongside.

"Not bad, am I right? No broken bones, no frostbite. It's perfect!"

"Well, not perfect," Deana commented, distinctly aware that Cross was just engaging her to open up. "The trees keep blinking in and out. And it really could be a lot cooler."

"True enough," he admitted. Even without his face, she could tell by his tone that he was smiling.

Just for kicks, she headed directly for a tree. The entire booth vibrated slightly as she passed right through.

"That's pretty cool," she admitted.

"Are you sure you don't want to try the ski jump? It'll take your breath away."

"I'm sure. I do have to ask how and why you're trying to sell these things door-to-door."

"Well, as you can imagine with anything Dippy and I do, it's kind of complicated.

"First of all, it's not door-to-door sales where they're walking up to people's homes with one of these monsters strapped to their back. What we do is commission bars and arcades to put up one or two of the models in their business. Our sales team then goes to the surrounding businesses and sets up a sales presentation, allowing the potential customers to try it out for free. Whatever the tube brings in from walk-up traffic is split with the house. If the bars end up selling any on their own, they get a flat commission."

"But why," she asked. She was beginning to maneuver more freely on the virtual slope. She was practically slaloming. "This seems to be a lot of trouble compared to just marketing it through standard retail."

"Danny and I have been toying with the idea of marketing something completely outside the mainstream. No store front, no web site, no employees. Hell, no patent for that matter."

"That's insane. You guys don't have a patent on this thing?" "All the components have patents on them. But no one outside the few hundred people who've bought them even know this technology exists. We're working entirely outside the FTC. We're launching something with no government interference whatsoever. It's just convenient that it was available to market about the time I was looking to drop out for a while."

Deana was winding around a tight curve next to a fairly long drop.

"What are you doing here, Jacks? What the hell happened?"

"I'm sorry, Deana. I just can't…"

Deana physically turned about face in the tube to look directly at the computer projection of her host.

"Then, y'know what Jacks? Fuck off! I want to leave! Now!"

"Um. Deana?"

"No, Cross. I mean it! I want to go!"

"I understand. It's just that…"

"What? *What* you manipulating, self-riotous, self-centered prick? What the fuck do you want from me?"

"I just wanted to tell you that you're going over a cliff."

Deana took stock of her environment. Sure enough, the simulation continued. The perception tilted as she slid off the edge of the mountain. She put her hand out and felt the side of the container, but the side appeared to be looking several stories straight down and into a canopy of pine.

"Oh, shit! Get me out of here!"

"It won't hurt! Enjoy the ride!"

"Fuck you, enjoy the ride! Turn it off!"

The treetops rushed up to meet her at an alarming rate. The tube began to shake violently. Branches crunched and snapped, while she continued to plummet.

"Cross!"

The ground looked real enough. Deana closed her eyes and braced for impact.

The flash of light that heralded the start of the program ignited once again. She opened her eyes.

Deana stood breathlessly in the dark booth. It took all the strength she had to not cry.

CHAPTER TWENTY-ONE

Kimberly was coughing and sniffling as she let herself into the apartment.

"I'm home." She meant to call it out, but what emerged was barely above a whisper. She heard Collene's voice from the other room.

"Lyle? Hang on. Kimmy just got in."

"It's ok! I'm just going to go to the guest room and die!" She coughed, summoning more fluid than expected, and ran into the bathroom.

"You sound terrible!"

"Good," she commented in-between hawking and spitting. "I'd hate to feel this shitty and sound like peaches and cream."

"I'm going to let you go, Lyle."

"No, don't! I'm just going to go to bed!"

"Oh, she's got the creeping cruds again. It's her usual summer cold thing. I'll give you a call back once I've got her under the covers." "Don't be a fuckin' perv. She's sick!"

Kim heard the phone hit the cradle. "Please don't make a big deal out of this."

"Shut up, sweety," Collene responded from the kitchen. "I'm putting soup on. I bought some juice while I was out. I figured you'd be coming home today from the shape you were in this morning. I also picked up some cold medicine."

When she was confident that there was no more phlegm to bring up, Kim stripped off her clothes and started running the water in the tub.

"You going to shower?"

"Uh-huh."

"Good. I changed the sheets so you'd be comfortable."

"I'm moving into the guest room. You don't need to get this shit." She checked the water temperature before stepping into the tub. "What'd Status have to say?"

"Nothing good," Collene shouted above the shower. "We've been able to prove that Don belonged to this church that was causing all the ruckus in Colorado. They're already under investigation for putting together the riots that week in February, but no one's charged them yet. Still not enough evidence."

"Do you really think a church would have somebody killed?"

"I don't know. They worked Lyle over pretty good that morning. He's been trying to track down that Max character again, but the bastard keeps moving. Supposedly, he's in California now. God only knows why."

Kimberly turned off the shower and stepped out. Collene was waiting with her towel.

"Still feeling crummy?"

"Better, but I've got to lie down."

"Sure, but you're laying down in our bed. I don't want to hear shit. If you get all phlegmmy and disgusting tonight, *I'll* move into the guestroom. Ok?"

"Fine." Kim put her head down and let Collene scrub her hair dry.

"Isn't it weird, though, that you guys are so busy looking for the killer when the body might provide the most information?"

"Your degree is what? Fine Arts? Let the professionals worry about it. Get into bed and I'll bring you your soup."

"Fine." Kim padded into the bedroom and pulled her pajamas out from the dresser. "I've been thinking about this, though," she called out to her roommate. "Tell me again why you're *not* looking for the body?"

"Because we're being paid to find the killer, not the kidnapper," Collene replied from the kitchen. "And when someone's paying you the kind of money we're getting for this thing, you don't ask too many questions."

"But, wouldn't it be easier to find the body first?"

"Possibly."

"It just seems to me like you could be tracking the body without your employer's knowing. Then, once you've found it, you might have an easier time with this case. I mean, what's it been? Six months?"

Collene stood at her bedroom doorway with a serving tray, looking strangely at her girlfriend.

"What?"

"Jesus. You're right! They've been leading us around by our noses, and we've been letting them!" She set the tray down on the dresser opposite to the bed. "I've got to make a phone call."

"Wait a sec.," Kim called out. "Give me the soup first!" She listened to Collene pick up the cordless phone in the living room. "Goddammit," she said, flopping back against the pillows. "I'm sick!"

# # #

"Well, *that* was pretty rude."

Deana and Holly weren't out of the warehouse parking lot. Deana didn't take the bait.

"I thought you were having fun," Holly continued to press as she drove. "You certainly looked like you were having fun. Then whammo! With the screaming and the yelling, and then total silence. I've *never* seen you like this."

"You've known me for like a year-and-a-half, Holly," the passenger snapped. "There's a whole lotta life I had going on before we met. And it ain't all sweetness and light." She stared up through the sunroof, gazing at the clear summer sky.

"What's that got to do with tonight," Holly inquired. "I'm trying to understand."

"You don't have to understand. You're making money, he's hidden away…again! Everybody's happy."

"You don't seem to be very happy."

"How I feel about things has never really mattered where Jackson Cross is concerned."

"Why do you say that? He seemed thrilled to see you again. And he also seemed genuinely concerned when you got so upset…"

"Fuck him! Genuinely concerned, my ass! The only person Jackson Cross is genuinely concerned about is himself. And that faggot, Epstein."

"Who is that Epstein guy you two were talking about, anyway?"

"Danny Epstein was this rich kid who was forced to go to our school after both of his parents died. His mom was Catholic, and he was left in the care of her sister and brother-in-law, who were raging Catholics. So he shows up Junior year at St. Ignatius Catholic High School in Ft. Wayne. And, of course, he was pretty much a target for any and all anti-Semitic feelings being harbored there. I knew how he felt. There were only a dozen or so black kids in the entire school when I went. I can't imagine how bad it would have been to be the only one. Not that that's an excuse."

"Excuse for what?"

"Well, the varsity football team was the worst. His uncle made him sign up to be the manager of the team? Y'know, this is the guy who gets a letter for picking up all the dirty jocks and towels and gets the balls back in the coach's closet. Not the most glamorous job under the best conditions, but I guess these guys were just brutal to Danny."

"Uh-huh."

"Well, Jackson pretty much can't stand to see someone discriminated against. It's the one endearing quality…well, never mind. Anyhow, Jackson met with Danny one day after a game when Danny was mopping out the showers, and asked him if he was ready to give some shit back. They hung out at the locker room for a bit, then they drove over to the mall. Now, this was a Friday night, so the mall was crawling with kids and cops. Jacks and Danny do a slow drive past a patrol car while trying to light a joint. Twice. The cops didn't see them the first pass.

"So these two geniuses get busted in front of practically the whole school. But, the thing is, when they get to the station, all crying and in hysterics from being arrested, they have the wherewithal to offer a deal to the DA. First, they were able to convince the cops that it was their first joint. Of course, this was several years before they legalized it."

"That was just two years ago, anyway."

"Right. So they take pee and blood tests and prove that they have nothing in their system. Second, they come up with their own plea-bargain. They give up their source, making it seem like this is the connection for the entire school, in return for clean records.

"Well, the DA can't resist, and asks them where they got the dope. And they tell him…?"

"The football team."

"The quarterback, to put a fine point on it. They return to the locker room with the DA and the cops and show them exactly where the stash is, which just happens to be the QB's locker.

"So, Ryan Collins, the all-star pride of St. Ignatius, gets hauled downtown first thing Monday morning, cuffs and all, in front of the whole school."

"But this guy Ryan didn't sell them the drugs…"

"Them? No. But he *was* a small time dealer. Whether or not he supplied Dopey and Dippy got pushed to the wayside. The two angels had to go into counseling for six months. Collins, along with half the starting line-up, got sent away to Juvie Hall. No prom, no scholarships, no frat parties, no nothing. And everyone in the school knew that they were set up, but no one would or could do anything about it. Danny and Jacks were inseparable from that point on. They were also protected."

"By who?"

"By the Source. The real drug connection for St. Ignatius and most of the other schools in Northeast Indiana. They appreciated the way Jacks and Danny eliminated the competition, and put the word out that these two were not to be fucked with. We were all pretty much untouchable."

"You were dating him at the time? That seems kind of crazy."

"What high school girl do you know that doesn't have a crush on the bad boy? Jacks was always on the edge. Hell, dating me put him on the edge. But he wasn't happy unless he was in somebody's face."

"So, what happened?"

"What ever happens?"

The two rode in silence. Holly fidgeted with the radio and the rear view mirror while Deana closed her eyes and pretended to fall off to sleep. By the time they were pulling into Deana's apartment complex, Holly couldn't contain herself anymore.

"Deana?"

"Hm?"

"What happened tonight? Why'd you go off like that? You seemed fine one minute and then, bam!"

"He hasn't changed, is all. It's the first time I've seen him in thirteen years, and the bastard hasn't changed. Did you know he was talking to me while I was in the simulator?"

"You mean, from outside?"

"No, he was plugged into my program somehow. Talking to me like you and I are right now. I asked him a simple question, in private, just between the two of us, and he still didn't care enough about me to give me an honest answer. It just brought up all the really ugly shit from the past, and I just wigged out, I guess."

"What'd you ask him?"

Deana remained silent until Holly found a spot in front of her apartment.

"I asked him what happened in Colorado."

"And you're surprised he didn't tell you? I mean, I asked and he didn't tell me. And I'm one of his best sales people."

"Did you ever sleep with him?"

"What?"

"Did you ever fuck him, Holly?"

Holly blushed. "No. I can't believe you…"

"Ok," Deana continued in a hushed tone as she opened her door. "So you've never fucked him. Never been pregnant with his kid. And he's never faked his own death to get away from you. See, all these years later, I think maybe he owes me a just little confidence at this point. But maybe that's just me."

Deana exited, closed her door and peered at her stunned friend through the sunroof.

"I'll see you tomorrow, Holly. I've had enough chatting for one night."

Holly silently waited and watched her friend let herself into the apartment before she drove away.

CHAPTER TWENTY-TWO

Nicki let herself into her Brooklyn studio apartment. Jackson was waiting impatiently at the door.

"Well," she addressed him. "What can I do for you? Hmm? Nothing? You just want to eat, don't you?" She stroked his ear, and he purred contentedly.

"Oh, no. Don't pretend that you're waiting here for *my* attention. You just want to eat." Nicki dropped her bag and mail at the door and walked into the kitchen. Jackson followed.

"It would be nice to think that you're greeting me because you love me, but I know better." She took a can of food out from the pantry, opened it and emptied the contents into a dish. Jackson rubbed her legs right up until she set the dish on the ground next to his water. Then he went to town.

"All men are exactly alike," she said to herself. She left the dining feline and walked back into the living room. The petite young woman turned her computer on before undressing as she walked into the bathroom. Moments later, now wearing a sweat suit, Nicki sat down in front of her keyboard. "Ok," she commented (still to herself). "Who wants to play?"

The first thing, as was her usual routine, was checking the emails.

"Crap." Delete. "Crap." Delete. "Hate mail." Delete. "Crap." Delete. "Crappy hate mail." Delete, delete, delete. Of the 18 messages waiting for her that day, only four survived the massive purge. "I'll get to mom and my sister later…who's this?"

The correspondence in question held the title *Practicing Crosstian,* and was from *Judas-Lover@AOL.com.* She read the title several times before double clicking on the note. The more she read, the more she smiled.

Hey there!

I hope you do not mind the intrusion, but I read your bio attached to the Jackson Cross Website and just had to drop you a line.

First of all, I think you are very brave. You must get a ton of crank mail from that site, so much so that you may never read this, but nothing is ever gained without a gamble.

Did you really meet Jackson the day of his Tom Green show appearance? And Danny, Darlene and Scott? I am so jealous! I think it is so cool that creating his Fan Club and Website was the main reason that you finally bought a computer! All I can boast is that I saw him live once. I am not exaggerating when I say that he changed my life forever! So many people do not (or even try to) understand what he is trying to say that it is difficult to connect with anyone and have a meaningful conversation about his unique genius!

Do not get me wrong. I am not some unstable jerk who is obsessed with this man. I just really like what he is trying to say and do, and I am tired of being harassed for it.

My name is Nick, by the way. I work in the City. I drive a cab right now, but that is only until I get my own book published (any day now, I hope and hope).

If you ever feel like no one else is listening, feel free to drop me a line. It does not even have to be about the Cross. It is just nice to know there is someone else out there who has got some common sense and who is not afraid to tell people.

I guess that is all I wanted to say. I hope this finds you well.

Thank you for your time,

Nick

Nicki read and re-read the note.
Nick, she thought to herself. *Nick and Nicki. Nicki and Nick.*
"Hi! I'm Nicki and this is my boyfriend Nick!"
She giggled at how silly she was getting from one email. She didn't know who this guy was, how old he was, or what he looked like. But the thought that she may have actually made a connection in the crazy, virtual cyber-world was just too romantic a notion to give up too quickly.
Jackson jumped up into her lap. He settled down, licking himself quietly. She petted him absent-mindedly as she moved the cursor over and around the Reply button.

# # #

"Hel-lo! I know you're ther-re!"
Holly felt ridiculous. She stood outside Deana's apartment, shouting through the kitchen window.
"Deana? You can't keep yourself locked up like this! How much work do you plan on missing because of this guy?"
"Go away." The weak reply came from the living room. All Holly could make out was the flickering light of the monitor in the dim dwelling.
"She lives! C'mon! Let me in! I've got *choc-olate!*"
"I don't want *choc-olate!* Go away."
Holly looked around. People coming home from work were averting their eyes as they approached their own doors.
"C'mon, Dee! People are staring!"

"Good. Maybe you'll take the hint."

Holly considered this for a moment. "What do I care? I don't live here! Let them stare!" She began projecting her voice away from the apartment instead of inside. "That's right! You go ahead and look! This is Deana Brown's place where she's been holed up for two days because of some *guy*!"

"Shut up, Holly!"

"Some guy she hasn't seen since high school! How pathetic is that?"

"Oh, I don't *believe* this!" Deana forced herself up and off the couch. She shuffled to the door.

"And I haven't even told you the best part!"

The door unlocked and Deana peered out, smoldering cigarette dangling from one lip. "Cut the shit, Holly. I'm up, alright? I'm fine. Go away."

Holly pushed her way through the door. "You don't really want me to leave, y'know."

Deana watched her young friend as she marched into the kitchen and began dispensing items from her grocery bag. "I don't?"

"Nope," Holly continued while retrieving two bowls and a pair of spoons. "You wouldn't have let me in if I was standing outside buck naked, screeching Barry Manilow's 'Mandy' through a megaphone. If you really didn't want to let me in, it wouldn't have mattered."

Deana shuffled back into the living room and collapsed on the sofa. "If you were standing outside singing 'Mandy,' naked or not, the neighbors would have killed you long before I would have given a shit."

"This place stinks! I didn't know you smoked."

"What you don't know about me could fill a biography."

"Even still," Holly continued, nonplussed by the insult. "We should air this place out." She gathered up the bowls of ice cream, the syrup and the bottle of sprinkles and joined her friend in the living room. "Whatcha watching?"

"News," Deana commented, taking her bowl of comfort. "Some big time Mafioso guy just died."

"Really? Was it a whack?"

"You mean a hit?"

"Yeah! Was it one of those?"

"I don't think so. It's kinda funny, actually. Officially, he died of a coronary. But what they've just discovered is that, when he died, he had this weird sex glove attached to his crotch. Keeled over in a crowded strip-club in Las Vegas. There were so many people around, the mob couldn't keep it out of the papers. Imagine being married to that guy?"

"Men are all pretty much creeps."

"Yeah."

The two ate their ice cream in silence.

Deana finished her bowl, placed it on the coffee table and grabbed her smokes.

"Ugh! How can you follow up Royal Fudge with a cigarette? It's disgusting!"

"Are you here for anything besides griping about my life?"

"Not really." Holly finished her own desert and straightened up on the couch. "Hey! You'll never guess what I did today. I quit my position in the IS-5000 program."

"Dammit, Holly! What'd you do that for?"

"What? I thought you'd be happy!"

"Why the hell would that make me happy? You're making good money, and you've got the new car to pay for now."

"I couldn't just keep working there. Not after what he did to you. I've got half a mind to go to the tabloids and tell them where he is."

"You don't really know what he did and didn't do."

"But, you said…"

"I know what I said. But that's only part of the story. You shouldn't be so rash."

"*I* shouldn't be so rash. I haven't been stuck inside my apartment for two days, all depressed and stinky."

"Man!" Deana turned off the monitor. "Look, I'm as much pissed off at myself as him. Just do me a favor and get your job back. I don't need the idea of your car getting repossessed weighing on my conscience on top of everything else."

"Well, I can't go back thinking about him the way I do now. If there's more to it, you're just going to have to share."

Deana puffed at her cigarette a few times, mulling everything over in her head.

"You want to know everything? Fine.

"The first thing to remember is that *I* got pregnant. He didn't *get* me pregnant. He didn't rape me or take advantage of me or anything like that. It was just a stupid mistake made by a couple of stupid kids."

Deana chuckled to herself. "Have to admit, the sex was great. He wasn't like the most caring or affectionate lover of my life, but by God I loved being with him. He was just like this presence, y'know? Even back then. I lived for him to touch me. S'funny, I've never been all that attracted to white guys, but Jackson was outside of that whole race thing. He was outside of the whole physical attraction thing too, being that he was kind of scrawny and pasty. Jacks was more like something out of nature. He was primal. A force. I would do anything for him back then. Including having an abortion."

Deana reached forward and stubbed out her stick. Holly was riveted.

"It was a mutual decision. I actually felt kind of guilty even telling him about it. I knew that he had some grand designs for his life. And I felt like my mistake got in his way. But I needed to pay for the procedure, and I sure as hell wasn't going to my parents. They were already down on African-American Teen Promiscuity, as my father lectured it. So I had to tell him. And, y'know what? He was great.

"He didn't get upset, he didn't fly off the handle, and he didn't bring up abortion as if that was the only real solution. He even offered to get married. I'm the one who insisted that this was the last thing either of us needed right then. It was our senior year in high school. I was not going to spend that year getting fatter and fatter and listening to all the sniping and bullshit. So we agreed that it was the best thing for everyone involved.

"Epstein paid for it. He had just turned eighteen, and had access to some, but not all, of his inheritance. That didn't sit well with me, having to rely on Danny. I mean, he and Jacks were joined at the hip by then. I just wanted it to be between the two of us, y'know? But money's never been something that drove Jackson. He was always broke. And we wanted to have it taken care of pretty fast. So I agreed to let Danny chip in.

"Things weren't all that different for the months afterwards. Well, we were pretty cautious about sex, but other than that it was like nothing happened.

"Then, one Friday night, I was home with the flu. It was about three months before graduation. Jacks and Danny went to a basketball game at school, which was surprising since neither of them liked sports at all. All I heard from everyone was how obnoxious they were. They were drunk and starting fights and making a general nuisance of themselves, which was also contrary to their usual behavior. They love to fuck with people, but they much prefer to do it from a distance. But not that night.

"So, after the game, they were involved in some kind of brawl out in the parking lot with some kids from the opposing school; Boone High, I think it was. Jacks actually threw a punch at somebody! The fight got broken up and Danny and Jacks took off in Danny's Camero. They were yelling and cursing and peeling out of the parking lot. Everybody was relieved when they were gone, I heard. Then, a few minutes later, this explosion happened blocks away. Everybody drove over to see what happened. They found Danny, crying uncontrollably, next to the fiery wreck of his car. I guess it was a monstrous inferno. The fire department didn't arrive for close to twenty minutes, and there was nothing but a cinder left by then."

"My God. What did you do?"

"Oh, I cried. I spent close to a month in hiding. I almost didn't graduate. Luckily, our relationship was common knowledge. One of my teachers made sure I got whatever extensions I needed to get through it."

"So, he faked the whole thing?" Holly asked before turning on herself. "Of course he faked the whole thing. I've worked for him, for the love of…" She shook her head and turned back to her friend. "How did you find out?"

"That he was alive? Shit, we always knew that. He left a note, telling his parents he was running away. There was no body found. Epstein claimed he was knocked out and woke up when the car exploded, but nobody really took him seriously.

"Technically, they fucked it up. Everyone knew he wasn't killed. But he became something of a legend. The kid who wanted out of high school so bad, he faked his own death mere months before graduation. And some people did, in fact, buy it."

"But you didn't."

"Of course not! I knew him well enough to recognize that it was a con."

"But, if you knew he wasn't dead…then?"

"Why cry and cry for months?" Deana pulled her cuff sleeve to her eyes to dab them dry. "Why get all down since he wasn't really dead? Well, let me ask you Holly: How bad of a person do you have to be for someone to think they had to die to break up with you?"

"Oh, honey no."

"No, I mean it. How hideous are you for someone to go to the lengths of faking their own death?"

"Now, I'm sure that's not the reason…"

"No, I know," she admitted while grabbing a tissue from the coffee table. "But, you have to understand just how bad it hurts."

Holly waited quietly for her friend to contain herself.

"God, I just hate him."

"I can understand."

"I mean, I've finally gotten to a point in my life where I thought I was okay with what happened, y'know? Then he's right there in front of me, smiling at me. He's aged well. I'll give him that. San Diego was good for him."

"San Diego?"

"That's where he went after high school. Danny helped him get a fake high school diploma. He went to college, dropped out, faked a degree, and started working in advertising. We were always supposed to go out West."

"How do you know so much about him if you hadn't seen him since high school?"

"Well, when his book showed up years later, all I had to do was read the Prologue and I knew that the Jackson Cross on the cover was the genuine motherfucker. I started following his career, just to see how far he'd get before screwing it up. It wasn't long before some cheesy publisher issued a hack biography. It's probably not terribly accurate but, with Jacks, it's not too hard to fill in the blanks."

"Which book?"

"Which book? *The Judas Conspiracy*?"

"Oh, that! The one everyone was so bent out of shape over last year?"

"I take it you never read it?"

"No. I don't read books so much. Should I?"

"You're asking the wrong person. I was hoping it would be terrible, but it really wasn't. I don't understand what's got so many people bent out of shape, but even that's starting to smell fishy. I guess whether or not you should read it depends on how open-minded you are. If you're easily offended, then the book will almost surely offend you. So why read it? If you're not easily offended, then it's just a weird, meandering, fuckin' huge book.

"It was everything he had been trying to say when we were growing up. He was convinced he was put on this planet to shake us up a little bit. It's a testament to his need to push people's buttons. Pure and simple."

"But, what's it about?"

"How much time do you have," Deana asked as she reached for another cigarette.

"As much as we need," Holly responded while making herself more comfortable on the couch.

"Then I guess we should start at the beginning."

And she did.

CHAPTER TWENTY-THREE

Back in Indiana, before we got all fucked up, Jackson used to talk about how he was going to rewrite Dante's *Divine Comedy*. Except he was going to call it The Big Joke, and make it a comedian going through Hell, Purgatory and Heaven. For a while, it was all he talked about.

It's been a few years since *The Judas Conspiracy* came out. I bought it that first week, read it and then threw it away.

It's funny. I'm not sure how much of this I'm remembering from shit he told me when we were stoned in the back of his car, or from the book itself.

To begin with, it's written in first person, so you're to presume it's Jackson, although the main character is only referred to as "Jay," and even that reference is rare. It's also written in three parts, like *Divine Comedy*.

It's Memorial Day Weekend, and Jay has decided to visit some friends of his who live in New York. Now, Darlene and Scott (a couple) know Jay from working at the same company as he did some years previous. Danny, as you now know, had been one of Jay's best friends since high school.

The story begins with Jay and Danny coming out of a peep show in Times Square. They're stoned out of their minds and are meeting Darlene and Scott, who've been watching a movie while the two boys were being boys.

I'm trying to remember exactly what happens next. I know they find the side entrance to some club, Boca Del Diablo, maybe, and Sam Kinison is acting as doorman. He's yelling at them for being late to the opening or some such. I mean, it's *really* Sam Kinison! The group thinks he's like a really good impersonator, but Jay knows better. This madman is the genuine article, he's sure.

He asks Sam how Hell's been treating him. "Hell? Man, I had three wives back in the world! Hell is fucking Club Med!"

Jay's so stoned that he's anxious to see where this leads. So he convinces Danny, then he and Danny coerce Scott, and all three of them pressure Darlene, and then there they go, through the door of this club and down some kind of brick stairs.

As they're descending this weird stairwell, Kinison prodding them on further and further (Oh, Ohhhh!! You know how he does), you find out a little about the group. Darlene is fairly conservative, not interested in conflict of any kind. Scott, on the other hand, can only express himself through hostility at times. Darlene and Scott have one thing in common, however. They both embrace a conventional lifestyle; no smoking, no drinking, nothing illegal. Living together outside of wedlock was the most flagrant disregard of convention either of the two had dared in their lives, and even that was going to have to come to a halt soon. Danny, on the other hand, never tried a drug he didn't like. Not that he was an addict. He was just committed to finding the best, most rewarding high. Not to mention the best, most rewarding meal, the best, most rewarding drunken experience, and the best, most rewarding fuck in recorded history. Moderation was not a word that Danny had been required to use in a sentence back in the fifth grade. He was strictly a person of excess.

Jackson, on yet another hand, portrays himself as walking pretty much down the center of those two personality types. The pompous jerk makes his character out to be the most level-headed, grounded, sensible human being...not just of this group! But the entire planet! That's how full of himself...well...

Anyhow, these personas come out during the grousing that goes on as they descend further and further down this brick staircase, having almost no idea where they're going. Finally, music rises up from several levels below. People talking, traffic noises; they could be coming back out onto Times Square if they hadn't just descended what felt like a dozen flights of stairs.

Sure enough, they start to see a doorway below, and they start to see a sidewalk with people walking by. Further back, there's a street with traffic. They walk through the doorway and find themselves back outside! But, it's definitely not New York.

The streets are narrower, the buildings are old, two-story tenements, instead of skyscrapers, and the people are simply *not* from the City.

Then Scott says, "What's that smell? It's like day-old urine and beer farts!"

And Jay realizes, "Holy shit! We're in New Orleans!"

[What?]

It's true. Kinison, who has…devolved somewhat, slowly transforming into a kind of demon, informs them that Purgatory filled to capacity some time ago, as the requirements for admission into Heaven have became so strict. So, at some point during the 20th Century, New Orleans became the wait-station for souls awaiting judgment.

[That must have pissed off New Orleans residents.]

I guess so. They turned around to see that they came out of a brick building and onto Bourbon Street. Sam kept the group moving forward. At one point, they get accosted by an old, frail black man, calling himself "the Chicken King." He claims to recognize the smell on those four. He says three of them are forever people. While one will meet Death on the best possible terms before the next morning. He tries to sell them incense, which he claims to be made of soap, but Kinison runs him off. Before he gets more than a couple of steps, he calls back. "Hey Jay," he says. "Don't make it bad!" Then he giggles madly and scampers away with this voodoo woman who had been standing behind them the whole time.

They eventually come up to this storefront that looks like it might be a bank or something. The sign over the entrance reads "Good Intentions, Inc." There's a revolving door that leads into the building, but all of the windows are tinted so severely, that they can't actually see inside.

Well, Darlene just about snaps. Everything that's happening just caves in on her, and she's telling Jay that there's no fucking way she's going through those doors. Jay confirms with Sam that they don't really have a choice if they want to get back to where they came from. And, besides, he's just dying to see what's going to happen next!

So, he reasons that if he goes through, then everyone else will have to follow. Because they're the best friends he has in the world, and no way would they leave him alone in some fucked up building in New Orleans while they traipse on back to the City.

Darlene warns him not to put that theory to the test, but by then Jay has already pushed into the rotating doors.

The door swings around and flings him out the other side and into a surprisingly small brick room. He hits the brick chair that's built into the center, turns around and sees that the door is gone. He's alone in this octagonal room made entirely of brick. I think he says something like, "Man. Darlene is going to be pissed at me."

[No kidding.]

So, he checks out the digs, and finds no way in or out. The ceiling is brick as well. He has no idea how it's lit. He starts to wig out a little. Then, after he's collapsed in the chair, Howard Stern just pops up behind him.

[That radio guy? The one who strangled the hooker?]

Sort of. He's actually Satan. He just shows up like Stern because it's both logical and more palatable than some giant, slimy, hairy thing with hoofs and horns. You can't talk to anybody if that's how you appear to them, They just start crying and wailing, and you're trying to explain the rules to them and it's just a mess. So, now he has a variety of images; Bill Gates, Michael Jordan, Trey Parker…there's a ton. It just makes everything run a little smoother.

Jay's concerned about the rest of the group, and Howard assures him that they're fine. Steve and Darlene went through together, so they're too busy fighting about how Darlene was right and they shouldn't have gone through the door to notice the fact that they're in Hell.

And, Danny's so stoned, he thinks he's really talking to Howard Stern.

[So, they were all there together?]

Well, they were all in the same kind of room, and were all talking to Howard, but they weren't exactly together. They were experiencing it separately.

[Weird.]

Howard has a proposition for Jay and his friends. Well, *most* of his friends. It seems that he and God are both calling it quits. Retiring. Going to the place where all washed out gods go. They'll lawn bowl with Odin, play pinochle with Ra, and just do whatever it is retired gods do.

Jay asks, "Why?"

[Of course!]

Of course! So, Howard lays this bit on him about how the human subconscious has the capacity to create it's own deities out of shear necessity. It's the "parent principle."

[Oh-oh.]

Very funny. The gist is that we can't function as humans unless we're scared shitless of some greater power who's gonna make us tow the line. It inevitable. We couldn't have evolved as far as we have as a species without this ingrained need to be told what to do and how to act. Even the appearances of rebellion against authority is an extension of the free will guaranteed by God. It's teen angst on a social scale. A forgivable offense in the course of natural development. But we won't be able to evolve much further unless we learn to let go of the overwhelming need for a parent/creator.

So, what Jackson tries to say is that all of our "gods" have been real, but only because they've been created by the group subconscious. As we evolve, we outgrow the reigning deity. So our collective subconscious creates a new, more malleable supreme being.

The thing is, the digital age has put the final nail in the coffin for current supreme beings. The Judeo-Christian God (and, by an extension, Satan) had become passé.

[More people pissed about that, I imagine.]

I'm sure. But, y'know, God and Satan are taking it like men. They're quietly moving on into the memory regions of our dream stuff. But, they need to set up a replacement for themselves before they go. They've tapped into the mainstream river of consciousness, and were able to determine what the next evolutionary step of a divinity should be.

The answer turned out to be a Triumvirate.

[A what?]

A trinity. But not in the Christian sense. And there would be no Devil. No Satan, watching us over our shoulders, ready to push us over the edge. "Yeah," Howard says. "Like I did any of that anyway." But he was psyched because that meant that Howard Stern would be the last recorded devil. And he laughed and laughed!

Anyway, this triumvirate would consist of the metaphysical representations of three very key…I almost want to say ideologies. I know that doesn't sound right, but these ideas are based on the general state of mind of the people at the time, most of whom decided their own comfort based on political or economic conditions. I guess that makes it ideological.

Sigh [Anyhow.]

Anyhow, the trio consists of Convention, Excess and Judgment. These are the three rules by which we are to abide. Well, two rules, one deliberation. See, these are the terms by which we will monitor ourselves. Either we live in excess (which is no good), or in convention (surprisingly, also no good), or somewhere in between (the goal). At the end, we will be shown how and where we either indulged selfishly to the pain of others, or refused to experience more of life due to fear of recrimination. These are the new sins. And we will be judged for them.

Unbeknownst to Jay and his friends, they were born into these roles. Darlene is to become the embodiment of Convention, Danny will take on the mantle of Excess, and Jay will become the Judge of Humankind.

[What about Scott?]

Scott had the bad luck of dating Darlene at the time that this went down. Unfortunately, no one gets out of Hell alive (unless your name is Paul Reubens), so he's going to be moving on, as they say.

[Poor Scott.]

Yeah. Jay wasn't too keen on that, either. But he was most put off with the idea of being responsible for judging souls. He had no interest in being the final say on people's eternal damnation (another division between Jackson and the character. Jacks is one of the most obscenely judgmental people I know! Never about race, never about gender, but just loved to judge those he deemed inadequate). Howard assured him that people would mostly be judging themselves. He'd be primarily a figurehead, only having to intervene over those who were either judging themselves too harshly, or not harshly enough.

Jay remained unconvinced. So Howard suggested they take a tour of the current Hell, and see if Jay doesn't think that things could be improved upon. He tells Jay to pick a brick, for the room they were in was, in fact, Hell. Every brick in the room represented a different faction of damnation.

So then they go on this tour of Hell. I forget most of it. I remember there was a telemarketing room.

[What?]

Seriously, there's all these lost, tortured souls making phone calls. People don't realize that about every third solicitation phone call they receive is actually coming from Hell. If they convince you to take the product they're selling, they'll get something like 20 minutes off their eternal sentence. It's pretty funny, because desperation is the worst way to make a sale and, let me tell ya,' these people are desperate!

They tour all the corporate offices of Hell, which just gets ugly.

[Upsetting even more people, I'm sure.]

Oh, it would've had to. He was pretty brutal, especially on Human Resources and MIS. And each of the different sections of Hell is monitored by dead comedians. Or at least the demons took on the form of dead comedians for the purposes of Jay's tour.

Now, Jay remains preoccupied with the proposal even while he's watching Lenny Bruce torture one victim in Addicts Hell, shooting up right in front of this girl whose own collapsed veins are laid out around her. He just can't picture himself condemning people, no matter how evil they've been in their own lives, to some kind of eternal torture.

He tells Howard that he's seen enough, and they end up back in the throne room. Jay declines the offer to be the final Judge. Howard shrugs and says that's fine. They'll use Scott instead.

[Just like that?]

Just like that. They're on a timetable. Satan was late for a poker game with Puck, Pan and Loki.

This drives Jay nuts! Scott, according to Jay, wants to incarcerate people for driving shitty-looking cars. He likes the idea of another world war, because it could open up the job market for himself. He thinks people who don't own dogs should be sent to a camp for re-education. As much as he loves Scott as a personal friend, this shouldn't be the guy in charge of humanity's souls, in Jay's opinion.

Howard couldn't care less. They needed three, if it wasn't the original three they wanted, they had a fallback, so Stern's job was done.

Satan vanishes, leaving Jay alone in the brick room, with no idea how to get out or where he'd go to if he did.

[What happened to Darlene and Scott and Danny?]

It's implied, I think, that they've agreed to this. I can't remember for sure. I do remember the music that starts playing while he's sitting on this brick chair in the middle of the brick room. At first he heard Every Breath You Take. Then he heard Like A Virgin and In The Air Tonight and My Sharona, all in Muzac form. Somehow, it made sense to him that the Muzac piped into Hell would be the best of the '80s. He was on the verge of freaking out when Paul McCartney shows up.

[The Beatle?]

There's more than one? Well, actually, there is. This was Death, arriving to take Jay on his next step of the journey. Remember; no one gets out of Hell alive.

[Unless you're Pee Wee Herman.]

So Death comes calling, and he happens to look exactly like Paul McCartney. He even ran into the group while they were in India with the Maharishi-Whatever-The Fuck. Turns out, they laid down the backwards vocals as a lark, but people got it screwed up. Instead of "Paul is dead," John was actually saying, "Paul is Death." And the Abbey Road cover? That was him. He regretted it later because, for a good twenty years, recently deceased souls kept badgering him to take off his shoes and smoke right-handed during their walk towards the infinite. It's not that he preferred the moaning and wailing and pleading for a second chance that came pretty much standard with the job, it's just that even celebrity can wear thin.

So Jay chats a little bit with Death, kind of whining and saying how much of a raw deal he's gotten. Y'know, it sucks! All he did was explore this weird doorway in New York, and now he's dead and not allowed to return to his life. He was also worried about where in Hell he was going to end up. I found it interesting at the time. He's barely concerned at all about his friends, even though they just made a deal with the devil! Yet no concern for their welfare at all.

[Um, he's dead. I think it might be okay for him to be a little self-involved right then. No offense.]

Whatever. Paul reassures him some. He tells him that his progression is determined within his subconscious, and that his soul has progressed to the point of reincarnation. That was kind of interesting. He's suggesting that we each have the capacity to construct our own afterlife, and that we can even decide to give ourselves another chance.

"It's not that big a bloody deal," I think Paul says. He leads Jay out of the throne room and into this preposterously bright light. He asks Death if he can request a particular life to be reincarnated into, and Paul just laughs. "Oh, the hubris of you monkeys. You'll go where there's availability. I can't even guarantee what part of the universe you'll pop up at, old son." I remember that after the long hall of light, they come out to this platform at the edge of existence. Death looks up at the millions of sparkling lights, points to one cluster in particular and says, "But I think you'll end up somewhere 'bout here."

The second book opens with Jay being reborn. This is where it gets kind of weird.

[*Now* it gets weird?]

Well, it wasn't easy to read, let alone explain. Apparently, our souls are tied to the subconscious, not the conscious. The problem is that Jay was reincarnated while still conscious, so his personality remained intact, when he should have been a clean slate.

[I don't get it.]

It's like this…If you were killed, you would stop being the person you think you are and would revert to your subconscious self. So, if you were reincarnated, you would have no memory of the experience of this life.

But since Jay remembered everything about his previous existence, it was impossible to break that tie to his human existence. And the planet he was reincarnated on was anything but human.

He goes into great detail to describe this incredibly advanced society which exists on a planet consisting entirely of water. They're essentially huge amoebas. They use every follicle individually and with tremendous precision. They are truly the masters of their own domain. But Jay is still essentially human. He doesn't have the capacity to grasp all the complexities of life on this planet. Or even to grasp all the complexities of his own body.

Worse still, they've become so advanced that they have no need for procreation. They've essentially created spare bodies for themselves to be activated in the event of some unforeseen catastrophe. So, Jay was revived as a replacement for someone who worked in a kind of kelp mining place, and was expected to take his place in society within a couple of days after being born.

But he just doesn't get it! He can't control this new body to do even the simplest of tasks. In this gorgeous, glorious planet, he's essentially the village idiot.

The worse part is, for all their advancements as a species, these folks are mean! He's the first flawed personality to come their way in like 1000 years. They don't know what to do with him, with the exception of belittling and hazing him. He doesn't even have parents to fall back on. And, even if procreation was allowed, they're asexual. He's so dumb, he can't even get himself pregnant. Imagine how that feels.

So, he spends something like twenty years on this planet...

[Twenty years?]

Yeah. I pretty much skimmed this part. He goes into serious detail about the culture and religions and everything. It'll bore you to tears. Eventually, however, they get tired of this idiot hanging around like a blight on their supposedly perfect existence. So they come up with a way to get rid of him.

It turns out that this race has been cultivating other planets, helping them evolve closer to the "perfection" that they have achieved. They've created a kind of astral projection whereby they separate the conscious self from the body and propel it across space and into the body of an inhabitant on another planet. This way they can work from the inside. The governing bodies decide that one of the emissaries they have on some mudball in the armpit of the universe could use an assistant.

So they load up the narrator into the hydro-powered machine and fling his consciousness out into the stars.

[Okay.]

In the third and final part of the book, his consciousness lands in the body of Judas Iscariot right about the time that Jesus is being baptized. Jesus, according to this story, was one of the creatures from that other planet, sent here to put us on the right evolutionary track. Essentially, he's here to reinforce that whole parent principle…

[Oh-oh.]

Thing. Please stop doing that.

[Sorry.]

Anyway…where was I? Oh, yeah! So he's been sent down to assist Jesus by assuring that he'll be martyred, thereby solidifying his place in the religious culture of a vast selection of this planet's inhabitants. But here's a guy who already turned down the position of ultimate judge. It galled him to think that some alien culture, one that treated him like shit for twenty years no less, was determining the course of our development. So he decides to *not* betray Jesus, just to see how we'd get along as a species without the crucifixion.

He hangs out with the apostles for the three years leading up to the main event. He sees where the miracles are sometimes the result of the alien technology, sometimes they're out and out fraudulent. More and more he's convinced that he's made the right decision to not betray this man, and is looking forward to the consequences.

Of any part of the novel, this captures Cross best. He's doing this because he'd like to see what's going to happen. He would deny millions of people their heritage…pretty much on a whim. Why not? He can't ever get home anyway? What's it to him? Do you see where I'm going with this?

[Sure. But the best news is that you're not bitter.]

Why are you here if you're not going to be sympathetic?

[Don't be such a baby. So, he's *not* going to betray Jesus…]

John and Peter put a wrench in the plan when they conspire to make sure that the betrayal goes off without a hitch. They set up Judas in such a way that, when the end finally comes, the general populace of Palestine is convinced that Judas rolled over on Christ. The more he denies it, the more he's accused of the crime.

Even his suicide at the time of the crucifixion is a travesty. A mob is stringing him up, claiming that he killed himself by turning against God.

[So, they kill him?]

Yep. He's screaming at Jesus, telling him to "get off the cross," while John and Peter put a noose over his head. They lynch him. But, just as he's heading for the bright light, again (!), someone extends a hand of comfort to him. He takes the hand, only to find that it belongs Darlene. She and Scott and Danny, all gods at this point, were graced with omnipresence upon taking the mantles of divinities. They pulled Jay out of the pain of his own execution and plopped him right back in the time and place that he started his journey.

They needed someone to spread the word about the new Order of things. It becomes his job to present this tale to the world and make us understand the new standards of Excess, Convention and Judgment.

So he goes to Scott and Darlene's apartment, sits down in front of their computer and enters all of his experiences from the last 2000 or so years, right up to the last word of the book.

CHAPTER TWENTY-FOUR

Roy Washington returned from his lunch with Spike Jonz at *Fishnets West*. His intercom was buzzing as he entered the trailer. His secretary informed him that he had visitors waiting.

"I don't have any appointments on my schedule, David."

"I understand that," the secretary confirmed through the intercom. "But these men have been waiting for a while, and are kind of insistent."

"Well, who are they? Are they players?"

"Not as far as I know, but they're convinced that you'll want to talk to him."

"Is either of them holding a script or something?"

"Not that I've seen."

"Thank Christ for that. Oh, what the hell. Send them in."

The two men entered Roy's prefab office on the Universal lot moments later. The Caucasian was slim, well dressed and pampered. His companion looked as if he might have been in prison as recently as that morning. Roy's church group would have blamed those thoughts on the Hollywood machine perpetuating the myth that all African Americans are convicts, but he knew a little better. Growing up in East L.A. taught him that some people (regardless of color) are criminals, pure and simple.

"Gentlemen," Roy greeted the two. "You're lucky to have caught me. My schedule's usually so full…What can I do for you today?"

"My name is Max Swanson," the first man offered while shaking Roy's hand. "This is my associate, Mr. Sims. We've come to offer our help with one of your productions."

"Mr. Sims," Roy shook the large man's hand. He did his best to continue smiling as the fingers of his right hand were ground painfully together in the monster's grip. "Easy, brother. I'm hoping we're all friends here."

"You can call me Nailz," came the reply.

"So, you'll have to enlighten me. I wasn't aware that one of our productions was in need of a hand."

"You're executive producing the film adaptation of *The Judas Conspiracy*?"

"That I am. We've got Terry Gilliam signed on to direct. He's scouted all the locations and filming begins next week. So, in what way do you think you can be of assistance?"

The tidy man took a seat in front of Roy's desk. Nailz continued standing behind him.

"We'd like to handle your extras."

"Beg your pardon?"

"The crowd scenes? My benefactor would consider it a personal favor if our company could be put in charge of getting the people put together for that shooting. Specifically, for Christ's trial before Pilate."

"Really?" Roy laughed a little too heartily for Max's taste. "That's about the strangest request I've had this year, and I do business in Hollywood!" He took a moment to contain himself. "Ok, I'll bite. Who's your benefactor?"

"That's not too important," Max stated. "You'll be dealing directly with me." He pulled out a check. "As you can see, it's worth quite a bit to us."

Roy's eyes lit up. He whistled. "Damn. You guys don't fuck around."

"We'd pay the salaries, insurance and transportation of the extra crew. All we're asking for is total access to the production."

Roy held the check. His eyes darted from the dollar amount on the paper, to Max, to Nailz, and back again.

"I'd like to take your money, gentlemen. Believe me. But I'm afraid things work a bit differently out here. First of all, I'm not even the person who determines from who and where we get our extras. That's casting. Second of all…well, it's pretty fucking weird, don'tcha think? I mean, who do you guys think you are? The mob?"

Max smiled broadly. "The Mafia? No. Why, if we were the Mafia, we'd probably show up with compromising photos of you and a transsexual prostitute down on Mulhuland Drive."

Roy smiled even more broadly than Max. "Maybe thirty years ago. Those pictures don't make squat today. Hell, a scandal would probably raise my stock in the industry." Roy leaned back and put his feet up on the desk. "But you guys amuse me. Thinking you can come in here and blackmail a brother, this day and age. What else you got?"

Max's smile faltered. "What do you mean?"

"Oh, c'mon! That wasn't your whole game plan, was it? Flash a big check and elude to elicit pictures, and that's it?" Roy leaned up to contact his secretary. "Looks like you boys came a long way just to have security throw you out."

Nailz reached over as if to grab the intercom before Roy could contact his secretary, just as the producer pulled a small caliber weapon from under his desk.

"Now we're talking *real* scandals," Roy commented. "You wanna play, my nigger?"

Nailz froze and looked back at Max. The minister couldn't believe how quickly he'd lost control of the situation.

"Hang on, hang on. We're getting terribly sidetracked here. We just want to talk business."

"Business?" Roy confirmed. "You want to talk business, you ask the Jolly Black-as-the-motherfucking-night Giant here to sit the fuck down. Then maybe we can talk like business folk."

Max nodded at his associate, and Nailz moved back to his position behind Max.

"So," Roy began, leaving the gun out on his desk blotter while still reclining. "You have something else to bring to the table?"

Max considered this. He cleared his throat before making his pitch.

"We have access to certain technology which may reinvent the way movies are experienced. We'd like to test it out on this film."

"Really? When were you going to let our studio in on this…or were we supposed to just figure it out after the bootlegs?"

"No reason to be coy, Roy. I'm offering you the chance to be this century's Al Jolson."

The black executive looked at his guests soberly. "Why the fuck would I want to be Al Jolson?"

"Well, y'know. He did the first film with sound."

"Yeah, but he didn't invent the process. I don't remember the name of the guy who did invent it, but it sure as hell wasn't some cracker in black face."

"Semantics, my friend. I'm not exaggerating when I say this will revolutionize the industry. And Universal can split the production costs with my church."

"You want a church to produce *The Judas Conspiracy* movie? Now *there's* some interesting press." Roy reached into a cedar box and pulled out a joint.

"I can assure you this, Mr. Washington," Max said while reaching across the producer's desk with a lit match. He regained at least some control of the discussion, so he was relaxed once again. "Life is only going to get more interesting from here on out."

# # #

Holly yawned and stretched.

"So, that's what's gotten everyone in such a twist?"

"That's it," Deana responded, stubbing out her spent cigarette. "Of course, it took about two years for people to get really bent out of shape, for some reason. Then that one guy got killed in Jersey, plus the whole Colorado incident. It's no wonder Dopey went underground again."

"Dopey?"

"Jacks."

"What?" The question came from the kitchen, specifically, the window.

The women jumped at the sound of a man's voice intruding on their conversation.

"Deana?" The voice continued, followed by a knock at the door. "I thought maybe we could talk."

Deana and Holly looked at each other.

"How did he…?"

"I don't know!" Holly insisted. "Unless…oh shit."

"What?"

"The register. I put your name and address in the book the other night when you came to the presentation."

"Holly!"

"What? I didn't know! It was before I knew who he was to you. I'm sorry."

"Please, Deana?" The voice called again from the breezeway in front of her apartment. "It's starting to rain."

"Good!" Deana called out, then she turned and spoke to her friend in hushed tones. "Christ, Holly. What do I do?"

They both got off the couch and slowly walked toward the door.

"You're not letting him in, are you?"

"I don't know. It's not like I'd be in any danger. He doesn't have that in him. He says he wants to talk. I don't know what to do. I'm so confused. After all these years, you'd think that I'd be ready for this."

"Well, I'm here. I'll stay the night if you want."

Deana unlocked the door.

"No. Thanks. We need to do this alone, I think. I'll see you tomorrow."

Deana opened the door. Jackson stood on the other side, dripping and disheveled.

"You're sure? You don't have to let him in," Holly stated right in front of the visitor. "Tell him to take a hike."

"Good evening to you too, Ms. Ferringer," Jackson responded with a smile.

Holly turned and kissed her friend on the cheek. "Call me tonight. Anytime you need." She walked past her former boss in silence, but stopped as she reached the steps. "Your book sounds stupid, by the way."

"Then I guess it's a good thing you didn't buy it," Jackson responded. "Drive safe!"

Jackson chuckled as the young woman flicked him off.

"She's a good friend," Jackson assured Deana.

"What's your point of reference," Deana asked before turning and walking away from the open door.

Jackson stepped in, wiped his feet and closed the door behind him.

"I brought whiskey. I thought we could both use a belt."

"Whatever."

He walked into the kitchen and hunted down a couple of glasses. She settled back on the couch and turned the monitor on.

"You have no idea how good it was to see you the other night," he said while pouring the drinks. "It really brought back good times."

"You must have discovered a new definition for the word 'good' during your travels that I'm unaware of," she returned while flipping channels.

He brought the glasses and the bottle out and set them on the coffee table before taking a seat on the opposite side of the couch and lighting up a cigarette.

"So," he stated, "Here we are."

"Here we are," she agreed, taking a sip of her drink. She thought better of it, and up ended the glass, emptying the contents.

"Jesus. Drink much?"

"Fuck you," she replied while wiping off her mouth. "What happened in Colorado?"

"That's what you want to know? We haven't spoken since high school, but all you're concerned about is six months ago?"

Deana stared at the monitor, refusing to meet his eye. "You want to stay and chat?"

"It's why I came."

"Tell me about Colorado."

Jackson up ended his own glass. Then he brought out a pack of joints. "Do you…?"

Deana looked at the pack before giving him an evil stare.

"No, I don't," she said, before snatching the weed out of his hand and lighting it.

Jackson looked at the monitor. "Did you hear about that mob boss?"

"Look, if you're not going to talk about what *I* want to talk about, you should just go," she said all this before exhaling her first hit. The coughing fit that came after was staggering. Jackson delicately took the joint out of her hands.

"I guess it has been a while for you, hasn't it?"

"Whatever," she said in-between hacking.

Jackson took a hit. "It was all a setup, y'know. I was pretty much just along for the ride. Sinatra picked me up that crazy morning at the radio station, and he had everything planned out already." He exhaled and coughed slightly. "I was just a magnet for the media."

Deana turned off the monitor, took the joint from Jackson and gave him her attention.

"It was a con. That's about all there is to say."

"What was a con," she asked between puffs. "They aren't really dead?"

"No. Are you kidding? If the ATF was really responsible for the death of those kids, I'd be marching on Washington daily. It just had to look like they died. It was the only way to get the Mafia off their backs."

"I don't understand," she admitted while passing.

"It's like this; the mob created these kids the way zoos breed animals in captivity. But they started with the most rebellious bunch of DNA they could have gotten hold of. As many of them escaped the lab as could travel. They knew that the mob would track them down no matter where they went. So they had this idea that, if they were dead, they wouldn't be hunted any longer."

Deana filled her glass to capacity and took another deep sip.

"So you didn't come up with the whole fake death thing? I mean, after high school, I just assumed…"

"Well, I don't know where they got the idea exactly. They may have read one of my bios. I'm not sure."

He handed the dark cigarette to Deana.

"So how did they get out," she asked after inhaling.

"There was an access tunnel that lead outside the compound to this old barn where they had the cars stashed. Once the Feds were committed to breaking through the gates, we hustled our asses out of there. The whole place was booby-trapped. It was wired to collapse if so much as a K-9 cop stepped on the porch. They had recordings to sound like screams and everything. We got to the barn and split up. Danny and I took that souped up SUV, while the kids and the bodyguards got into these vans and headed up north. I think they're somewhere in Canada."

"Why didn't you tell me all of this the other night?"

"'Cause it wasn't safe?"

"Jackson!"

"No, I'm serious! Y'know that mob boss I was talking about? He was the ringleader of the whole thing. Now that he's gone, I don't feel so bad about letting a few choice people know the story."

"Let me guess; you two killed a Mafia boss."

"Oh, that was Danny. I came up with the Trojan Horse scenario, but his tech people came up with the device. And, technically, we didn't do it to kill him so much. I mean, we knew that whoever used the glove would be putting their nervous system through the ringer, and multiple uses would probably be fatal, but we had no idea that the first victim would be the boss. That was just gravy."

"I heard the feds found evidence of even more clones in a lab in Las Vegas. All executed."

"Sinatra told me there was more of them. We were hoping that there would be time for the feds to save them. Y'know, to make up for the debacle in Colorado?" Jackson took a drag and sat in silence. "I still have nightmares, thinking about what those kids were put through. It fucking kills me."

"I bet." Deana said this in such a way that Jackson couldn't determine whether or not there was sarcasm in the statement.

He poured himself another drink. The two of them quietly sipped and smoked.

"So," he stated again, "Here we are."

"Here we are," she agreed.

CHAPTER TWENTY-FIVE

"For the last time! I don't have any more information on the Don Owens case! Now fuck off!"

Lyle got up from his chair but didn't motion as if to leave the captain's office.

"Look, I'm being paid to hang out in this town and get to the bottom of this case!"

"I've got *real* cops on this case! I don't need your interference!"

Lyle looked out of through the window and noticed that almost the entire squad room of the Edison Homicide Division was glued to the exchange he was having with their boss. He leaned over the desk and dropped his tone.

"I'm not some gumshoe wannabe, y'know. I could be of some real help."

"The help of some out of town dick, I don't need! Do you need to be removed?"

Lyle dropped his card on the captain's desk. "Give me a call when you get around to having your head removed from your ass." He turned and left the office.

He wasn't three steps out the door when a derelict bumped him, spilling coffee on his shirt.

"Oh, for the love of…"

"Oh! Hey! I'm sorry about that, boss!" The bum began wiping Lyle down, using his own jacket to mop up the spill. "Let me get that for ya'!"

The stench coming off the transient was staggering. "It's ok! It's fine! Thank God it wasn't hot."

"Fuckin' cops never have hot coffee. No sense either. Cops around here don't got no sense!"

"Shut it, Caesar!" The detective shouting out the command, Lyle noticed, never even looked up to see with whom "Caesar" was speaking.

"Y'see that? No fuckin' respect from these fuckers! And with all the help I've given them."

"Yeah, well, things are tough all over. Excuse me." Lyle tried to maneuver past the vagrant, but Caesar jumped back in his path.

"I know things," he confided, glancing around with paranoid intensity.

"Really?" Lyle wasn't listening so much as calculating the odds of getting the coffee stain out of his polo shirt. They weren't good.

"Caesar! Freeload time's done! You making a statement, or what?"

"Gimme a sec!" He called out to the desk sergeant. "I'm conferring here!" He dropped his voice and got up close to Lyle's ear. "I know 'bout that stolen body you're looking for."

Status stopped fussing with his shirt immediately. "What did you say?"

"Caesar! This ain't no flophouse! You got a statement, you make it now!"

"I'm comin'!" He looked back at Lyle. "Fuckers. They didn't believe me, cause I was in detox, but I know what I saw and I know what I heard."

"Caesar," the massive, uniformed officer (the only uniform on the floor) walked up and grabbed the derelict by the arm. "Stop bothering the out-of-towner. You came in to make a statement?"

"Yeah! I got the goods on that fire downtown, in the old Sears warehouse. Gonna get me some big bucks for that!"

"That's great," the sergeant appeased. "Detective Duvall is ready to talk with you about it."

"Fuckers! He won't believe me. No one believes me. Not even the bats."

The vagrant shuffled in the direction of the detective's desk. Lyle stopped the desk sergeant.

"He's one of your regulars, I take it?"

"Caesar? Yeah. He's always coming in here, looking to roll over for coffee and a couple of bucks."

"How reliable is he?"

"Maybe 50%. He's gone downhill since the new acid."

"How's that?"

"The new acid. Sugar Magnolia? Comes on sugar cubes. These idiots have been frying their brains on the shit for about three or four months now. Supposedly more intense than all of the 60's LSD combined. Caesar's information isn't what it used to be, what with him throwing in giant bats and cockroaches and Gandhi in the middle of his statements. Ironic since he was in Dumont County Mental Hospital *before* Magnolia hit the streets."

"That *does* limit his credibility, I guess."

Lyle focussed his attention back to his shirt and began to walk out of the precinct. He was passing the detective's desk where the bum was issuing his statement.

"I know what I saw! The firemen came before the fire! They looked like astronauts! Fire-breathing astronauts!"

The detective wasn't writing or typing. He was preoccupied with trying to find a paperclip that fell down under his desk. Caesar looked up at Lyle as the private eye was making his way past the desk.

"This fucker don't believe me," he said to Lyle. "Maybe you don't either."

"I believe you just fine."

"No you don't. You're all fuckers. Never changes. Just cause I was in the loony bin, don't mean I don't know what's what! Don't mean I don't got ears!"

"Settle down, you old crank," the detective commented from under his desk. Lyle noticed a whole box of paperclips in his drawer, but the man was committed to finding the lone strangler. "I'll be with you in a sec."

"Nobody got time for old Caesar. I told them months ago. They brought in that body. Middle of the night. And they took his head for collection purposes. Nobody should loose their head, man."

Lyle stopped. "What do you mean, 'collection purposes?'"

"Some nasty fucker wanted the head for his collection! What'd I say? Nobody deserves that. That's why I'm a gonna be cremated. Burn me up! Nobody getting' my head!" Caesar dropped his gaze down. "Fuckers."

The detective found the elusive clip and sat back up straight. "Ok, Caesar. What were you saying? Who set the fire? The bats again?"

"No! You dirty bastard! The bats are controlling everything, but they don't do the dirty work!"

Lyle quietly left the station house.

# # #

Jackson, in stocking feet, was standing on Deana's couch, while his host was doubled over in a fit of hysterics.

"Okay, so picture this. Darlene is standing on top of the kiosk counter, holding a camera and screaming, 'OJ! Over here, OJ!' Click. Nothing. 'Shit!' she screams. 'No film!'"

"Oh, no!" Deana laughed and wiped the tears out from her eyes.

"So she throws this camera down, smashing it to pieces," Jackson said, while gesturing the described motions. "Having no idea whose camera it was! Then she grabs somebody else's camera out of their hands. But he's already finished playing the game and he's leaving our booth."

"What did she do?"

"What *could* she do? She standing three feet above the crowd, screaming like a banshee, 'OJ! Don't leave! Look over here! OJ!' I, on the other hand, am standing firmly on the ground."

"Oh, Christ. What'd *you* do?"

"The only logical thing. I tackled him."

"No you did not!"

"Are you kidding," Jacks asked as he sat back down on his end of the couch. "I made like I was tripping and threw my shoulders into the backs of his knees. The man folded like a deck of cards."

"Well, duh!" Deana was laughing so hard, she could barely talk. "What was he then, like 60? What'd he do?"

"Oh, he was pissed. You could tell he just wanted to kill me. But he'd already gotten away with it twice by then, and this was in a crowded convention center, so he had no choice but to just shake it off."

"Remind me why it was so important to get a picture of this guy in your booth?"

"File it under No Such Thing As Bad Press. It all seemed like a good idea at the time. But, when Darlene and I got back to corporate, they had our walking papers ready for us."

"Well, *that* sucks."

"Fuck 'em. Have you ever even heard of Titanic Entertainment?"

"Can't say as I have."

"See? Maybe if the Associated Press ran more pictures of me tackling famous celebrity homicidal maniacs, the company might have made something of itself."

Deana nodded in agreement as she reached for the bottle. It took a few passes before she could center her glass properly, and several seconds after that before she realized nothing was coming out.

"Tell me we didn't drink this whole bottle. Shit. It's not like I can stay home tomorrow. I've got to get some sleep."

"Why can't you stay home tomorrow? C'mon! When's the last time you stayed up till dawn?"

"No. Seriously. I've been out for two days this week already."

"Oh, I'm sorry. Are you sick?"

"Something like that."

The two lapsed into contemplative silence. Abruptly, Deana drew in a long, cleansing breath.

"When's the last time I stayed up till dawn? Probably thirteen years ago, waiting for you to come back to me and tell me that it was all a big joke." She considered this and decided. "Yep. I'd say that's about the last time. Waiting for you to tap on my window and tell me to come with you. Enticing me to run away with you and start a whole new life together. I must have stayed up till dawn for three months or more."

"You wouldn't have come, y'know," Jackson pointed out while lighting a cigarette.

"Maybe," she agreed without looking him in the eye. "But I would've liked to have had the option. Was that why you never came? You were so sure I wouldn't come? 'Cause, from where I stand, that's pretty fucking lame, Dopey."

"I'm not trying to give you some kind of excuse. There's no logical reason. I was a kid. I needed to see if I could pull it off."

"You didn't, you know."

"I know. But it taught me important lessons about going underground that have proven useful later in life." He said this with a smile, but understood immediately that she wasn't in the mood to kid, and he blushed. "It's not like I could have just waltzed back to Fort Wayne, y'know. I was embarrassed and ashamed."

"*You* were embarrassed? Did *your* girlfriend fake her death just to get away from *you*?"

"See, it wasn't like that. It didn't have anyth…" Jackson stopped the sentence mid-word.

"What? What? It didn't what, Cross? It didn't have anything to do with me? Is that what you were going to say?"

"It's not what I meant."

"Fucking prick! Do you have any idea how much therapy I've had to go through? Have you ever even considered how fucking crushed I was? I love you, you motherfucking bastard cocksucking cunt of a degenerate asshole!"

"Jeeze. Sounds like my bio."

"Well it should! It's what you are, and you're never going to fucking change. I wish you *had* died!" Deana got up and ran into her bedroom, slamming the door behind her.

"Dee!" He got up and walked over to the closed door. "Don't do this."

"Fuck you! I want you to leave!"

"But I don't want to leave. I want to…"

The door violently swung open. "It's all about *you*, isn't it asshole? It always has to be about *you*! God, I fucking *hate* you!"

She began hitting him then. Chest. Face. Shoulder. Arm. Anywhere she could connect. At some point, her crying became more fierce than the blows she was trying to inflict. When he was sure that she was done striking him, he took her by the shoulders and guided her to the floor. They sat, Indian style, each on the other side of her bedroom threshold. He was crying almost as freely as she.

"I'm sorry. I've wanted to say it for thirteen years, but couldn't bring myself. I was afraid you didn't want to hear it. Afraid it would do more damage. I don't know. I guess I was just afraid. I don't know why I did it. I don't know why I've done just about anything; before or since. But I want you to know that I didn't do it to hurt you or get away from you. I'm sorry, and I love you too."

"Don't say that to me!" More slaps to the face with little-to-no force. "You can't ever fucking say that! Not to me!"

"I don't know what else to say! Maybe I shouldn't have come."

"Maybe you shouldn't have," she agreed, wiping her nose with the sleeve of her robe.

Jackson pushed against the door jam to stand up. "Oof. I'm pretty drunk." He looked down to see Deana, still sitting cross-legged, covering her face as she sobbed.

He squatted next to her then, his face inches away from her ear. "I'll never forgive myself for leaving you. But loving you was the one thing in my life that I didn't fake, and I think that was too much for me to take back then."

"Whatever."

Jacks stood back up and staggered out of the apartment.

CHAPTER TWENTY-SIX

Danny's intercom was buzzing as he let himself into his Park Avenue apartment.

"Yes, Manny?"

"You've got a guest down here at the desk, Mr. Epstein."

"Is she wearing a plaid skirt, penny loafers and the little socks with the balls on the heel?"

"Um, that appears to be an accurate description."

"Perfect. Go ahead and send her up."

He let go of the intercom and pushed the messages button. An electronic voice chimed over the speaker.

"You have three new messages. Message One:

"Hello Daniel, this is Ira. I sent you an email earlier today, but you haven't read it. Something's going on with the IS-5000 orders. We've just gotten tons of requests, with some weird-ass ship-to locations. New York and California, mostly. Orders are getting into the thousands..."

"Son of a bitch," Danny commented to the empty room.

"We're going to have to move into the expanded facility faster than we thought. But that's not the problem. This is huge. I think the secret's out, and we're not ready.

"Also, before you read about it in the news, one of the lab tech's died today from using the glove..."

"Are you kidding me? Idiot!"

"It's not that we didn't warn them, but he had to go back for just one more..."

"I'll read the email tonight." Danny hit the delete button.

229

"Message One erased. Message Two:

"Mr. Epstein? This is Collene Sons, from Status and Sons…"

"Not too interested in listening to this, right now." Danny hit the skip button.

"Message Three:

"Hey there Daniel. It's Scott."

"No shit?"

"Listen, Darlene and I got this weird package in the mail. It's got something to do with Jackson. Give us a call when you have a chance? Thanks."

Danny absently deleted the last message before walking into the kitchen and pulling a beer out of the fridge. Standing over the sink, he drank his beer and lit a joint. He turned on the monitor over the stove.

"We're back with the highest rated program on FOX television; Who Wants To Kill A Millionaire?! The only show that allows the poor and indigent the opportunity to hunt down and kill rich, successful people who are currently facing the death penalty. It's the chance to serve the community, while directing all the feelings of worthlessness and self-pity toward fantastically wealthy people who were stupid enough to throw away their own posh lifestyle by committing capitol crimes. We call it karma-tainment!"

The knock came as Danny was about half-way through both his beer and his joint.

"It's open!"

A leggy brunette (dressed exactly as Manny had confirmed) let herself into the enormous apartment.

"I still can't get over how huge this place is! You could fit like five of my apartments in here!"

"Hey, Cynthia! I'm in the kitchen!"

Cynthia made her way into the massive kitchen area.

"Hey, hot stuff! Haven't heard from you in a while."

"I've been traveling. I'm probably going out of town tomorrow too, so I've got a lot of shit to take care of tonight."

"That's fine," Cynthia said while unbuttoning her blouse. "Are we talking the usual?"

"Well, we can start with a blow job. I'm not sure if I can take the time to fuck. I need to check the ticker." As he said this, he scrolled down the menu on the monitor and highlighted Finance. Stock figures began to pass across a bar at the bottom of the screen.

"Are we doing this in here, or do you want to watch the monitor in the living room?"

"Here's fine," he said. Without looking at the girl, he reached down and unzipped his pants.

"I can do that," she said, slipping off her skirt. "But we need to take care of something first. $500 will do to start. If you're in the mood for anything else, you can pay as we go."

"Hm?" Danny asked distractedly. "Oh! Seriously? Jesus, Cynthia. You've been here what…four maybe five times? I can't just pay you before you go?"

"Do I tell you how to run your business? Things happen." She walked over to him and reached into his open fly. "Besides, I can be so much more attentive when I don't have to worry about getting paid."

"Fine, fine." Danny reached into his wallet and pulled out eight $100 bills. "Here. This way if I get in the mood to bend you over, I don't have to stop and pay a fucking toll."

"And if you don't feel like bending me over?" She asked as she folded up the bills and slid them into her purse.

"Then I've taken care of the tip early, haven't I?" He left the scrolling ticker on the bottom of the screen, while flipping through other news windows.

"Do you have a dish towel?"

"What? Eight big ones and you can't even swallow? Keep this up and I'll think we were married."

"For my knees, you asshole. This is tile in here."

"Oh, sure," he said apologetically, reached back and handed her one off the sink.

Danny finished off his beer and applied a clip to his roach. He continued to drag while Cynthia knelt down.

"Hey, I'm rude! Did you want a hit of this? Y'know, smoke a joint before you smoke my joint?"

"Maybe after," she said before conducting her business.

Danny leaned back against the sink. He turned up the volume and flipped to the entertainment site.

"You're watching *Entertainment This Very Second.* In an exclusive announcement to ETVS, Roy Washington, Executive Producer of the upcoming *Judas Conspiracy* film adaptation, announced today that his movie will be the first ever feature filmed for the new IS-5000 Total Environment System."

"What! Ow!"

"Don't jump like that, then!"

"Hang on a sec. This is important." He turned the volume up.

The smiling, vacuous image of the ETVS correspondent continued. "Little is known about the IS-5000. It's parent company, Eptech International…"

"Holy shit."

"…has opted to test-market the device in small regions in the Midwest. It has been confirmed to be the first total environment system, immersing an individual in a completely digitized environment. Mr. Washington had this to say…"

The image pixeled in with a fairly young, black executive.

"This is a *very* exciting time in the history of entertainment! If we pull this off, and I'm confident that we will, this will be the first-ever, truly interactive film. We're starting soft, allowing the user to be a spectator within an actual movie. But soon, you'll be able to step into Humphrey

Bogart's shoes, kissing Ms. Bergman goodbye on the tarmac. We're very proud to be the first Hollywood studio to embrace this new age!"

"I'll fucking bet you are. But who gave you the right?"

"Daniel Epstein, President and CEO of Eptech International, has been unavailable for comment…"

"Somebody asked me to comment?"

"But, if the American viewing public takes to the technological wonder of the IS-5000 as Universal Studios apparently has, Epstein will in all likelihood be one of the richest men on the planet this time next year. I'm Truman Farly, reporting live from Hollywood with *Entertainment This Very Second.*"

"Hey," Cynthia asked while holding Danny's penis to the side of her face. "Were they talking about you?"

"As a matter of fact."

"You don't seem all that excited."

"I'm stunned. Nothing, and I mean nothing ever fucking seems to go as planned. How did this happen?"

"Does it matter? You're rich!"

"I've always been rich. That's not the point. I need to make some calls."

"Do you want me to leave?"

"And lose my deposit? I didn't get this rich by flushing cash down the toilet, baby. Well…some." He looked down and smiled for the first time since getting the news. "Ever blown a billionaire?"

"Are you kidding? This is New York." Cynthia went back to work.

# # #

After three consecutive tries, he was able to get his keys into the car door lock.

"Jackson!"

He looked back to see Deana, fuming from the second floor landing.

"What? You forget another name you remembered to call me?"

"You can't leave! You're too drunk!"

"Well, I can't stay here!"

Another voice came from the kitchen of someone else's apartment in the complex. "You could damn well shut up!"

"Fuck off!" The two yelled this in unison, looked at each other and cracked up.

"What do you want me to do, Deana?"

"What I've always wanted, you moron! Come back!"

Jackson left the keys in the door as he ran back up the stairs.

"You're sure about this?" He asked even as she greeted him with open arms.

"I love you, I've hit you and I've told you off. I don't need you to go and get yourself killed by driving like an idiot."

They hugged like a couple who survived a mid-air collision.

"However," she commented, sniffing back tears. "I fucking *hate* the beard."

"It'll be gone in the morning," he promised.

She led him back inside.

CHAPTER TWENTY-SEVEN

"So! Did you guys do it?"

Deana almost spilled her coffee.

"Holly," she avoided, in mock embarrassment. "Why would you ask me that?"

"Why wouldn't I," Holly returned, taking a seat opposite her friend at the table in the office break room. "You sashay in here like an hour late (which you never do), you've had this goofy smile on your face all morning and, not to be too frank about it, you've got the smell of sex on you."

"Oh my God! I do not!" Deana looked around sheepishly. "Do I?"

"No. It was a *trick*! So you *did* sleep with him!"

Deana smiled. "Well, yeah…"

"And?"

"And? And what? What sort of sordid details are you looking for?"

"Well, considering the fact that you hated his guts when I left the two of you yesterday, I guess what I'm looking to find out is; was it worth it?"

"Well…yeah!" Deana smiled even broader. "The man has aged *very* well. He's traveled and gained both confidence *and* experience." The two women laughed giddily. Deana lowered both her head and her voice before continuing. "Did you know they can get bigger?"

"What? What do you mean?"

"I mean if he was standing next to his seventeen year-old self, naked in line-up, you would barely be able to tell it was the same organ."

"Did he have surgery?"

"I don't think so. I'm pretty sure I would've been able to tell."

"Weird."

"Yeah," Deana agreed thoughtfully. "But in a *really* cool way."

"So? Does this mean you've officially rekindled that old flame."

"Well, last night went a long way to repair quite a bit of damage. I mean, I don't trust him entirely yet…"

"I would hope not, considering the history you two have."

"But I can't tell you how good it felt, Holly. The years of doubt and rejection just washed away…after I gave him a black eye, of course."

"Of course," Holly replied with a smile.

"But, I figure maybe we can start over again, taking it a little slower than we did last night."

The intercom next to the door buzzed obnoxiously. Avril, the receptionist, called out.

"Deana?"

"Yeah, hon?"

"You've got a visitor up front. He's got flowers."

"Go ahead and send him back, Avril."

Holly looked impressively at her friend. "Flowers after one night? You couldn't have been so bad yourself, girl."

"It's amazing how well you can channel pent-up aggression."

"Well, I better leave you two…"

Jackson was at the doorway before Holly even rose from her chair. He was clean-shaven which meant, for Holly, he looked close to ten years younger.

"Jesus," Deana commented. "Did you sprint back here?"

"Almost. I'm glad I caught you both. Here you go Ms. Ferringer."

Holly accepted the flowers with quizzical amusement. "These are for me?"

"I found out that you resigned from the IS-5000 program. 'Lo, darlin'." He leaned in to kiss Deana.

"Sure, Holly gets flowers and all I get is a kiss," she faux pouted.

"Patience. I have gifts to spare. First things first. Can I change your mind about leaving the company, Holly?"

"I'm…I don't know. Why?"

Cross took a seat with the two women. "Why? Because things are blowing up, and anyone at ground zero's going to be rich within a couple of months. Think about it. I've put a call in and your position is guaranteed for the next few weeks. All you have to do is show up."

"Wow. I guess I shouldn't have called your book stupid."

"Oh, don't worry about that. You were probably right."

"Jackson."

Holly blushed. "I'm sure it's not stupid. It seems to have caused quite a stir."

"So would a pile of shit in a punch bowl, but that don't make it art. No, if you really want a good yarn with good writing, there's tons better stuff out there."

"Jackson," Deana repeated with bemused impatience.

"Like what?"

Jackson's eyes did a slow burn from Holly to Deana and back again. Deana just shook her head.

"Well, just to give you an example, there was this fabulous book that came out a few years back.

"This writer traveled from California to Maine, crossing fifteen states. From every state, he sent a postcard to ten different friends, meaning he had written ten different postcards per state, you follow?"

"Yeah."

"Well, each postcard was, in fact, a piece of a short story. But the friends didn't know that from the beginning. They just kept receiving these odd, sometimes almost incoherent correspondences from different states. About one a month.

"So, at the end of the journey, each of his friends have fifteen postcards. He invites them all to dinner to celebrate this trek that he's made, and asks them to bring the postcards with them. Now, these people are each friends of the writer, but they don't actually know each other very well. But, when they get together, they compare notes.

"They're waiting for the writer to show up for dinner, and they start talking about the postcards, and they realize that they each have different parts to a much larger puzzle. By the time the writer arrives for dinner, they've put all the postcards together to create fifteen short stories about traveling across the country.

"That's when the writer reveals that he was late for the dinner on purpose. He'd intended to publish the stories that he'd given his friends but, if they had figured out the puzzle, then they (being his ten friends) would evenly divide the proceeds of the anthology."

"Seriously?"

"Oh, sure. It's called *America In Pieces* and it's written by Alan Gaiman. *That's* great writing. Compared to that, my stuff is a kind of elaborate writing exercise. At best."

"Jackson," Deana finally interrupted with conviction. "What are you *really* doing here, besides trying to get Holly to work for you again? Or was that it?"

"Not at all," Jacks confirmed. He reached into his back pocket and removed a pair of paper sleeves. He handed them to Deana.

"What's this?"

"Airplane tickets. Ms. Brown, would you accompany me to the major motion picture production of *The Judas Conspiracy*?"

"These tickets are for today," she noted with a frown.

"We've got just enough time to get back to your place so you can pack. We fly into Phoenix and drive something like two hours out into the desert where the sets have been constructed. We get to hang out with Terry Gilliam. They're trying to get Johnny Depp to play Christ, but I'm still pulling to get a brother cast."

"But, what about my job here?"

"What about it?"

Deana looked soberly at Jackson. She knew instinctively that he was serious.

"Look, I *have* to do this. But I'm not about to take off on you again." He leaned back and splayed his arms, indicating their surroundings. "Is this what you want? Coffee in an 8 x 10 break room twice a day? Lunch from the cafeteria? Worrying about how many personal calls you're making? Being laid off on a whim? This isn't the life we saw for ourselves as kids."

"No, but it's the life I was able to make for myself once I picked up the pieces you left me."

"Maybe I should go," Holly stated as she got up from her chair.

"Hang on," Deana said, also rising. "My break's about over."

Jackson leapt up. "I don't understand. I'm making a commitment here. I thought after last night…"

"Last night was fantastic. It was exactly what I needed, but it wasn't nearly so much about you as it was about me feeling human again. I've never felt so good in my life as I do when I'm with you, Dopey."

"Then what's the problem?"

"The problem is that I should feel that way without you too. And maybe, because of last night, I finally have a shot at that." She walked over and kissed him. "You go to Arizona and bask in the glory of having your movie made. I'm not denying you that…"

"But I want you to go too," Jacks' voice cracked. It was almost imperceptible, but it was enough. Deana teared up a bit.

"How many times do I have to say it, Jacks? It's not always about you."

"Can we pick this up when I get back?"

"*If* you come back, you'll just have to call me to find out."

Jackson picked up his tickets from the table and slowly walked away from the break room.

"I don't get you," Holly whispered. "I've never seen you as happy as you were this morning. Why would you give that up for this place?"

Deana chuckled. "You don't get *me*?" She looked up and called out. "Hey Dopey!"

Jackson turned around.

"That book you were talking about? *America In Pieces*? Is that real?"

Jackson smiled. "Not yet. I just thought of it on the way over here. Sounds pretty cool though, doesn't it?"

"Pretty cool," Deana agreed and watched as he turned back around and left the office.

"I don't understand. What's that got to do with anything?"

"You mean besides the fact that you don't get *him* either? It means he's the same adolescent misanthrope that he was thirteen years ago. He may *never* change. I'll love him until the day I die, but I won't die of neglect for him. Not again."

She looked over at her friend. "C'mon. Let's get back to work."

BOOK FOUR

Revelations

Chapter Twenty-Eight

Deana stepped out of the electric limousine and onto the red carpet that led into the Eptech International Los Angeles Headquarters. She walked alone amidst an explosion of light bulbs. It wasn't her first media circus since Jackson Cross came back into her life nearly two years ago, but she still felt unaccustomed to the claustrophobic feeling of being the center of attention.

"Deana!"

Everything was so bright! She squinted in the direction of the familiar voice and eventually made out a figure running to greet her from the building entrance.

"You made it!"

Holly was almost on top of her before she recognized her. She'd gained weight, but looked great in a very elegant strapless evening gown.

The two women embraced while a flurry of shutters captured the event.

"I didn't know you were going to be here," Deana commented after taking her friend's arm and escorting her back inside the immense structure.

"This new Regional VP position has some perks," Holly admitted. "Once I found out you were scheduled to attend, I just *had* to come!"

The paparazzi continued its onslaught even after the glass doors separated them from the outside. Deana stopped to take in the grandeur of the cavernous glass and steel lobby. People mixed and mingled throughout the four-story complex of offices. Buffet tables and open bars were sprinkled about haphazardly.

"Is this your first trip to LA?"

"Yeah."

"Isn't it something?"

Deana took a cleansing breath. "It's pretty amazing. Who knew all the schemes and conniving would lead to something like this?"

She looked at Holly and smiled a sad, contemplative smile. "Y'know, for all their faults, Jacks and Danny should be here for this. I almost feel guilty."

"I know, honey," Holly sympathized. "But they *are* here in a way. C'mon! Let's get hammered!"

They moved carefully through the crowd and found a bar near the giant fountain in the center of the massive gallery.

Deana took the glass of champagne being offered by the bartender, turned and narrowly missed bumping into the chest of a Suit.

"Oh! Excuse me," she tried to apologize while making sure she didn't spill on the gentleman's obviously expensive jacket.

"No harm done," the dark man replied while extending his hand. "I'm Roy Washington with Universal. I believe you're the elusive Ms. Brown?"

"Deana. Pleasure to meet you." Washington's handshake was firm and confident. "So," she continued, taking a sip of her drink. "I have a reputation?"

"Only with the people trying to get your approval for this thing. You've surprised us, y'know. Considering the success of the *Judas Conspiracy* movie, this little venture should blow people out of the water. It's going to make you tons."

"I've been rich for over a year now, Mr. Washington. Being even more rich doesn't have as much appeal as you might imagine."

"Even still…" A slight vibrating hum interrupted his redress. He pulled out what looked like a credit card and pushed the corner before talking into its face. "Washington."

"Sorry to bother you, Roy," said the voice emanating from the face on the card. "We've just gotten the contract back from Leo. He wants 45 million for *Hell's Harbinger*, and he claims to need to know tonight or he's walking."

"Fucking prima donnas," he said before looking up sheepishly at the two ladies present. "That was rude. I apologize. Can we pick this conversation back up a little later this evening?"

"By all means," Deana offered, but Roy was already walking away.

"Welcome to Hollywood," Holly snickered.

"Hm," Deana considered. "Nice ass, though."

"Plenty of that here, m' dear." Holly took her friend by the arm once more. "Tell you what: We've got a few hours before the formal launching festivities. Let me show you something."

Leaving the hustle of the party and entering the dark, empty conference hall felt eerie to Deana.

"Should we be doing this?"

"Hel-lo? You're the president? You could be smoking crack while riding the banister on the spiral staircase and no one's going to say shit to you."

"Oh, good. Because that's what I planned on doing for my big speech later."

They walked to the front of the auditorium (which struck Deana as very reminiscent of the warehouse setup back in Indiana, but considerably better made), and onto the stage.

"I don't know about this, Holly."

"C'mon, Dee. I know for a fact you haven't tried the program. It's amazing."

"I've got the thing at home now. I can do this whenever."

"You're going to be conducting a press conference launching this new program in a little while. Wouldn't you at least like to know what you're talking about?"

"I've faked it pretty good so far," she said as she slowly approached the pod. "I can't honestly say I'm ready for this."

"Nothing to worry about," Holly assured her. She turned on the unit and waited for the control panel to warm up. "It's a reenactment, remember? Most of the original footage was destroyed by the acid rain, if any of it really happened. I mean sure, they're being called Jacks and Danny and Lyle and Max (the prick), but it's just actors playing parts. Don't you want to know what really happened that night? Or Jackson's version at the very least?"

"I've always assumed if I was supposed to know, then I would've been there. Besides, do you really think a reenactment is going to provide some kind of closure? I don't."

"This is taken directly from Jackson's notes, and people who were there have all said that experiencing this program is exactly like being in Arizona when it all went down. Except for the end, of course. Jackson's the only person who really knows what happened in that regard. And, in a way, this is even better than being there because you get to experience it from the perspective of the different participants individually."

"Really," she responded dryly. "They get all that from his journal?"

"Well, they've embellished some for dramatic purposes."

"Uh-huh."

"Take off your high heels and give me your purse."

Deana did as she was told. As much as she fought the concept, part of her was almost compulsively curious about seeing Jackson as portrayed by some unknown actor.

"If and when I say to turn it off, you turn it off. Got it?"

"Are you kidding? How long's it been since you've tried this? There's a whole interface for you to control. You can pause it, skip ahead, rewind, or stop it entirely." Holly gathered the small train of Deana's evening gown and tucked it inside the booth. "When you want to change perspectives, you just tap on the image. All set?"

"I guess," she confirmed, trying to ride through the slight nausea. She slid her hands delicately over the walls, which were covered with even finer ball bearings than she remembered. "Let's get it over with."

"That's my girl," Holly said with a smile and closed the pod door.

Deana anticipated the flash, so she closed her eyes and waited. The brilliant light, however, remained long after the initial program start. She peeked through squinted eyelids, and found herself in a desert. The image was amazingly fluid when compared to her first experience with the technology.

She virtually stood at the foot of a moderately large dune. She heard voices on the opposite side of the hill but, before she could even step in the direction of what sounded like a small crowd, the scene moved of its own accord. Suddenly, she was swept up and over the crest of the mound.

I'm flying, she thought.

As she gained speed and altitude, an orchestra began to play a deep, melodic selection, which she immediately imagined to have a shattering crescendo at key dramatic moments in the film.

The river was the first thing that caught her attention. Next was the crowd on the shore. Two men had waded out several yards and were speaking to each other, but Deana couldn't make out what was being said.

Why is this so familiar?

One dark man lowered the other into the muck. An instant after raising the baptized man up again (*Is that Will Smith?*) a high-pitched, piercing sound erupted from the sky. Deana closed her eyes as everyone present was immediately blinded by a flash of painfully bright light. She opened up her eyes to see each of the men sprawled out on the shore.

This is the movie. Why start the program like this?

Instinctively, Deana reached out and tapped the image of one of the actors on the interface. The environment swam around so violently, she thought her nausea might return. When the all-encompassing image clarified, she was looking up from the ground. She gazed around from the perspective of the man she'd chosen.

Okay. That *was kind of cool.*

Will Smith approached her from off shore. The music gained momentum as he came to stand over her, extending his hand. Then everything stopped.

People stopped moving, even breathing. The breeze halted. Confused, Deana looked around to see if she had inadvertently paused the program somehow.

It took a bit of looking before her eyes found the cue box floating over the environment just below her waist. It was scrolling a single name continuously in about twenty-point type. On a hunch, she spoke the name.

"Jesus," she said with something like reverence.

The program continued.

"Let me help you, Judas," Smith offered.

The environment began moving on its own again. Like an out-of-body experience, Deana's view was lifted up above the group and began floating across the desert.

She was swaying with the sensation of flight when a man's voice disrupted her revelry.

"When the major motion picture *The Judas Conspiracy* opened Memorial Day Weekend of 2013, it was immediately embraced by audiences worldwide as an iconoclastic masterpiece. The tale of humanity's second chance to take control of its own destiny appealed to the jaded, post-millennium generation."

The flight path carried her across miles of desert, toward an ancient city. Storm clouds gathered as she closed in on the immense town.

The music toned down so as not to drown out the invisible narrator.

"As much as ticket buyers loved the big screen version of this now-classic tale, more breathtaking still was the predecessor of the Digital Environmental Unit, originally called the IS-5000. Programmed to take viewers directly into the movie, sometimes even making them a participant, *The Judas Conspiracy Experience* premiered as the first-ever fully interactive motion picture."

Rain began to fall. Deana felt grateful that actual rain didn't fall in the booth, and smiled at the irony. She remembered criticizing Jackson because the mountain air wasn't cold enough during her very first program. Floating above dirt alleys and market streets, she realized that the town was nearly barren. But then the faintest rumblings of an angry crowd reached her ears, and it appeared to be coming from the direction to which she was flying.

"But the events surrounding the making of both the motion picture and virtual program are steeped in rumor and innuendo. Hollywood insiders say that, were it not for the commitment of Executive Producer Roy Washington (*Name dropper. Wonder how much Roy paid for* that?) to be the first to introduce this new interactive form of entertainment to moviegoers, neither film might have been made."

The roofs of the dwellings gave way to a huge courtyard outside a palace. What appeared to be hundreds of livid people were crowded into the yard. A much smaller group of men were standing on a balcony overlooking the mob. Deana recognized Kevin Spacey as Pontius Pilate, standing next to Will Smith and addressing the crowd.

"Why are you persecuting this man? He's committed no crime."

"Crucify him!" The masses demanded.

"No!" A lone, dissenting voice broke from the crowd. Deana finally remembered the actor's name who played Judas, being Don Cheadle, as she picked his image up in the throng. She briefly considered taking the scene from his perspective again, but thought better of it. She didn't need the responsibility of reciting lines in the midst of a mob. Instead, she singled out the actress, Alfre Woodard, who was portraying Mary Magdeline and standing right next to him. The flowing, swirling dissolve of the scene and change of view didn't effect her as badly as the first time. She even began to enjoy it.

"You don't have to do this!" Judas railed. "There's no reason on Earth to kill him!"

The commoners in the courtyard stared in disbelief. Two men (Ice T as John and Michael Clarke Duncan as Peter) rushed at him from different sides.

"I have the authority this day to free a man from Roman incarceration," Pilate continued, oblivious to the squabbling below. "One of your brethren, a lifetime criminal named Barabas, is scheduled for crucifixion. It makes no difference to us. He mostly steals from you poor idiots anyway. I'll free the despot Barabas, or the teacher you call Christ. I leave the decision in your incapable, inbred hands."

"Free Barabas," John called out while trying to subdue Judas. The rain intensified, making the dirty section muddy and slippery. John almost lost his footing. He steadied himself, called out, "Barabas!" and then continued to chase Judas through the crowd.

"Barabas! Free Barabas!" The masses agreed.

"What?!" Judas skirted the grip of Peter and ran toward the palace gates. "This asshole is a *murderer*! Jesus' only crime is conceit! He's no *criminal*, for Christ's sake! What's *wrong* with you people? Why do you need a lamb to slaughter *so badly*?"

"Crucify the Lamb of God!" John retorted.

"Crucify him!" The flock agreed.

Pilate shook his head in disbelief. With a motion, the criminal Barabas was set free. Pilate walked to the edge of the balcony and stretched out his hands to catch the rain. Then he began to scrub them.

"The Jewish Nation, in keeping with a history of outstandingly asinine decisions, has made its choice. Rome has nothing to do with it from here on out." Pilate looked back annoyingly at his guards and shooed them. "Well? Go on! Take him away!"

The music stuck another high.

"Oh, this is bullshit!" Judas exclaimed as Peter and John dragged him away from the security of Rome's diplomat.

Deana once again floated above the crowd.

"It was during the filming of this pivotal scene that an entirely different kind of trial was taking place. Jackson Cross, author of the original *Judas Conspiracy* novel, was to defend himself and his ideals in a parallel circumstance to Christ's own prosecution."

Deana flew up and over Pilate's complex before heading toward the outskirts of Jerusalem.

It's like watching a trailer for the movie. It's just giving me the highlights.

She swept down over a small mob that was dragging Judas, kicking and screaming, outside the city. In the distance, about half a mile away, the crucifixion was taking place at the same time.

"You don't have to do this," Judas screamed out in the direction of the *other* execution. "I know you can hear me Jesus, you sanctimonious *fuck*! You can stop this anytime you want!"

"You're only getting yourself in deeper," John observed with an evil smile.

"What? You going to hang me twice? Fuck you and fuck him!"

"We're not killing you, Judas," John noted as he prepared the noose. Peter held the condemned man in a bear hug. "By betraying our savior, you've damned yourself."

"Oh, I don't *believe* this shit!"

John slipped the rope over his thrashing head. Peter held the struggling prisoner aloft to provide his fellow apostle with sufficient slack.

"Fucking get off the cross, you bastard! Let *us* have some say! You're not always right, y'know!"

"Let him go, Peter."

The rope pulled tight. The music rose dramatically. Judas kicked and danced in the air.

"You've killed yourself, Iscariot," John concluded before leading the group back toward the crucifixion site.

Deana floated uneasily above the dying man.

"Rumors abound regarding the circumstances of one particular night on the set. Two hundred people were hospitalized, two people found DOA, while only one *actual* murder had been committed. And, most interesting of all, three of the participants vanished that evening, never to be heard from again. How did everything get so far out of hand? Could this have been some elaborate prank gone awry? Or could it possibly have been the night Jackson Cross would have you believe; wherein the course of human development was changed forever. Who exactly orchestrated the event and who has been held accountable since?"

The desert scene faded to black. The feeling of floatation passed. The music settled into what could have been a television show theme score. Footfalls proceeded the image of a man in a business suit approaching her.

"Come with me, and maybe together we can get to the bottom of one of the most notorious nights in Hollywood history."

The handsome, confident man walked up to what seemed like arms reach away from Deana. The music approached yet another crescendo.

"I'm Ben Dover, and you're experiencing Hollywood's True Unexplained Scandals."

Ben looked to his right. Deana followed his gaze and watched as the words materialized in thin air:

Roy Washington Presents
In Association with Universal and DEE Pictures
An HTUS Film
Desert Maneuvers:
The Trial of Jackson Cross

CHAPTER TWENTY-NINE

"Strangely enough, our story begins on a dark and stormy night at a mental institution in New Jersey."

Thunder rolled. A lightning flash illuminated the change in scene. Deana felt the rollers brush up against the back of her legs, and took the hint to sit down. The image of a sedan interior washed up around her. She was sitting in the passenger seat. Ben was standing outside.

Type scrolled across the windshield.

Dumont County Mental Hospital…Thursday, August 30th, 2012… 9:58 P.M…

The driver's door opened and a portly, balding man stepped in behind the wheel, shrugging off the rain. Deana's own seat shifted under the weight.

"Lyle Status, Private Investigator," Dover introduced.

That's supposed to be Lyle? Boy, he must have been pissed when he saw that.

"Status' agency was commissioned to investigate the death of one Don Owens. Owens was widely considered the mastermind behind the Christian Riots that previous February. He was murdered in his hotel room the morning of the riots, and his body disappeared from the Dumont County Coroner's office the very same evening. Six months later, Lyle gets the tip of a lifetime."

Lyle (or at least the poor substitute used in the program) picked up the car phone and dialed.

Man, they didn't even use his headset.

While waiting to be connected, he looked past Deana and glanced into the backseat.

"We doing alright back there?"

Deana looked behind to see a body dressed in ragged clothes, slumped over and curled up, with its back turned toward the front seat. The lump grunted in response to Lyle's query.

"Great. Hey, Collene?"

"Collene Sons was Lyle's partner in the agency."

"Listen, I need you to find out where our illustrious benefactor's going to be this weekend, and then I need two plane tickets to wherever that may be." "That's right, two tickets. Plus you need to get there to meet us." "What?" "Oh, I've done better than that. I've got an eyewitness you'll have to see to believe. I'll fill you in when we meet up. Call me with the info."

Status hung up the phone and turned on the ignition.

On a lark, Deana tapped Lyle's image. The program abruptly paused. Ben's image leaned in through the closed window and looked Deana directly in the eye.

"A perspective change at this juncture may potentially spoil key plot suspense. Try again later!"

Dover phased back through the doorframe and resumed his position next to the car as the program continued.

Fine, Deana thought. *But did you have to be so damned creepy about it?*

The car backed out of its parking spot in the gravel lot. Deana remained stationary, which meant that she appeared to be sitting in mid-air as the car pulled away. Ben stepped up next to her.

"More on that development later. Let's meet a few more participants in this tragedy."

The image of the mental hospital spun and swirled. The atmosphere unfolded to reveal both daylight and an interior view. She was sitting in what appeared to be the smoking section of an airport. Dozens of people walked to and from the gates just outside the regulated pen. Text scrolled across the glass partition that separated the innocent travelers from the evil nicotine addicts.

Phoenix International Airport…Saturday, September 1st, 2012…3:45 P.M…

The digital man sitting next to her smoked while occasionally glancing at the clock on the wall. He was ruggedly handsome and obviously in very good shape. Deana watched him hot box the cigarette.

Who the hell is this supposed to be? Smokes like a pansy.

"Jackson Cross…"

"Get out!" Deana blurted.

"…dropped out from the public eye immediately following the Grand Ravine Tragedy. It had been rumored that he was in Africa, retracing a safari route of the late Earnest Hemmingway…"

Where do they get this stuff?

"…when he returned to the U.S. to oversee the production of *Judas Conspiracy*."

An obnoxiously sweet and friendly voice called out over the airport P.A. "Delta is ecstatic to announce the arrival of Flight 517 from LaGuardia at Gate 32. Passengers using this flight as the connection to Los Angeles should be prepared to board this delightful aircraft sometime in the next eight to ten minutes. Thank *you!*"

The man who would be Cross stood up, stubbed out his smoke and proceeded to the gate. Deana stood and waited for her makeshift seat to be absorbed back into the wall of the tube before following.

Ben was waiting for them at the ticket counter.

"Darlene Tyler and Scott Lloyd were the real-life friends whom Jackson incorporated into his book. They were flying in to visit the set and get a behind-the-scenes view of the making of a motion picture. They had no idea what they were really getting themselves into."

I guess not.

Deana couldn't take seeing Jackson, even if it was only an actor. It wouldn't be all that great seeing Darlene and Scott either, both knowing and *not* knowing what was to come. But they were the lessor of two evils right then, so to speak. She touched Jack's image and became swept up into his perspective.

"Jacks!"

Deana looked over to see a bubbly, vibrant couple step off the walkway. The woman rushed over to embrace Cross. She felt a pang of jealousy as her virtual image hugged the attractive girl back.

Stupid cow, she chastised herself. *They were only ever friends.*

The program stopped. Deana glanced down and understood.

"How was the flight," she recited.

There was a brief glitch before the actress began speaking.

"Oh, it was fine. Scott got into a fight with the stewardess, but that's nothing new."

"I paid for a first class flight," Scott defended. "I wanted slippers. They had them on *Seinfeld*." Deana was put-off. They gave him Scott's self-involved, passive-aggressive manner of speaking, but the actor was trying to be ironic by saying everything with a smile.

"The movie studio paid for our flight," Darlene pointed out.

"Even still."

Without warning, a window opened next to the actors playing the friends. Deana recognized the image of the real Scott Lloyd's mother immediately.

"It was no surprise that Jackson and Scott were barely civil to each other at that point. Oh sure, they used to be best friends. But then Scott and Darlene moved away and Jackson put them in that stupid book…I don't know. Scott just couldn't let it go. And I, for one, don't blame him. Especially now."

The window closed as quickly as it had opened. Deana was on the ball for her dialogue. "How're we doing, Scott?"

"As well as can be expected, Jackson," the actor replied without missing a beat.

"Y'know, not for nothin'," Darlene interjected. "Nicki was *so* jealous when she found out where we were going."

"Nicki?" Deana inquired as Jacks.

"Remember? She was at the apartment when you and Danny were on the lam from the Tom Green debacle."

"Danny being Daniel Epstein," Ben quickly interjected. "Life-long friend of Jackson's."

Like I didn't know that *already,* Deana thought with some irritation.

"Oh, right," she spoke for Jacks. "My number one fan. How's she doing?"

"Ok, I guess. She's dating some guy she met through the Website she started for you. Get this…his name's Nick."

"Nicki and Nick," Scott noted sardonically. "It's just too damn cute for words."

Now Deana felt as if someone had punched her in the stomach. She tapped the interface and ejected from Jackson's perspective.

"C'mon. Let's get your luggage," Jackson suggested of his own accord. He took Darlene's arm and led her away. "I've missed you, y'know."

"Yeah?" she replied with a smile. "We've missed you too."

The three actors walked away from the gate. Deana stood still as harried, virtual travelers rushed around and through her.

Jacks knew. He knew who he was. I mean, maybe they hadn't met before, like officially or anything, but still. Christ.

"Meanwhile," Ben segued. "Back on the set."

The scene dissolved into the mass of psychedelic swirls to which Deana had become accustomed. The score turned menacing.

She stood atop a hill overlooking Pilate's palace. The change from the movie scene she'd experienced only a few minutes previous was subtle. It wasn't until she heard and saw trucks moving and crowds being directed by megaphones that she realized that this represented a more contemporary sequence.

"The set was all-but a ghost town by this time. It was Labor Day Weekend, and the primary cast was off for the holiday. The second-unit director was finishing up crowd sequences for Christ's trial, which was scheduled to be shot the following week."

Deana felt the familiar sensation of being swept up. She flew over the set in a series of swoops and dives before landing on the roof of one of the modular offices. Upon landing, Ben stepped up next to her and motioned toward the street below where two men were speaking.

"Maximillian Swanson, known by some as Minister Max, plays an odd part in this tale."

The program paused. A window opened next to Deana and Ben, revealing a photo of a toddler.

"Born in Utah in1972, Max was the only son of Rob and Loren." The picture cut to a young, clean-cut man standing behind an altar and raising what could only be a bible high over the congregation. "Rob Swanson was a television minister whose ministry was stripped from him in the early 80's. To his credit, he merely embezzled funds from his God-fearing flock, as opposed to the sex scandals surrounding such infamous televangelists as Jim Baker and Jerry Falwell. But unlike his brothers of the bible, Rob couldn't live with the guilt and shame he had brought upon both his family and community." The picture dissolved into a crime scene photo of a garage interior. "In the Spring of '86, while Max was attending advanced classes at Oral Roberts University and Seminary, and with his wife Loren passed out from her nightly abuse of alcohol and prescription pain killers upstairs, Rob Swanson left his Cadillac to run in gear while he sealed off every conceivable source of ventilation from inside his garage. Max withdrew from his classes the next day."

The men talking on the road by the trailer finished their discussion. Deana just assumed one of them represented Max. Sure enough, the more slender and charismatic of the two men stepped inside the trailer upon which she and Ben were standing. Almost immediately, they began to sink through the roof. The window (which now displayed a picture of a mid-to-late teen backpacking with friends) descended into the trailer office with them.

"Max went off to find himself then, taking a cursory look at most of this world's popular religions." Another picture cropped up while the actor portraying Max got on the phone and began bellowing orders. The picture showed a young adult preaching in what had to have been a prison of some kind. "Upon his return to the United States, he began a new ministry, having almost nothing to do with his father's failed congregation. But those within his flock described him as driven to the point of madness. He returned with the conviction that Christianity was the only true faith, and would entertain no opposing views whatsoever."

The window disappeared and Deana could concentrate on the discussion Max was having over the phone.

"You're going to have to trust me, Roy." "No, I know the studio is responsible for anything that happens on the set." "Listen, I'm telling you that these people have no place to be, and they're staying here of their own free will. I have nothing to do with it."

Someone rapped on the door. It opened before Max could respond, and a rather imposing figure stepped up into the trailer. Max nodded in the large man's direction and motioned for him to take a seat.

"Walter 'Nailz' Sims was an ex-convict hired by Max. He was responsible for the minister's personal protection…among other more distasteful responsibilities."

"I understand your concerns Roy. We're covering all the expenses at this point. You just enjoy your weekend at Lake Tahoe. I've got everything under control here. See you Tuesday!" Max hung up the phone. "Control freak." He looked up at the giant sitting across from him. "Well, m'man? What's the good word?"

"I just got a message from the limo driver. They're on the way."

"Excellent. You want some gum?"

The large man waived him off. "Tell me again why I'm not just putting a cap in the back of this motherfucka's head?"

Two people I hate most, Deana considered to herself. *Racists, and assholes who give racists a reason.*

"No finesse, my friend. We have to break him in order to show others the error in their ways. Believe me, after tonight, people will remember what it's like to have the fear of God in them. They'll be too busy wiping themselves to even consider the possibility of God *not* existing. This is it. Everything I've been working toward for the last three years comes down to this night."

Max smiled a broad smile, unencumbered by a hint of conscience.

"Are you *sure* you don't want some gum?"

Chapter Thirty

Deana sat in the limousine next to the faux Jacks and across from the actors portraying Darlene and Scott. She looked out the window and marveled at how natural the environment felt. They were on a two-lane stretch of blacktop, driving northwest—adjacent to the setting sun—passing the occasional truck stop and trailer park.

"So," Darlene disrupted the quiet. "Where's Dippy anyway? I just assumed he'd be here for this."

"Danny had to sit this one out," Jacks replied while still looking out his window. "He's taken on a lot of projects over the last year or so, and can't fly off like he used to. I guess we're growing up a little."

"'Bout time," Scott pointed out. Darlene gave him a disapproving look.

"Well, how've things been on the set? You've been here how long?"

"Just a couple of days," Jackson said before looking back at the driver. He reached up and pressed the button that lifted the privacy divider. Once it was secure, he looked back soberly at his friends. "They all *hate* me here."

"What," Darlene was stifling a laugh until she understood that he wasn't kidding. "I don't understand."

"I'm not sure I do either," Jacks admitted as he pulled out a joint and cracked his window. "And I'm not just being psycho paranoid."

"I didn't think you were," she said.

"I did," Scott admitted. Deana was relieved to see the actor taking Scott's derisiveness more seriously.

"Shut up, Scott."

"Seriously, though," Cross continued. "Everyone's been pleasant enough, but it's all forced. It's like they all secretly want to kill me, but have to wait for some reason. I swear to Christ; they're even signaling one another. It's like being in that old movie, *The Sting*? Every time they see each other, they're tapping their noses or rubbing their chins. It's driving me apeshit."

"Sucks don't it? When people are always doing stuff to annoy you?"

"Scott…"

"No, I'm serious. You've made some kind of career out of pushing buttons, Jackson. I'm finding it hard to feel sympathetic when people begin pushing yours."

"Look, we're here to have fun this weekend. Now that we're here, you don't have to worry about people conspiring against you."

"I'm not so sure," Jacks admitted while eyeing Scott.

"Oh stop it, assholes. We're here to celebrate! They're making a movie from something you wrote! Isn't it something?!"

"It's something," Jackson agreed before gazing back out the window and withdrawing once again into silence.

Deana and Ben stood in a trailer and watched as Jackson let himself in. The text scrolled across the windowpane in the door.

Desert View, Arizona…Saturday, September 1st, 2012…10:45 P.M…

"The friends had a quiet dinner together at the studio commissary built especially for the film crew. Everyone involved was tired from the traveling of the day, and they agreed to turn in early."

Deana watched uncomfortably as the Jackson in the program sat down and began making notes in a journal at his kitchen table. The phone rang.

"Cross." "Hey! How are you?"

She winced.

That's me. He gave me his number when he first arrived, and I decided to call him that night. He was talking to me.

"Jackson had recently rekindled a romance with a sweetheart from high school. According to his journal, things were going well."

Son-of-a-bitch.

When the knock came at the door, Deana almost stopped the program. Her breathing became labored and she began sweating in the temperature-controlled tube.

Don't answer it, Dopey.

"Hang a sec., hon. I've got somebody at the door."

Deana shuddered as he set the phone down. The program maneuvered her behind him, so she was looking directly over his shoulder when he opened the door to the several dozen angry-looking extras from the film all glaring anxiously at him.

No one from the mob said a word. Neither did Jacks. He turned stoically and picked the phone back up.

"Honey? I've got some people here who need me on the set. I've gotta go." He pulled the receiver close. "I love you."

"I love you, too," Deana said as she wiped a tear from her cheek.

Jackson barely had the receiver back in the cradle before the hands were on him, pulling him out of the safety of the trailer and into the mocked-up streets of Jerusalem.

The music pounded in Deana's ears as she was swept up and over the streets of the movie set. She could make out Darlene and Scott being removed from their trailer in the same unceremonious manner as Jackson. All three friends were being directed/carried toward Pilate's Palace, in the center of the set. Flying over people's heads while listening to the persistent bass and fast beat of the program's score began to take its toll. She decided to lock into Darlene's perspective, hoping that she wouldn't be forced to speak very much.

Once she was firmly in Darlene's skin, she realized that the situation wasn't much improved by being a participant. The mob pushed and prodded her and Scott roughly through the streets. They met up with Jackson at one of the alley intersections.

"What is all this, Jackson?" Scott demanded.

"Somebody's pushing my buttons?"

"Are you kidding? You're joking while we're being led to a firing squad?"

"What do you want me to tell you, Scott? I'm sorry? I'm sorry a bunch of narrow-minded cunts have it out for me because I question their…"

The punch to the stomach could have come from a half-dozen people at least.

Deana yelled, "Hey!" which was fortunate as that was exactly how the program anticipated Darlene to react.

"I'm alright," Jacks said between coughs. "Plenty more where that came from, I'm sure."

The closer they came to the center of town, the louder and more ominous the score became. They also began to hear a kind of chanting coming from the court outside the palace.

"What the hell are they yelling in there?" Scott questioned.

"Tear down the wall?" Jackson pondered.

"Jesus Christ, man. Your ego knows no bounds at all."

"Blow me, you whiner."

"Whiner? We're being kidnapped, for Christ's sake!" Someone moved in to strike Scott, but was waived off by the large black man who met the group at the mouth of the courtyard.

"Just another day at the office," Jackson said, apparently both to Scott and Nailz simultaneously.

"Maybe your last day," Nailz commented with a grin.

"Whatever." Jackson seemed beyond reaction. He became more and more withdrawn as the three were herded more closely together and ushered toward the palace gates.

"Can we just for a second focus on surviving this thing?" Deana recited with all manner of sincerity.

"I am sorry you guys got dragged into this. I figured these idiots were bored with me by now." Another blow. This time to the back. "Oh, that's *very* Christian!" Jackson tried to yell, but his face was contorted in a wince.

Angry voices began singing out from the crowd. The temper of the mob was rapidly overtaking the camaraderie. It wasn't until they were in the middle of the ruckus that the chant, "Bury the Cross," became clear.

"My fans," Jacks chuckled. He kept his head low and followed the direction in which his group was being moved.

Deana couldn't stand it. She ejected from Darlene and floated up and onto the balcony overlooking the yard. Max was there (as she was confidant he would be), looking out over the pandemonium he had created.

A wave of deja vu washed through her. The crowd was dressed almost entirely in period costumes from 2000 years ago, crying out for the destruction of a man whose primary crime was trying to change the way people thought. The only difference being that this demonstration was taking place in the dead of night.

Floodlights began to kick on with deafening thuds. The trio at the center of the consternation was taken inside the mock palace. The mob quieted down as the environment was systematically illuminated.

The score died down to heighten the anticipation.

A final spotlight assaulted the balcony.

The three friends appeared from behind garish curtains.

And the crowd went wild.

CHAPTER THIRTY-ONE

Two of the stadium lights flared, and Deana instinctively lifted her hands to shield her eyes. When she lowered them, the lights belonged to a car coming to a stop directly in front of her, outside the perimeter of the set. The flash was a different form of dissolve.

What the fuck? There's a scene break now?

Two people emerged from the sedan. She recognized one almost immediately as the actor playing Status. Deana wished she had the ability to turn off Dover as he stepped up behind her to tell her what she had already figured out.

"Lyle Status and his partner, Colleen Sons, arrived just as the events were unfolding…"

I don't buy it. They must have tweaked that to make it more dramatic.

"…accompanied by a very important player in this little drama."

Colleen and Lyle were both trying to block out the light coming from the direction of the small coliseum.

"What the hell's going on there?"

"No idea," Lyle offered. "But I'm going to be pretty conspicuous if I drive through *those* streets to get there." He considered this further. "A pretty good target, for that matter. Let's give our friend here a hand up, and then let's start hoofing it."

"Of course," Colleen agreed as she slammed her car door home and opened the door to the back seat. "*You're* not wearing a mini-skirt and high heels."

Oh-My-God! Deana was stunned. *Colleen must have shit two bricks when she saw this! Who wrote* that *crap!?*

Deana was still astonished at the audacity of the script when the scene began to dissolve. One moment Status and Sons are helping a derelict of sorts out of their car, the next she's standing behind Jackson, Scott and Darlene as they were being held captive on Pilate's balcony.

Which of the guys subduing Jacks and company is the one that freaks out?

She carefully eyed each of the six men who were holding the friends in place.

Max, in the meantime, coolly approached Cross. He spoke low and directly into his ear.

"If you act civilized, we'll make it painless."

"Monkey do as monkey see, Max," Jacks answered while trying to free his arms from the two men holding them behind his back. "Who's been *un*civilized up till now?"

Max smiled at this and motioned for the men to free their hostages. "You know who I am?" Max inquired, continuing to speak low.

"There isn't much about Colorado I *haven't* committed to memory."

"You should have burned with the kids you killed, my friend. You would have done yourself a favor."

"You have no idea."

Max approached the edge of the balcony. He turned on the microphone attached to his collar before raising up his hands in triumph.

"My fellow, God-fearing children of Christ! Three years ago, *this* man tried to destroy the very faith system that makes us who we are…and failed! We are still here, are we not?"

A roar of approval erupted from below.

"But the question remains…What right do people such as these have to belittle our God?"

"Hey!" Scott called out. "I didn't belittle anybody! I didn't even want to be in the stupid book!"

"Jesus Christ," Jackson swore to himself. "Did anybod*y like* the fucking thing?"

Nailz approached Scott, appearing ready to forcibly remove the skinny, white man's head from his shoulders.

"Do you disavow this man?" Max asked Scott while pointing at Jackson. "Deny him, join us, and you'll be free to go on your way."

Scott looked from Max to Nailz to Darlene to Jackson.

A window opened next to Deana in the program. Mrs. Lloyd's face appeared again, looking frustrated. "How could he? He wasn't going to leave Darlene there by herself. And, regardless of everything else he'd done, Scott claimed that Jackson was one of the best friends he'd ever had in his life."

Deana wasn't enthralled with the distraction. She touched the top corner of the window on a hunch, and drew her hand down. This action reduced the window (and Scott's mother) to the size of a postage stamp. She turned her attention back to the program.

"I won't turn my back on my friend. I don't feel much like defending him, but take a look around here for a second. It's like a Nazi-youth camp with bibles. You think you're in control, but you'll never make me turn on my friend."

Scott closed his eyes and braced himself for the pummeling that he felt was sure to follow. Nailz moved in so close that Scott's body became engulfed in the giant's shadow.

"It's not about control, Mr. Lloyd. Whatever happens here is outside of mere mortal control. We're the tools of the one true God. Whatever happens is His will."

"Then so's this!" Jackson screamed as he lunged for Nailz before anyone could grab him. Jacks threw his shoulder into the big man's waist, knocking him off balance. Cross kept his momentum going until he felt the monstrously large man fall backwards. Huge hands clawed at Jacks' back as the convict tried to stop himself from tumbling over the edge of the balcony. Grasping hands finally caught the rail, and Nailz held himself some twenty feet above the gasping crowd.

The men who had been holding Jackson recaptured his arms and began to drag him back from the edge, but Cross wasn't hearing of it. He surprised them by lunging at the railing once again, kicking at Nailz' exposed hands.

"Fuck all of you! I'm tired of taking your shit!"

The big man let go. He dropped straight down to the dirt and weed covered courtyard. The crowd opened a hole, preventing him from crushing anyone with his fall, and then closed it back up again.

"Well," Max said while trying to determine how much damage his bodyguard had suffered. "That's unfortunate, but…yes! It appears he's fine!"

Deana glanced over the edge to see the man get up. He staggered a bit before regaining his senses. Then he pulled a gun out from a holster behind his back and took a bead on Cross several feet above.

"Hang on there, friend," Max insisted. "I'm confident *that's* not our Lord's plan. We will not lose this night to such emotional responses."

"Are you sure, Max?" The voice came from the same speakers which amplified the minister's own speech. Everyone looked around to find the source of this new intrusion.

"You have no idea the powers at work here, Swanson. You never have."

As if on a cue, huge machines and fans began to switch on, seemingly of their own accord. Something slightly more oily than water sprinkled lightly at first, before raining down on the congregation in sheets. The several hundred followers stood in the downpour, each looking more confused and scared then the last.

Darlene stood with the others under the cover of the balcony. "Um, what the hell's going on?"

She looked over at Jacks, but he appeared to be just as dumbfounded as the rest.

"It's the rain machines," Max instructed in as calming a voice as he could muster. "They're here for the movie. Someone's playing a joke, is all." He looked back at his three prisoners. "It's them! They're trying to distract us again!"

"Don't look to lay blame, minister," the mysterious voice commented. "You've been the only instrument in your own destruction." The voice became deeper, more malevolent. There was a flash from behind the palace. An image was projected against the wall of rain falling on the crowd. A red, bearded and horned face floated over the congregation. It began to laugh maniacally. A percentage of the people on the ground fainted dead away.

So much was happening so quickly that Deana could barely take it in. She saw a shadowed figure in a fedora and trench coat quietly enter the balcony from behind. He held what appeared to be a weapon and stood squarely behind the men holding the three friends. The darkly clad man cleared his throat. When the guards turned, he fired what looked like a ray gun of sorts at the half-dozen or so men. Electricity attacked the watchmen. Jacks, Scott and Darlene, hardly aware of what was transpiring, instinctively jumped away from their captors as the men began to jerk and spasm from the shocks.

Max's attention was held down in the yard. People began screaming and moaning. Some of his followers fell to their knees and beat their heads against the dirt ground.

"What's wrong with you people? It's just a bunch of smoke and mirrors for the love of…Get up!"

"That's not entirely true, Max." The demon continued laughing as Max turned to see whom among his captives could be so bold. It was only then that he understood how far events had shifted from his control.

There, in front of his unconscious men, stood Jacks, Darlene, Scott and one more.

"Epstein?" The minister shook his head and attempted to clear his thoughts as the man who subdued the guards revealed himself. "What are you doing here? You said you didn't want to be involved."

"Oh, c'mon Max. The idea of betrayal *never* crossed your mind?"

Max turned his back on the group and looked out at the crowd that had been reduced to quivering putty. "But, how did you…?"

Deana was quickly swept up and taken for a flight across the heads of the crowd.

What? I don't want to be doing this now!

But the journey was brief. It lasted just long enough to for her to see people shrink away from the demonic image and tear and claw at their own clothes. Some simply stared at the water running down their own hands and shrieked in bloody terror. Others pointed at the floodlights and laughed and laughed.

She swung back up onto the parapet just as Jackson and Danny flanked Max from either side. The three men stared at the bedlam below.

"Isn't it gorgeous, Dopey?"

"What did you do?" Max asked in a voice barely above a whisper.

"What did I do?" Danny flicked a switch on the microphone on his collar. "Ladies and gentlemen! Your esteemed leader just asked me what *I* did! What he fails to realize is that you people brought this on yourself!"

Cries of "No!" and "It isn't true!" wafted up from below. Others simply held their heads and wept.

"Ohhhh, yes!" Epstein persisted. "All that crap about doing it, 'for Don.' You people don't give a shit about Don! Hell, you don't even give a shit about Jackson! You just want to lord over everyone else's thoughts. We've had *enough!*"

"Danny?" Jackson was looking at his friend as if he'd never seen him before in his life. "What the hell *did* you do?"

"He killed Don! This is all just some elaborate distraction! But he killed him just as sure as I'm standing here!"

"Nice try, Minister Moron. But there's someone here who might disagree with your accusations." Danny spoke directly into his mike. "I'm looking for Status!"

"Right here, Mr. Epstein."

Everyone on the precipice turned to see two men and a woman walk onto the balcony from the palace entrance. Max's legs shook so badly he had to brace himself.

"It can't be."

"Oh, but it is!" Danny assured him with an exaggerated grin. He pulled out a remote and, with the flick of a couple of switches, turned off both the rain machines and the projector casting the demon face. "If I can have your attention please! It is my great pleasure to introduce tonight's Guest of Honor…the late, great Don Owens! Let's give him a hand!"

Don shirked away from Collene's grip, and avoided everyone's gaze, The silence was deafening.

CHAPTER THIRTY-TWO

Jackson peered out over the teeming cacophony that resembled a sort of live Hieronymus Bosch painting, then he looked back upon the broken, disheveled figure of a man who was supposed to have been dead for the last six months, and then he looked back at Danny.

"Can I get a cigarette off of you?"

"What?"

Everyone on the balcony looked at Jacks as if he'd just asked Mother Theresa for a blow job. Deana just smiled.

"They yanked me out of my trailer before I could grab my pack. I could really use a smoke right now."

Danny sighed and handed Jackson his pack, which wasn't easy since he was concentrating on holding the stun gun on Max. Jackson took the first stick jutting up from the soft pack.

"Light?"

Danny sighed more deeply, put his cigarette pack back in his pocket and retrieved his lighter. Jackson puffed at the flame to get the stick lit, then took a long drag. He leaned against the railing with his back to the courtyard, exhaled, and took another. No one spoke.

Finally, he pointed in the direction of the two detectives.

"Did I hear correctly? Danny called you 'Status?'"

"Status and Sons," the private eye offered. "Discretionary investigations."

"I'll bet. Listen, do you think you could do us a favor and keep an eye on our minister friend here?"

"He won't be going anywhere." Lyle moved up next to Max. "And where's that gorilla friend of yours? I still owe him some lumps from

Colorado." Max didn't answer. He stared out at the mass of writhing humanity that was once his congregation.

"Great." Jacks looked over at Danny again. "I think you and Scott and Darlene and I need to have a chat."

The four meandered over to the far side of the parapet and huddled close.

"Ok, what the hell is going on here?"

"You're asking us?"

"No, Scott. I'm asking Daniel. I just assumed you wanted to hear this too, since you've got something of a vested interest."

"No shit! I thought that big fucker was going to hand me my ass!"

"So, I ask again. Danny, just what the hell is going on here?"

"Which part?"

"Let's start with the lost scene from Caligula playing out down there."

"Well, now *there's* a funny story!"

Deana walked over with the group and listened intently, but she began to feel like a fifth wheel. She looked around her tube and noticed a tiny control button next to the dialogue box. The button read "Menu." She tapped on it, and called up a selection of commands.

Exit Program

PIP

Scene Selection

Run Credits

She pressed PIP, and a picture (approximately a foot square) of the four friends blinked on to her right.

●

Danny: I was playing poker with some Suits a few years ago, and found out that there are these funeral directors keeping their own collections of celebrity body parts. It turned me off, mostly, until I heard that someone had kept a vial of Tim Leary's blood.

Jackson: That's kind of cool.

Danny: That's what I thought.

Deana climbed up onto the railing and stepped off. She floated/drifted down to the ground below. She looked around at the wailing, laughing, psychotic group on display before her.

Danny: So I…liberated a sample, and had some of the chemists on my payroll break it down. As I suspected, Leary's constant experimentation changed his chemical make-up on a fundamental level.

Deana watched as a man tried to burrow down through the weeds and mud. She tapped on his image.

Danny: We manufactured a component to recreate the exact same chemical deconstruction on everyone. All I had to do after that was convince you to write the sequence in *Judas Conspiracy* to include rain during Jesus' trial. Remember?

Jackson: I'll be damned! That *was* your idea!

Deana's environment phased into the perspective of the digging man. The window with Jackson and company remained. When the atmosphere swam into focus, all she saw was worms. Giant, squiggling, crawling worms. That and the birds circling above, seemingly prepared to swoop down and gobble up anything writhing above ground.

We're all worms, waiting to be devoured, she realized.

So she dug.

Jackson: But, I wrote the book over three years ago. You've been planning this the whole time?

Danny: Pretty much. I mean, I didn't actually get hold of the blood until last Spring. But the idea was kicking around since just before you started writing the third book in the *Conspiracy*.

Deana got bored with digging. So she looked up at one of the other worms and tapped their image.

Darlene: So, you're trying to tell me that the water poured on those people down there was really…

Danny: Literally acid rain. LSD derived from Timothy Leary's blood. We just put 200 right-wing, fundamentalist Christians on the acid trip of a lifetime.

She fazed into the new perspective, only to be surrounded by breasts. Big ones, small ones, firm ones, floppy ones. Everything and everyone was composed of tits and nipples. There was no escaping it. She looked up for some relief, and noticed the sky was one giant vagina.

Danny: So? What do you think?

Jackson: [Pause] It's brilliant.

Deana quickly grew tired of all that was mammary, and began trying to find someone else to phase into. This proved a more difficult task than initially imagined, due to the fact that virtually the entire world was comprised of pink, fleshy globes. She probably tapped on a pillar or cart or any number of scenery dressings before finally picking a person.

Scott: Brilliant? You're out of your minds!

When the atmosphere came into focus, she found herself in a world populated by old, black-and-white, 1930s cartoons. There were horses and mice and ducks flailing about, all with big white eyes and exaggerated mouths.

This is awesome!

Jackson: Oh, it's insane. But the fact that he pulled it off is *absolutely* brilliant. So what's the story with Lazarus over there?

Off Screen: Where's the fuckin' cracker what tried to off my ass?

Deana broke away from the euphoria of the animated world when she heard the threatening voice. She tapped the corner of her PIP view, and immediately returned to her place on the balcony.

●

Nailz stormed onto the landing, gun thrust out. The second he stepped across the threshold, Don started screaming.

"Oh my God! He's come to kill me again!"

Nailz looked at the screeching derelict with disgust.

"What the fuck is this? What kind of sick fuckin' game is goin' on here? I know you're dead you fuck!"

Don, who had been standing off by himself in the corner, loped across the floor toward Status and Sons. "Help me! He's gonna kill me again!"

Nailz took a bead on the panicked, sickly man.

"You're already dead, bitch!"

Oh my god.

The top part of Don's head evaporated mid-stride and mid-scream. Offal flew onto Scott and Jacks.

"Jesus Christ!"

Nailz never had the time to pick another victim. Collene had three fingers of her right hand buried into the big man's throat. He gagged and dropped his gun just before the petite woman grabbed both of his ears.

"C'mere!"

Those not wiping blood out of their eyes winced uncontrollably as she tugged Nailz's head down and threw her knee up. All Jacks and Steve heard was the crunch of pulverized bones.

Now that's *Collene!*

She hauled the semi-conscious giant over to the balcony edge, but stopped as Lyle stepped up to intercede.

"This gentleman and I have an appointment."

Colleen allowed the convict to fall to his knees. "Be my guest."

Lyle bent down close. "Hey there, butter-cunt. You've been a bad rim-licker."

Status grabbed Nailz by the collar and smashed his face into the marble rail.

"You've got the right to remain unconscious, you fucking waste of spunk." And he cracked the man's skull again.

Jesus. I've known Lyle for over a year now. He's nothing *like this!*

Scott was flicking the blood from his face. He was close to tears.

"What the fuck is going on?"

Danny, in the meantime, approached Lyle as he was administering Band-It™ cuffs to the semi-conscious, beaten psychopath.

"Careful with him. He must have one fuck of a constitution to have kept it together after the acid shower."

"He won't be a problem," Collene assured her boss. "We called the Arizona State Police as soon as we arrived. They should be here any second."

Max's head jerked up. "The police?" His eyes darted about crazily. "None of this is my fault! None of it!" He backed away from the accusing eyes surrounding him. His voice lifted several pitches as he pointed at Epstein. "He set it all up! It's all his doing! He's the one who killed Don!"

Max hung his head shamefacedly when it became apparent that he could find no sympathetic ear in the party. That's when he noticed Nailz's gun. He dashed quickly, stooped, picked up the revolver, rolled and pointed it at Danny as if he'd been a member of the Green Berets his entire life.

"Max," Jackson spoke in calm, quieting terms. "You're not a killer… are you?"

The minister considered this for a few seconds as everyone held their breath. "I can't stay here! I've got to get out!"

Max lunged for the rail, stepping squarely on the back of Nailz as he jumped over the side.

"What is he crazy?" Darlene wondered out loud.

"Do you doubt it?" Scott responded.

The group gazed down on the courtyard. Max didn't take the fall nearly as well as his bodyguard. With one leg twisted unnaturally, Swanson tried to drag his own body through the undulating remains of his followers.

"Max?" One of the group recognized him through the trippy haze. "Help me, Max! I'm on fire!"

"Where are you, Max? Where did you go?"

Max's name spread like a communicable disease through the crowd.

"Max! Help me, Max!"

"Keep away from me, Goddammit! I've got to get out!"

But his followers would hear nothing of it. Body after body began to pile on top of the broken minister.

"Please! Stop! It hurts so bad!"

Jackson, Danny, Scott, Darlene, Lyle and Collene (and Deana) watched with something akin to horror as the Christians smothered their fallen leader.

After several seconds, Jackson turned back to Danny.

"Seriously, Dippy. What the fuck just happened here?"

"I'm surprised you don't know, Dopey," Epstein replied. "It's all *for* you."

Chapter Thirty-Three

Danny walked over and stood next to the second corpse of Don Owens.

"What was that supposed to mean, Dippy?"

"Y'know, we broke the rapid aging code in the cloning reproduction. Within three weeks, he was the same exact same age that he was on the day he was murdered. And we found out something else."

"Danny? Why is it all for me?"

Deana began to feel creeped out. As a measure of defense, she phased into Darlene. In a strange way, it meant she wasn't going through this alone.

Danny knelt down. He reached out and lightly stroked the edge of the head, where the bullet left the skull.

"If you catch the cells soon enough after death, they'll have memory stored within them. That, combined with the rapid aging process, allowed for an exact duplicate. Every scar, every mole, every callus; we sat back and watched him gain and lose weight in a matter of hours, all reflecting his original progression. I guess at one point he was a real porker. Do you know what that means?"

"I'm trying to understand what any of this means, Dan."

Darlene reached out and grabbed Jackson's wrist. Deana was glad that no words were coming up on the display. She was just trying to subtly tell Jacks not to press Danny too much too soon.

Danny was still captivated by the hollow skull.

"But there was something that got lost in the whole process. I mean, to my core I believe that Frankie, Deano and the others are complete, total human beings." Danny laughed and looked back at his friends.

"Do you know how much of a computer whiz little Sammy is? He'd stolen files from the lab where they were raised. If it wasn't for those files…well, everything would have been different. But, hell, this isn't exactly going as planned either."

"What *was* the plan, though? Did you know about the kids before Sinatra picked me up? I'm trying to understand."

Danny stood up and walked over to the far end of the balcony. Deana watched as the men who Danny had stunned earlier were beginning to stir.

Shit. I don't know if I can watch this.

"Frank and the Pack were one fucking bizarre diversion, but I had nothing to do with it. I was as grateful for that little *deus ex machina* as you were, believe me." He threw his legs over the rail, first one then the other, and sat contemplatively above the madness.

"I'd been sponsoring Max from just about the time you sold the manuscript."

"What?! What the fuck for?"

Danny looked back at Jacks and yelled.

"What the fuck do we *ever* do this shit for, Cross?! We've wanted to start a revolution together since we were sixteen! Well, take a peek, buddy-boy! Your revolution is calling!"

"You've gone insane."

"And you pussed out. What the fuck did Deana do to you back in Indiana?"

Jackson dismissed the attack with a slight wave of his hand. "Don't put this on her, dude."

Yeah! Fuck you, Epstein!

He approached the railing and stood a few feet away from his friend. "This isn't revolution. This is…I don't know what this is. Nihilism? What exactly do you mean by 'sponsoring Max?'"

"I did some research on these fly-by-night ministries, and found this guy whose primary converts were convicts. He was this angry, desperate, charismatic guy. I convinced him that you were the devil, and that we needed to take you down. And, since I was your best friend, I needed someone outside the circle to formulate the attack."

"Holy shit," Scott piped in. "Max wasn't kidding. You did orchestrate the whole thing. You may as well have killed Don over there."

"Not true." Danny never looked away from the direction of the gyrating crowd. Deana followed both Epstein and Cross' glances and made out police lights flashing in the night, still some distance from the movie set. "I never told him to kill anyone. Hell, I had nothing to do with the whole radio station thing. He was so ready to make you a scapegoat that he didn't want to wait for my plan anymore. The only reason I didn't get killed in the stairwell is because they knew not to mess with me. It'd be like the Roman's knocking Judas around." Danny opened his arms over the throng. "But *this!* This is the scene I was trying to set up from the beginning. I was going to get this movie made for you, Jackson. We were finally going to make the kind of impact we'd always wanted."

"It's artificial, y'know. Making people hate me to belittle them later…I don't know. It feels kind of mean somehow."

"What was I going to do? Wait and see what kind of reaction the *Conspiracy* was going to get? C'mon, Dopey. It wasn't *that* good a book."

"Jesus-*fucking*-Christ! Did *anybody* like the fucking thing?"

"Nicki and Nick think it's tits," Scott said without a hint of sarcasm.

"Honestly, though. People wouldn't have given two shits about the thing if there wasn't some kind scandal wrapped around it. And, besides, it's not like I'm your fucking sidekick or something. We're partners! We always have been! I was just doing my job to make sure that our newest project had the impact it deserved."

"Back-up, Dippy. 'Our' project? That book was mine. You didn't help me write it. I'm not even convinced you ever read the whole fucking thing when it was finished. I only wrote it to try and kickoff a standup career. What's this 'our' shit?"

"He might have a point, Jacks."

Jackson heatedly looked back to stare at Darlene and Deanna simultaneously. Deana felt flushed, but decided she'd follow this new twist to the end and continued to recite.

"It's always been you and Danny. Always. I'm not sure it'd be all that fair to Danny if you were to cut him off from the single biggest achievement you'd accomplished to date. To be honest, I'd just assumed you were both behind *all* this shit somewhere."

"And don't you think you were being presumptuous?"

"Now? Sure. But I'm just saying that maybe it's a little presumptuous of you to think that you can just drop Danny from your goals and plans and expect him to say 'ok.'"

"What? Scott, help me out here, I'm beggin' ya'!"

"Help you out! I'm standing here covered in blood, you idiot! You're your own worst enemy, Jackson. Always have been. You're lying to everyone, including yourself, if you're trying to say that you didn't want something like this to happen once you wrote that book. You just don't like being taken to task for it."

"Oh-my-God! Everyone's gone insane!"

"I have to say, I agree with Cross." Everyone looked over to see where this new contribution came from. Lyle stared in disbelief.

"Collene? I don't think it's our place to…"

"Fuck that, Status." Sons pointed at Epstein. "This guy manufactured a hate-machine against his best friend, hoping against hope that he could put the kibosh on it before anything serious happens, just so he gets to look like the hero. And now all their friends are trashing *this* guy," she said after moving her pointing finger to indicate Jackson. "I mean, I've just met most of you people, but that sounds messed up to me."

"Thank you," Jackson acknowledged with a slight bow. "But, something else just hit me. If you had nothing to do with Don's murder, how did he end up here tonight?"

"What? Pinning a murder on me will put you in the clear?"

"Just answer the question."

"I suspected Max had Don killed, but I was too busy going to Colorado with you to confront him about it. I knew he wasn't going to leave any evidence that would tie it to himself. So I made some phone calls on the plane and had the body picked up. I was originally going to play the clone off as a resurrection, start up a whole new church around Don. But we found that the accelerated growth prevented other kinds of development."

"You mean, like mental? He seemed pretty out of it."

"As far as we could tell, he didn't have a soul."

"What the hell do you mean by that," Scott demanded.

"He was fully developed. His brain was probably in better shape than before the bullet went through the original. But he had no...drive. No compulsion to eat, drink, bath, communicate. He'd answer direct questions fine, but there was just no spark in him. No essence. *That* pissed me off."

"Why," Jacks inquired. "Because you couldn't use him for some false idol like you'd planned?"

"I can't explain it to you right here, man. But just *think* about it. Think about the fact that we created a soulless person. Then tell me how it'd make *you* feel."

"I'd like to ask a question," Lyle mentioned. "Why the hell did you have us look for the murderer all that time, when you could have simply told us that you had Don?"

"Honestly? Oversight. It never dawned on us to do what you did once you found him."

"What'd he do," Jacks inquired.

"I asked him who pulled the trigger," Lyle said dryly.

"Seems logical. What'd he say?"

"Max's nigger," Danny responded.

Jackson considered this. "Goes a long way to proving that bigots don't have souls."

"That's what I thought! It was just life's fine symmetry that got them here tonight."

The police vehicles stopped at the edge of the courtyard. The crowd's undulations had subsided somewhat, but the massive pile of humanity was still an unexpected site for the officers present.

"Best thing to do is just sit up here and wait for them to find us, I guess," Jackson suggested. "Well, one things for sure. You can afford just about any damn lawyer you want. Maybe you could even clone Johnny Cochran five or six times. Make a one man dream team of lawyers with no souls. Not that the idea's entirely novel, but…"

"You need to shut your mouth right there," Deana had to comment for Darlene. "You're joking about skirting the system and getting away with murder."

"You heard him. He didn't plan on Don getting killed." Jackson looked back over the courtyard and the cops milling their way through the bodies. "Besides…he did it for me." He looked over at his friend sitting next to him on the rail, reached over and punched him lightly in the shoulder.

"For us," Danny good-naturedly corrected.

"For us," Jacks said with a nod.

"Partners," they said together.

"Scott?" Darlene looked at her boyfriend. "Do you understand what they're doing here? Do you know what's going on?"

"What do you want me to do about it, Darlene? This is how they've always been. I couldn't believe it when Jackson seemed to have gotten a conscience all of a sudden. I've always said they were getting out of hand. And, up till now, you've always defended them."

"But now someone's dead."

"Everybody dies, lady."

Everyone on the balcony turned to see to whom this new voice belonged. One of the guards that had been subduing Jacks, Scott and

Darlene, and who had been stunned unconscious by Danny, stood with a gun raised and pointed at Epstein.

"My union connections told me what was going on with this shoot, so I figured you jagoffs would show up here sooner or later."

"Jesus," Jackson stated as he slowly turned around. "Who the fuck are *you* now?"

"Doesn't matter who I am."

"But it does."

The program paused. Ben stepped in between Deana and the assailant.

"Vince Vega was the uncle of a reputed mob boss; the notorious…"

"I know who he was, asshole!" In frustration at the intrusion, Deana swung at Dover's image. He glitched a bit, looked at her in surprise, shrugged and stepped back. The program continued.

"Turn around, Epstein."

Danny did as he was told, stepping off the balcony railing as he did so.

"Think carefully about what you're doing now, friend," Lyle reasoned. "My partner and I each have you in our sites. Plus about half the Arizona State PD is just downstairs. You're not getting away with anything here."

"I'm not here to get away with any-fuckin'-thing. This is for my nephew, Sally!"

He got one shot off before Status and Sons leveled him with three hits each.

"Oh, shit! C'mon!"

Jackson was kneeling next to Danny before the blood began to pour from Epstein's stomach.

"Jesus," Danny coughed. "Nothing goes like you plan it. Eh, Dopey?"

"What, you mean you didn't set this up too?" Jackson asked sarcastically.

Deana heard the police scrambling up the stairs in response to the gunshots. The music turned tragic and melancholy.

"Man, this really fucking hurts."

"Good. That's better than the alternative."

Lyle and Colleen held their weapons high, barrels down, and waited to be asked questions before explaining what was happening.

"I'm so close to the Last Laugh, Dopey."

"Don't even start with me about that. We're going to get you to a hospital."

"No, I mean it. I'm nearly there. Or, you are now."

"What are you talking about?"

"The money, Dopey. It's all yours now. But, you've got to do the Last Laugh. You've got to."

"It's impossible, Dan. It was a stupid stoner's dream."

"Fucking asshole. Couldn't even give me that."

Danny coughed up a bubble of blood, and expired before it burst.

"No. No, I'm sorry, Danny. I'll do it, ok? I'll do it!"

Law men pulled Jackson free of his friend and began administering simple resuscitation measures. Deana overheard one of the officers say that the ambulances were a good twenty minutes away.

Jackson went limp in the cops' arms, allowing his body to drag until he proved to be too much dead weight, and they let him fall prone to the cold marble floor.

The guttural cry began low in his throat before he raised himself up, like a hand being pulled into a fist, until it was released as a staggeringly loud howl of pain and damnation.

The music stopped.

The sound was something like thunder. It started very low before building; not coming from any particular distance, yet growing in intensity as if closing in on the unconventional gathering.

The air became electric. And, as every strand of hair on every person's body tugged skyward, it finally dawned on everyone present that something was approaching from above.

In unison, Collene, Lyle, Jackson, Scott, Darlene/Deana, all the representatives of the Arizona Sheriff's Department, and any of the congregation

still coherent enough to register that a noise was approaching, snapped
their eyes toward Heaven. They were immediately blinded. To a man.

Deana unclenched her brow enough to assess the damage through
the slits in her eyes. Everyone with the exception of Jackson had been
laid out on the floor. Since he was already on the ground the moment
the sky ignited, he was the first person able to rise. He turned and surveyed his surroundings.

"Where *are* ya'!" he demanded. "*Who* are ya'! Show yourself!"

Deana followed Jackson's gaze around the room, and realized that not
only was Jacks the first person to stand, he was the only person conscious.

Her own view was that from the floor. She was standing in the booth,
but everything was turned sideways.

Darlene's out cold too.

"Come on, you bastards! You're not fooling anyone!"

"Calm yourself, Jackson Cross."

Jackson spun around. Deana left Darlene's perspective and walked
freely toward him from his right. Don Owens approached him from
the front.

"There's no need for hysterics," Don reprimanded. "No one else can
hear us. It's just you and I."

"Which one are you?" Jackson peered closely at the features, trying to
ignore the shattered, gore-ridden skull peaking from Don's scalp. "Do I
know you?"

"I am of the council. You and I have never officially met, but I rec-
ommended you for the journey to Earth."

"What?!" Deana screamed in her tiny chamber.

Jackson's knees unhinged. He fell backwards, landing inches from
Danny's body.

"What are you *saying*? What was *I* saying? Why would I *know* you?"
Jackson clenched his hair and pulled his knees in. "I did it. I pushed
myself over. I'm a fucking loon." He rocked himself on the marble.

"What the hell is going on?" Deana asked herself.

"You know exactly what I'm saying. You've known since you came back." He looked back in the direction of the unconscious bodies of Darlene and Scott. "Perhaps our mistake was providing you with the means with which you could ignore the truth. We wanted to give you time to adjust. It's obvious now you may never face the truth without some…prompting. That is why I've come."

Don leaned in to catch Jackson's attention from his fetal position. "You've hidden from this long enough. Time to get on with it."

"You're wrong. You're lying." Jackson began to scream. "You're an hallucination!"

Don slapped Jackson with enough force for Deana to see sweat spray from Cross' face.

"This is bigger than your fragile little psyche. Don't screw this up!"

"Christ! What do you want from me?" This came purely from anger. Deana hated to see him being knocked around but, as Jackson glared at Don, she understood it was necessary. He motioned to get up, and would have gone through the fatally-wounded man if he had to. Jackson had flipped out for a second, but he was back in control the moment he was back on his feet.

"You've got to tell them."

"I did. See all this?" Jackson motioned across the courtyard. "This is what I get for 'telling them!'"

"No," Don corrected. "This is the legend."

Jackson rubbed his face. "You're pretty fucking lucky you're dead…," Jackson warned. Then, under his breath, "…slappin' me and shit. Damn."

"The myth is comprised of your journey."

"When I went to Hell, your planet and back in time," Jackson confirmed.

Don nodded. Drops of blood dripped from the top of his head as he did so.

"Exactly. Every religion is comprised of both Myth and Legend. But after your experience in Jerusalem…"

"I didn't want to be part of it anymore," Cross commented while looking over at the prone bodies of friends and strangers.

"Exactly right."

"Exactly bullshit!" Jackson reasoned. "If I lived the *Judas Conspiracy*, what the fuck are Darlene and Scott doing here? How could Danny have been killed if he's really the personification of Excess?"

Don smiled a dead-man's smile.

"You know these beings aren't your friends. Don't you?" Don gestured toward Danny. "You know they're merely props. Shadow puppets, placed here to help you acclimate."

Jackson looked over to see Danny's wounds completely healed. His shirt wasn't tattered, or even bloodied.

"Dippy." He spoke the name quietly. It made Darlene sad.

"But you've had enough time to get used to the idea, in my opinion. Time to sink or swim."

Don gestured again, and Danny's image began to dissolve.

"Hey, c'mon." Cross looked back at his other friends. Deana also looked. Sure enough, Darlene and Scott both faded like melting snow.

"Why are you doing this?"

"Because it needs to be done." Don rubbed his neck. He suddenly seemed very tired. "It's almost time."

"Time for what?" Jackson rushed up to the corpse. He couldn't bring himself to assault the animated thing with half a brain. "Why are you doing all this?"

"You need to make an impact. You need to create the legend that will support the myth, as every great religion has before. Tell people about this night. It's all part of the process. It's time for me to go."

"What?" Jackson swung at empty air in frustration. "Jesus!"

Don stopped and turned to give Jackson a stern, blood-filled eye.

"You know, I *have* to say, I opposed using one of your own species to promote the next development. I felt that our own associate in the field did a tremendous job last time. That paradigm held for two thousand years, which should be considered exemplary. Of course, I was overruled, but that's neither here nor there. What I'm trying to say is; I knew Jesus. You're no Jesus. You're nothing but a stupid, stupid little ape creature. I really think you should stop throwing his name around all the time."

Jackson stood without expression.

"Hey, Fuck YOU!"

Don's corpse collapsed, while Jackon's spittle ran down its face like tears.

Jacks stood stock still while everyone regained consciousness. The camera pulled back from the balcony as Ben's voice crept into Deana's ears.

"Darlene Tyler, Scott Lloyd and Daniel Epstein were never heard from again. The Arizona State Attorney's Office brought charges against Cross, but no evidence of foul play was ever found.

"Although no charges were filed against Lyle Status or Collene Sons for the shooting death of reputed mob Capo, Vince Vega, due to the overwhelming evidence and testimony that he was there to conduct bodily harm, there is absolutely no evidence of Vega shooting and killing Daniel Epstein, as Status and Sons have insisted in wave after wave of deposition.

"As for Cross answering for Epstein's, or anyone else's disappearance, he was still under indictment when, Friday, February 15, 2013, the writer was…"

Deana found the Menu button again. She touched the **Exit Program** option.

Holly jumped as Deana stepped out from her pod.

"Oh, you've got like another ten minutes of the program to go. Y'know, Ben talks about Nailz starting his own ministry on Death Row, and how they found Max, clinically insane but still alive under all those people…"

"And they talk about Jacks."

"Well, yeah, honey. But I thought you'd be okay with that by now."

"I thought so too, but it turns out we were both wrong. Do you have my shoes?"

Holly handed her friend the belongings with which she had been charged.

"Are you ok?"

"Hm? Oh, yeah. I'm not surprised Jacks never wanted to talk about that night, though. That was pretty out-there. Plus, just before the end, it seemed like even his friends were attacking him."

"Yeah? I thought so too, but it seemed like they were saying the same things you've always said about him."

"I suppose, but I didn't expect it to be all confrontational like that."

"And now, after experiencing it supposedly from his own words, I have to wonder where his head was at. I loved him. Did I love someone so deeply troubled as to believe something like that could *actually* have happened?" Deana shivered and gave the interaction tube a disgusted look. "Hard to believe what passes for entertainment now-a-days."

"Wasn't the interface something, though?"

"Oh, it's a pretty good ride," Deana answered off-handily as she put on a shoe. "That much I'll admit."

One of the doors to the auditorium swung open.

"Ladies! I thought I saw you sneak in here while I was on the phone!"

"Just giving our president here a taste of the merchandise, Roy."

"Ah. Well, just remember, Madame Presidente, the first one's free. You'll have to find some kind of payment for the rest."

"I won't be needing more than one visit, Mr. Washington. Trust me."

The Suit strolled up to the stage where Deana and Holly stood.

"The band has begun playing in the courtyard outside, and I've got America's heartthrob in my next interactive program. Anyone care to dance?"

He was extending his hand in Deana's direction, but she passed with a wave.

"Not me, thanks. I've got a speech to give in a little bit, and I need some time to absorb that whole thing. You go, Holly. You don't care how you look."

"Oh, you bitch," Holly responded with a smile. "Well, I *will* go. And we're going to tear that dance floor *up*! Mr. Washington?"

Roy's demeanor faltered when the acceptance of his invitation came from an unexpected source, but only briefly.

"Allow me, Ms. Ferringer," he offered, along with his arm.

"That speech better be flawless, Ms. Brown," Holly warned on her way out of the grand room. "Our third quarter earnings depend on it!"

"Whatever," Deana replied with a bemused smile.

When she was alone in the auditorium, she sat at the edge of the stage, allowing her feet to dangle, just as Danny and Jacks had done on the balcony.

I don't know, Dopey. Am I supposed to hate you or feel sorry for you? Just don't tell me I'm supposed to believe you.

She didn't cry. She didn't yell. She simply swung her legs back and forth, and watched her shadow dance across the carpet.

That, and she wished that life came with it's own soundtrack. She was in the mood for something bittersweet.

EPILOGUE ONE

A dirty-gray morning in Manhattan—Friday, February 15, 2013. Jackson, Lyle and Colleen rode uptown in the magnelimo, passing the crowd with the neon blue faces.

"This is completely out of our way, and we're already late."

"Jesus Christ, Lyle," Jackson observed as he tapped his cigarette through a tiny slot in his window. "You're beginning to sound like a publicist."

"Don't mind him, Mr. Cross. Since we've taken on your security, he's decided that people are going to judge *him* by *your* conduct. You'd think he'd be happy; getting Katy back and everything."

"Is that true, Lyle? You think people will judge you by how I act?"

"I'll tell you what's true, friend. They complain about how you never open up, suckering you into what any rational human being would consider a private conversation, offer some tedious and insipid piece of their soul—like they masturbate too much…"

"Oh! You *are* a prick!"

"—and you, in turn, say something private just so that they can blurt it out at the first inopportune moment." He took a breath. "That's what's true. Also, we're about to pass your skintique on the right."

"A moment of silence, please."

"—."

●

Excerpted from transcripts:
The Tom Green Radio Hour
Friday, February 15, 2013

Tom Green: OK, I think we're finally ready. My next guest is…aw hell, like you don't know. Jackson Cross, ladies and gentlemen.

Jackson Cross: Sorry I'm late, again. Hey there, Billy. I kinda figured you'd have given up radio by now.

Production Mike: Hey there, Dopey! It takes more than a riot to scare me! Bring them on!

JC: Don't do that.

Prod. Mike: Do what?

TG: Call him Dopey, ya' pinhead. What are ya'? Blood brothers? Get off my web space. I need to talk to my friend here. So, Jacks. Here we are.

JC: Here we are.

TG: First of all…what do you think of the new place?

JC: Well, the fact that you've strung dildos across the ceiling like Christmas lights is an interesting touch.

TG: Don't even try it. Our listeners have web camera access to like 90% of the booth's interior. That way we got 6 million people to call 911 when the angry villagers arrive again.

JC: 90%? Is that the same math you use when you tell the chicks you're hung like the horse William Shatner died on?

TG: Ouch! Someone's in a mood.

JC: Well, you're probably right about that.

TG: Let's get the plug in before the riots break out. What're you working on?

JC: I'm in town to record my HBO special this week.

TG: Finally!

JC: Finally.

TG: So, this is the comedy show at last?

JC: Not exactly. It's more of a dialogue. Think Spaulding Grey.

TG: Who?

JC: Exactly. It's essentially me sitting on stage talking about what happened last August in Arizona.

TG: You've never made a public statement about that.

JC: I haven't even told my girlfriend about most of it. It was a difficult night. But I think I'm ready to set it down. So I'll be at the Neil Simon Theater tonight through Sunday. It's called *Jackson: A Cross To Bare*. And you'll appreciate the title more when you read it on the program.

TG: Well, the good news is that it doesn't sound pretentious at all.

JC: [Laughs] You'll have to trust me when I say that I address that in the show. Sometimes painfully so.

TG: Well, what kind of thing can you tease us with so we'll go see the show?

JC: It'll change the nature of human theology, but it'll take about 400 years, so don't expect to get it the first time through. Other than that, you'll have to come down or watch it on HBO.

TG: Oh, c'mon. Let's be fair to the people out there still looking for a reason to hate you, if that last egomaniacal statement wasn't enough.

JC: That sounds suspiciously like you're fishing, Thomas. Is there something you'd like to know?

TG: Well, yes, since you asked. One of the few things leaked out about that night, besides the disappearance of your close friends—which I'm very sorry for your loss.

JC: Thanks. I won't pretend that my explanation makes sense. People will just have to believe that it's the truth. Consider it a leap of faith.

TG: Well, regardless of what happened after everyone lost consciousness, the reports have been published with the testimonies of the Sheriff's deputies present on the scene just after Danny Epstein was shot.

JC: All right.

TG: Anyhow, [sighs] it's been discussed that his last request of you was to "do the Last Laugh." What's the Last Laugh?

JC: [Chuckling] Oh, my God. Is that what people are talking about? Jesus. The Last Laugh is something we came up with in college. He was astonishingly rich already by then. His parents were loaded, but Danny had a preternatural feel for the stocks. So, as he's getting richer and richer, I say, "Wouldn't it be funny if you had enough money to give every person with a bank account in North America, whatever funds they required to meet a level balance of two million dollars?" Effectively, everyone wakes up one morning a millionaire. The way I had it figured back then, this would be catastrophic for Western Civilization. Who would show up for work? Are you going to flip burgers with $2,000,000 in the bank? I doubt it. Are you going to pump gas, work a conveyer line, wait tables…Hell, are you going to put on a badge and risk your life if you're a multi-millionaire? Chances are slim. And all you would need was the right computer program plugged into the banks, and someone with an account fat enough to pull it off.

TG: And, y'know, when you *were* talking about doing this, when were you *planning* on doing it? Just so we can finally have a definitive date for the apocalypse.

JC: Oh, God. Probably when one of us died. But, I mean, the variables are staggering. And, as much money as I have now, being president of Eptech Corporation and all, it's still nowhere near the funds required.

TG: The rumor is that you actually promised to do this.

JC: My friend was dying. Truth to be told, he'd been dead for years. I was stupidly trying to comfort both of us. I mean, he might have it great now, being all omniscient and everything. But I just probably grabbed for that one last straw of the past, y'know? If you think about it, we're just like Jesus and Judas. We're just playing parts. Doesn't matter who's perceived as the good guy or the bad guy. You've got your part and that's what you do. All that's left now is the martyrdom.

TG: Woof. Heavy stuff. But I have the strangest feeling that opening up the phones will lighten things up a bit. Billy? Who's on line 1?

Prod. Mike: Line 1 claims to be Beth, Jackson's former publicist.

JC: Oy.

●

Stu Peterman walked Jackson and his entourage of two to the building's reception area.

"I think the show went well, considering no one stormed the station."

"Yeah," Jackson agreed absently. "Can't hit a home run every time, eh Stu?"

"Um, no," Stu replied uneasily. He breathed a sigh of relief when they reached to revolving entrance. The crowd couldn't have been more than a couple of dozen, all primarily autograph hounds. It looked silly for four cops to be out there for that, but Stu felt it was more than justified.

"Well, thanks again for coming back on the show, Mr. Cross."

"Thanks for having me, after last time." He patted the short, junior-Suit on the back. "You should have relaxed, Stu. What were the odds, really?"

"Too close to call," Stu whispered to himself as Cross and his friends left the building.

"I should go first," Lyle insisted.

"Sure thing, boss. But, look around, they're pretty much harmless."

Lyle, Jackson and Collene emerged from the revolving doors and started down the path toward the curb and the waiting magnecar.

"Dopey!"

He heard it from the left. He turned, made eye contact, and smiled like an idiot. Lyle about had a coronary when he realized that Jackson wasn't behind him, but was instead off talking to someone on the sidelines.

"Deana! What are you doing here?"

"I wanted to come see you! I've been planning this since you told me that you were going to be on Broadway. They wouldn't let me in the building, but I knew you'd be coming down, so I waited and hoped to catch you."

"That's fabulous!"

Lyle grabbed Jackson's arm. "Mr. Cross? What's going on?"

"Oh, Lyle, this is my girlfriend, Deana. Deana, this is Lyle and Collene. Danny bought their detective agency and I kind of inherited them as bodyguards. So, how long have you been out here?"

"Just a couple of hours. I've met someone who says she knows you."

"Oh, yeah?"

Deana moved aside to reveal a petite blond with heavy mascara, who rushed up to hug him.

"Jacks!"

Jackson thought furiously before it finally hit home. "Nicki!"

Lyle moved to separate them.

"It's fine, Status. She's fine," he said before pointing to the man behind her. "He's fine. They're fine. Pretty much everyone here is fine."

"Oh, this is my boyfriend, Nick. He's like the biggest fan. I mean, even huger than me!"

Nick put his hand out, but Jackson held up one index finger.

"Hang on a second there, Nick," he said before looking past him. "Honey? I'm going to a book signing now. Do you want to come?"

"No, I hate those things," Deana shouted. She was being edged away from Jackson and his party. "I'll be bored. I just wanted you to know that I was here. I'll go to the apartment. You've got me on the doorman's list, right?"

"Absolutely. He'll let you in." He pressed up closely to Nicki's boyfriend as he shouted toward Deana. "I love you!"

"Love you, too," she said with a wave.

Jackson quickly turned. "Hey there, Nick," he said as he looked the strange, buttoned-up man in the eye and shook his hand. "I've actually heard something about…"

Nick clasped Jackson's hand and walked with him back toward the magnelimo.

"She really did it. I prepared and everything, but I didn't ever really hope."

"I'm sorry?" Jackson understood that this man wasn't letting go of his hand and was rushing him toward the open door of his car, but he couldn't quite grasp the significance of it.

"Nick?" Nicki shouted above the small din of the crowd. "What's going on?"

"Hours I waited in that club. Waiting for you to come back and acknowledge my free will."

Club? Free will?

Jackson's thoughts became somewhat fractalled even as the two rushed past the limo driver who held the door open.

"Jackson?" He heard Lyle call, but from way too far in the distance, he knew.

"You stole everything that night."

The man's jacket unbuttoned, revealing a small cube of putty with wires. His left hand rested on a small, black button on top.

Is that plastique?

Makes sense. He could never get a gun onto the Island.

"Well, now I've decided that *I'm* the comedian and *you* have no free will."

As the two clumsily entered the car, they rolled off the back seat and onto the floor. Nick landed on top. The men looked into each other's eyes.

Deana.

"Stop me if you've heard this one."

And he pressed the little black button down.

EPILOGUE TWO

C'mon boy, go thou across the ground. Go moan for man. Go moan. Go groan. Go groan alone. Go roll your bones. Alone. Go thou and be little beneath my sight. Go thou and be my newest seed in the pod. Go thou. Go thou, die hence. And let this world report you well and truly.

Jack Kerouac "On The Road"

And so I died. Which kinda sucked.

Fishermen don't know squat about hanging a guy. I had to dance around like some idiot marionette until I ran out of air. Thankfully, most of the faithful were too curious about how their Lord looked up on that big old cross to stand around and watch me kick it. The last face I saw was Mary Magdeline's. She was trying to say she was sorry, but I was in no position to tell her it was ok. She laid a small bag at my feet and I immediately knew that, although *I* never paid her to have sex with me on the foothill of Gethsemane the night of Passover seder, she had definitely been compensated. It's embarrassing to realize that I had 2000 years of evolution on John, and he was *still* able to trap me with sex.

I started moving for the bright light...again. If you consider the transference into the ameba pod, and then being ripped from there and getting shot across the cosmos, this would be the third trip in memory. This time, however, a hand came out from just before the light. An inviting hand. A friendly hand. I took it.

Darlene pulled me onto the platform at Hell's gate. I remembered standing there with Death (*NOT Paul McCartney*, I had to tell myself) when he decided my fate after I declined on the Judge position. Scott was with her. So was Danny. They were all wearing flowing robes and had very intense glows about them. It was sort of obnoxious.

"You could have timed that a little better."

"Don't be a grouch. We couldn't take you when you were still alive."

"Of course. That would have alleviated a small amount of my suffering, and who wants that?"

"I told you he wouldn't be grateful."

"Shut up, Scott."

"What are you guys doing here, anyway?"

"Funny that," Danny stooped over Scott to say. "Seems that when we became omnipotent, we became omnipresent. Now we existed before consciousness began. Wrap your brain around *that* for a while."

"So, you existed before the Creator?"

"See, that's what we needed to talk to you about," Darlene began. "There is no Creator, in the sense everyone's been so focused on for the last few thousand years. God was a creation of the human consciousness."

"But then, who created the human consciousness?"

"That's what *you* have to find out."

"Me?"

"Not you personally, you dope," Danny chided. "Humanity. You have to give up the shackles of the old deity, and embrace this new Trinity. It's the only way you'll evolve to the level of maturity required to finally learn the truth."

"So, we're close?"

Darlene smiled. "That would be telling." She leaned in to kiss his cheek. He felt something fall into his hand, and he clenched onto it instinctively.

"Go now. You're the crier and the prophet, the disciple and the harbinger. You must get the word out that there's a new set of laws. They will be Judged almost solely on the affect they have on those around them. Positive and negative alike. Go back to the Conspiracy. Everything they need to know is in there."

I turned to leave, and remembered which door this was.

"Hang on. This is leads back to Hell and, I have to say, I'm just not in the mood."

Danny laughed. "Like you're the cartographer of the metaphysics. A door may lead to many different places, Dopey."

"Fair enough," I agreed and entered the doorway.

"We love you, you know," Darlene called out.

"Yeah? I love you guys too."

I descended a couple of the brick landings before one of the platforms led to stairs going back up. This threw me, so I turned back to the last group of stairs I had descended. They led up to a magnestop. A familiar one at that. I turned around and went back to the other stairs. Sure enough, they now led outside too. Turns out I was in a magnerail connection tunnel.

I raced up to the surface. It was dark. It felt like early morning, predawn. I turned and read, "Bronxeville" off the station wall.

Son-of-a-bitch, I thought. *I'm back. Back when I started.*

I walked along the apartment building adjacent to the stop, and started to pick up my pace. I was wearing 2000-year old rags. I didn't want to get caught outside. I had no wallet, no money, no ID. But, as I hustled up to the building's entranceway, I did have one possession that made all the difference in the world.

Darlene and Scott's key. Darlene had slipped it to me when she kissed me goodbye.

I let myself into the building and slowed my pace. I didn't want to wake anyone or draw suspicion. I made my way down the hall and up to the elevator. I stood, half naked and conspicuous, waiting for the elevator, when the immensity of my task hit me.

She wants me to tell everyone, I realized. *She wants me to convince everyone.*

How do you do that? I'm asking you! How do you convince everyone that the selfishness has to end? How do you tell everyone that we're one planet, one species, and we're costing ourselves everything by not accepting responsibility for our own individual sins against one another?

Better still, how do you convince everyone that we're better than the trappings we've set for ourselves? What's the best way to tell people that they don't need to conform to the established, prejudiced religions, or the self-serving corporations and government that controls us more every day, or the media and celebrities who dictate what's important and/or fashionable. And how do you get noticed?

I thought about it in the elevator, and was obsessed about it by the time I let myself into Darlene and Scott's apartment.

I crept down their hallway and glanced inside their bedroom. I can't describe what it felt to see them, asleep and spooning in bed.

These aren't your friends, I told myself.

Why aren't they, I inquired.

Because your friends are gone forever, I reminded.

Maybe not, I grasped.

These things are here so you don't go insane, I informed. *If you actually thought that everything that's happened to you has any basis in fact, your brain would leak out through your ears.*

And I understood.

I watched myself writing this book, selling it, and promoting it. I watched my very own Judas conspire against me, putting me in danger, all for the success of this book. I watched fate turn itself on its ear, making the most implausible possible, just to bring attention to this book. I watched myself die...and more. And through it all, all I could think about was how I was going to write this book, and get the word of the Trinity out to the people. Out to you.

So I sat down at Scott's computer, and I typed. I typed everything that happened in New York and New Orleans, and everything that happened in Hell and on that shit-hole of a paradise of a planet. I typed everything about Jesus and his Board of Directors.

And I tried. I tried to make you understand that it's now time to overthrow the old thoughts. I tried to make you understand that being true to yourself and not hurting others is the only paradise.

I tried to reach you while I typed it all. Right down to this last word.

Jackson Cross
The Judas Conspiracy

About the Author

James Allan Fredrick endured 12 years of formal Catholic education. This experience prompted a smattering of horror short stories which he published in various 'zines throughout the '90s. He pays the rent by writing advertising copy for the corporate machines (or did, before the Suits got wind of this thing).